THE ISLAND OF HOPES AND DREAMS

KATE FROST

B
Boldwood

First published in Great Britain in 2025 by Boldwood Books Ltd.

Copyright © Kate Frost, 2025

Cover Design by Alexandra Allden

Cover Images: Shutterstock and iStock

The moral right of Kate Frost to be identified as the author of this work has been asserted in accordance with the Copyright, Designs and Patents Act 1988.

All rights reserved. No part of this book may be reproduced in any form or by any electronic or mechanical means, including information storage and retrieval systems, without written permission from the author, except for the use of brief quotations in a book review. This book is a work of fiction and, except in the case of historical fact, any resemblance to actual persons, living or dead, is purely coincidental.

Every effort has been made to obtain the necessary permissions with reference to copyright material, both illustrative and quoted. We apologise for any omissions in this respect and will be pleased to make the appropriate acknowledgements in any future edition.

A CIP catalogue record for this book is available from the British Library.

Paperback ISBN 978-1-83603-902-0

Large Print ISBN 978-1-83603-901-3

Hardback ISBN 978-1-83603-900-6

Ebook ISBN 978-1-83603-903-7

Kindle ISBN 978-1-83603-904-4

Audio CD ISBN 978-1-83603-895-5

MP3 CD ISBN 978-1-83603-896-2

Digital audio download ISBN 978-1-83603-898-6

This book is printed on certified sustainable paper. Boldwood Books is dedicated to putting sustainability at the heart of our business. For more information please visit https://www.boldwoodbooks.com/about-us/sustainability/

Boldwood Books Ltd, 23 Bowerdean Street, London, SW6 3TN

www.boldwoodbooks.com

For my wonderful readers
Thank you for helping to make my author dreams come true.

1

Clutching a bottle of rosé champagne to her chest, Lola Wild dragged her suitcase along the uneven paved path towards a wood-clad beach house. After feeling queasy from the train journey from Paddington followed by fifteen minutes in a taxi with a chatty driver, the Cornish air was a tonic and a reminder of carefree summers when she was a child. St Ives had been a pain to get to on a Friday afternoon, but away from the town, she couldn't fault the location; perched above a rocky bay and nestled between grassy hills, there was nothing else in sight besides the sea.

Lola reached the bleached-wood front door and paused. The light was fading and the humidity of the mid-August day had been dispersed by the breeze rolling off the Atlantic Ocean. Animated chatter drifted towards her and she assumed everyone was outside, gin and prosecco flowing as her friends made the most of the summer evening. She was the last to arrive. Her long and delayed journey had been broken up by the frequent updates popping into 'Mirabel's hen weekend' WhatsApp chat. She'd seen the photos of her and Mirabel's room and the rustic kitchen piled high with snacks and drinks, plus a selfie of everyone on a terrace with just the glinting expanse of ocean behind them. All day she'd been longing for the journey to be over and to finally arrive, yet now she was here, her nerves fluttered and her heart stalled at the thought of being sociable, of pretending that she was okay. Holding it together was exhausting.

Lola took a deep breath, put her game face on and navigated her way round the side of the house, past a border packed with coastal grasses that sighed in the breeze. And then her senses were assaulted by raucous chatter, the mouth-watering aroma of burgers grilling over a fire pit and Mirabel twirling on the terrace in a lemon-yellow midi-dress holding up a champagne glass.

Lola forced her tired frown into a beaming smile as first Mirabel, then the others, clocked her, their chatter morphing into welcoming cries.

'You finally made it!' Mirabel greeted her with a kiss, her smile as tender as her hug. She looked effortlessly cool in oversized sunglasses and bare feet. Her long chestnut-brown hair was enviably glossy – every bit the bride-to-be.

With the hen do this weekend and a leaving do at the end of the month before the epic Sardinian holiday and wedding in September, this was the beginning of the end – at least that was how Lola felt about her best friend moving away. For Mirabel, it was the start of an exciting new chapter.

Holding a bottle of prosecco in the air, Deni was next to greet her with a cry of, 'The party has officially started!' before she wrapped her arms around Lola.

Entertainment lawyer Deni was usually straight-laced and serious in a smart trouser suit, so when she did let her hair down, she did it with abandon and could be rather full on. She was easy to bounce off though, particularly when Lola wasn't feeling quite so bubbly.

Lola was introduced to Mirabel's old school friend Jenny, the only person she hadn't previously met, before Mirabel whisked her away to dump her luggage and swap the clothes she'd travelled in for a floaty summer dress.

'Sorry you had such a hellish journey.' Mirabel hooked her arm in Lola's as they strolled back through the beach house to join the others.

'It was to be expected on a Friday. If it hadn't been for the album launch, I'd have headed down this morning with the rest of you.'

'It went okay though?'

'Like a dream.' Lola chuffed a laugh. 'I might be all partied out, though. Those girls know how to have fun.'

Mirabel snorted. 'They're the hottest pop band in the world right now; I would expect nothing less.'

They reached the living room. Sliding doors opened onto the terrace and the glow from the fire pit flickered across the happy, drunken faces of their friends, who were silhouetted against the sunset wash of pink and orange and the rippled silver of the sea.

'Won't you miss that side of things, all the socialising when you're miles away in Sardinia?' It was a question Lola had thought of asking many times over the last few weeks as Mirabel's wedding inched closer and her time as a music agent at Rhythm was wrapping up.

'Maybe. Probably.' Mirabel sighed and tightened her grip on Lola's arm. 'But let's not talk about stuff that's going to leave me an emotional mess. Tonight is about celebrating and spending time with my friends.' She tugged Lola towards the joyful laughter on the terrace. 'And *you* need a drink.'

Lola was swept up by the merriment, but she was way behind

on the drinking and felt on the periphery; that sense of detachment had constantly followed her in recent months. So many of her friends had moved on in their lives, whether through a career change, getting married, starting a family, buying a house or making a commitment to the person they loved. Mirabel getting married and moving away was a loss and as heartbreaking as an actual break-up. Yet Lola was happy that her friend had found Fabs, her Italian husband-to-be, who was the nicest man ever, an all-round good guy with the looks to match. Mirabel finding happiness gave Lola hope that not everyone out there was a bastard – even if that was pretty much her experience of men and romance.

'Lola will be next to get married.'

At the sound of her name, Lola switched her focus from her thoughts only to be confronted by five pairs of eyes.

'I'm the only one left who's not married, that's why,' she said coolly before taking a swig of champagne.

She glanced around. Mirabel, of course, was just weeks away from marrying the love of her life, while their mutual friend Polly, who they'd first met at a spin class, was happily married with two young children. In her early forties, Deni, a colleague at Rhythm, was the eldest of the friends, married but childfree through choice, while Sarah – a close friend and neighbour of Mirabel's, who Lola had got to know well over the years – was married with two teenagers. Jenny was also married – whether she was happy or not was another matter. All it did was showcase how far away, at the age of thirty-two, Lola was from having a functioning, normal relationship, let alone a blissfully happy one.

She raised her glass to her lips again. 'But getting hitched requires having a boyfriend first.'

'I'm sure we can help with that – again!' Deni said with glee.

'Yeah, because you all did so well the last time you set me up!' Lola covered her discomfort with a laugh, but her insides churned at the memory of the last wedding she'd been to in May – one that had ended in disaster, knocking her already dented confidence when it came to men.

Jenny leaned forward with wide eyes. 'Ooh, do tell! What happened?'

Lola shook her head as Deni and Sarah started to tell the story. With her cheeks getting hotter and hotter, Lola escaped inside to raid the fridge for a cold drink. She didn't want to relive the mortification of ending up in a situation she was never going to live down, particularly when it was still fresh in her mind – fresh in Deni, Sarah, Polly and Mirabel's minds too, unfortunately. Nope, she didn't even want to think about it.

'Anyway,' Sarah was saying as Lola returned outside with a large glass of gin and tonic, 'it gave us all a laugh, even if Lola here missed out on a helluva night with a sexy groomsman.' She turned to Lola as she sat back down. 'Although, to be honest, I was gutted when you split up with Jarek. I really thought you'd found "the one".'

Lola gulped back a heady rush of distress and shifted in her seat. Mirabel met her eyes and gave a subtle nod, a soothing look that said 'talking about him doesn't mean anything bad will happen'. Because Mirabel had been the only person Lola had told the truth to about what had happened between her and Jarek. Actually, the semi-truth because even Mirabel didn't know everything. There were some things Lola had kept to herself because they'd been too hard to talk about, as if saying them out loud made them more real than they had been when she was still trying to understand how someone she believed had loved her could have behaved in such a destructive way.

'Although, the silver lining is,' Sarah continued, oblivious to

Lola's distress, 'if you'd stayed with Jarek, then you'd never have got up close and personal with Dax and we wouldn't have the best story *ever* to remind you about—'

'For all eternity. Yeah, yeah, I get it,' Lola said with a sigh.

'And oh my goodness was Dax hot!' Sarah wafted her hand in front of her face.

'So damn hot Lola only went and sabotaged things by cooling the situation down in the most spectacular way!' Deni reached across and squeezed Lola's knee. 'We promise we'll find you someone even better in Sardinia. Imagine all the sexy Italians we'll get to drool over *and* hook you up with. Right, Mirabel?'

Lola rolled her eyes and groaned, while inside she was squirming at the attention despite their good-natured teasing. *Let them laugh, let them tease. Let it not bother me*, she thought. She'd taken one for the team, so to speak, a story that would undoubtedly be retold at every social get-together until someone else did something worthy of being gossiped about.

So no, she didn't mind the teasing, she wasn't overly bothered that she'd made a fool of herself, but she was struggling with the attention so firmly focused on her love life – or, rather, her lack of one. They were living vicariously through her as the only single friend. Deni and Sarah in particular had their hearts set on finding her love when that was the last thing she wanted. To try to get them to back off would invite the inevitable questions about why she didn't want to be matched with anyone, much less be in a relationship again. She was doing just fine on her own. Actually, that wasn't true at all; she may be happy being on her own, but she was hardly fine.

Lola downed her gin and tonic and went inside to the bathroom, anxiety still swirling around her stomach. She rested her hands on the edge of the bronze sink and stared at herself in the mirror. The caramel tones running through her choppy blonde bob no longer made her face look quite so washed out now the travel sickness had eased and the colour had returned to her cheeks.

Laughter filtered in from outside, with Sarah's guttural snort overpowering the others. When they'd first met through Mirabel, she'd seemed quiet and mild-mannered, but she had a wickedly naughty side that was released at social events when an extrovert emerged.

Lola ran her fingers through her hair to give it more volume and patted her hot cheeks with cool water. She tended to brush things off when she felt uncomfortable, instead of telling her friends to back off. What she needed to do was switch the focus back on to Mirabel. She would shrug off the teasing, forget about their promise of finding her a man and just enjoy being together. Because she knew the truth: there was no perfect man for her, despite her friends all having found theirs.

* * *

After a long, tiring and hot journey, it didn't get much better than sitting out on the deck of a beach house, a breeze rippling through the long grass and the sun melting into a pool of burnished red and gold on the horizon. With good company, tasty burgers and a bottomless supply of drinks, Lola finally relaxed. They had the whole weekend to enjoy each other's company, with a trip to Porthtowan planned for wild swimming in its natural pool, then lunch at Blue Bar by the beach.

The excitement for the upcoming wedding and the promise of adventure in Sardinia was at the forefront of their minds. Lola was relieved when the attention was finally off her and she could shrink into the shadows – quite literally when the sun disappeared. Only the glow from the fire pit and the string bulbs decorating the front of the beach house were left, casting warm light onto the wind-blasted wood.

The arrival of darkness and night-time insects was the cue for everyone to move inside to lounge on the comfy chairs and sofas. The lamplight kept it cosy, while the breeze drifting off the ocean tempered the summer heat. After such a humid day, it was fortunate it wasn't raining, but it wouldn't have mattered because the house was cool and eclectic, with velvet sofas, a mix of white walls, exposed stone and stripped wooden floors stained dark oak. It reminded Lola of a larger, more glamorous version of her loft apartment in London. She loved city living and a job that took her to cool places, but how incredible would it be to have somewhere like this, somewhere away from the rat race, to share with friends, to relax and recharge.

'So, Mirabel.' Clasping her champagne, Sarah leaned forward. 'Have you found a house for you and Fabs?'

'Not yet.' Mirabel sighed. 'We've been looking, but it's difficult only seeing a place online. It'll be easier when we're there, I'm sure.'

Moving to Sardinia had been something Mirabel and Fabs had talked about from the minute they'd become a serious item, but it was Fabs taking over the management of his family's business with its portfolio of holiday villas and an award-winning vineyard and winery that had instigated it.

'It's a dream move,' Jenny said. 'Remember at school sitting at the back of a physics class making plans for our future? I don't think yours included moving to Sardinia, but you definitely wanted to move away from Chorleywood. You also wanted to marry Ryan Johnson.'

'Thank goodness that didn't work out!' Mirabel laughed.

'Mmn, you couldn't have done much better than your Italian

husband-to-be,' Sarah said with a sigh. 'You already live a dream life, but starting your married life in Sardinia is the ultimate dream.'

Polly reached across and grabbed a handful of crisps from the bowl on the coffee table. 'I dream about not being woken up at 5 a.m. every single day, which is ironic considering how bad my sleep is.'

Jenny huffed. 'I just wish I could go to the bathroom on my own without being followed by a two- and four-year-old. That's not too much to ask, surely?'

'Oh, I hear you!' Polly swallowed her mouthful of crisps. 'One day!'

'Remember this when they're teenagers and no longer want to be in the same room as you, let alone actually talk to you.' Sarah gave them a knowing look. 'I dream about the day we'll have an empty nest and the freedom to do all the things we've put off because of the kids or being tied to school holidays, but at the same time I know I'm going to bloody hate it when they're off to university fending for themselves.'

'And returning in the holidays with piles of washing and attitude.' Deni raised her glass of champagne. 'And you wonder why I've never had kids.'

'It sounds nice to be wanted, though,' Lola cut in. She glanced at Sarah. 'Or even not wanted by your teenagers. Don't go putting Mirabel off, when marriage and kids is next on her agenda.'

Mirabel slipped her bare feet beneath her on the sofa and gave Lola a soft smile. 'Marriage first, find our new home and set up my business – that comes before kids, but it's true I don't want to put off starting a family for too long.'

'What about you, Lola?' Polly asked. 'What's your dream?'

Secretly, Lola wanted her confidence back. She wanted to not feel constantly worried when she was finally free of a damaging relationship, but eight months on from ending things with Jarek, she still berated herself for having been so easily deceived. She wanted to learn to trust again, to be open to meeting someone new rather than terrified of the idea of opening up her heart. Finding her way back to who she used to be was what she dreamed about. Not that she was going to say any of that.

'I'd love to get a dog.' She breathed in the warm ocean air and took in the freedom of being surrounded by green open space. The darkness beyond the open doors was vast, the clear night pitted with stars. She loved being by the sea, felt at home in a place away from real life and the reminders of a relationship she was desperate to forget but couldn't. 'I longed for a dog growing up, but my parents never wanted the extra tie – probably why they didn't want another child either. I was enough. But I was lonely and wanted company. So a dog would be nice, but it's not exactly compatible with my life. I'd love to spend time by the sea, maybe travel more—'

'Really?' Deni said. 'You already travel loads!'

'Yeah, to some incredible places for work for photo shoots and interviews, sure—'

'Like Starlight's album launch last night.' Mirabel raised her glass.

'But I'd like to have the chance to travel on my own terms, rather than in the guise of a PR manager and only seeing the inside of the venue and my hotel room.'

'Ah, you're young and single.' Deni batted her hand. 'There's plenty of time for both of those things. What you should concentrate on is having fun, if you know what I mean!'

Lola refrained from rolling her eyes. Deni had her best interests at heart; all of her friends did. They just weren't aware that a man was not what would make her happy. Most of all, she wanted somewhere that felt like home. It used to be her apartment, until it had been infiltrated by Jarek. It was hers and she'd ended things with him, yet there were reminders everywhere. The safety and comfort of home was missing. It was a simple dream, yet one she didn't feel able to voice even to her friends.

Lola looked pointedly at Deni, whose cheeks were flushed with drunkenness. 'What is it that you want?'

'I want my husband back.' Her easy smile disappeared.

Everyone stilled. The upbeat pop track overpowered the pause in the conversation.

Sarah glanced at the others, then turned back to Deni. 'Way to go to dampen the mood!'

'What do you mean you want him back?' Mirabel's tone was soft and her frown matched the worry Lola felt.

'We're fine, but not fine.' Deni shrugged as if that explained everything. 'I love him, but we've drifted.'

'Is he okay with you coming to Sardinia on your own?' Mirabel asked.

'He's relieved I'm doing something other than working. And he'll be with me for the actual wedding – the important bit.' Deni reached for Mirabel's hand. 'I need to work on us. I don't mean we have to do everything together, but we do need time that's meaningful. My dream is to get our relationship back to how it was ten years ago. But there we go, such is life.' She let go of Mirabel's hand and drained her champagne. 'But you're already living your dream and it's only going to get better!'

Gone was the brief moment of seriousness as they all raised their glasses with a cheer. Sarah busied about topping up everyone's drinks and Mirabel cranked up the music. It was good to talk to her friends and open up a little bit, even if she didn't feel able to share everything.

Lola's phone pinged. Out of habit, she immediately picked it up and clicked on the message before realising it was from a number she didn't recognise.

> Enjoying the hen do? Cornwall in August must be delightful. I bet Sardinia in September will be even better.

Dread shivered through her. She understood exactly who the message was from as she read it a second, then a third time. Innocent enough words that could be perceived as her ex just being nice, but she knew better, because this wasn't the first time since she'd left him that he'd contacted her. He was always careful to not write anything that could be deemed as confrontational or untoward. The reason the number was unknown was because she'd blocked him. Bar reporting him to the police, which she hadn't done because she didn't think she'd be taken seriously, she'd done what she could to remove him and his damaging influence from her life, and yet...

Her stomach twisted as she reread the message and her earlier anxiety returned with a vengeance.

They're just words, nothing more, she tried telling herself. Yet he knew where she was and where she'd be next month. However careful she was about what she put on social media, she couldn't control what her friends shared and she had no idea who he was following... Who he was stalking, more like. Her heart raced. She tried to push down the fear and concentrate on the here and now. She was with her friends and safe. He just got a kick out of tormenting her because that was who he was.

Mirabel was saying something – making a toast. Lola swiped off the message and forced her eyes from her phone to her friend.

'Here's to love and happiness for everyone.' Mirabel raised her glass and looked around, her gaze lingering on Lola. 'And dreams coming true. Thank you, Lola and Deni, for organising this. Spending time with you all away from the madness of life in London means the world. I can't wait for you to all join me in Sardinia to celebrate Fabs and me getting married.' She lifted her glass higher and her face lit up. 'I'm getting married!'

Lola desperately wanted to be happy, yet being away with a wonderful group of women celebrating the good things in life managed to highlight all that was wrong with hers. At least Mirabel had found a man worthy of her; Fabs was as kind and loving as Jarek had been conniving and controlling. He didn't deserve a second more of her thought, yet months after she'd left him, he was still managing to needle his way into her life. She shouldn't allow him to spoil this weekend, and yet somehow he already had, and she knew that had been his very intention.

2

Rhys Strickland didn't know if he was pleased that the stag do was taking place in Bristol so he didn't have to travel or disappointed that it wasn't happening somewhere further afield; he could have done with a weekend in Prague, Amsterdam or Dublin. Anywhere really besides the city he'd thought of as home for the last fifteen years. It was a nod to their university days, and it made sense for it to be somewhere Fabs had lived for a chunk of time in his late teens and early twenties. They'd met in Freshers' week and had cemented their friendship with countless nights out. It was a long time since he'd been on a pub crawl up Whiteladies Road, drinking to excess with his university mates, who'd scattered all over the place once they'd graduated. Whether they'd be able to recapture that optimism and 'don't give a shit' attitude of youth, he wasn't sure, but it would be good to try.

Catching his reflection in the hallway mirror, Rhys paused. He hadn't known what to wear for a night out like this. A couple of drinks in the local pub with his new friendship group was his usual Friday evening, while this was a nod to the past, out with friends he hadn't seen in a long time. Yet his nerves were shredded because Zoe would be there: the token woman and his ex-girlfriend. She'd always been one of the lads and as much a friend to Fabs as anyone else, so of course she'd been invited; it didn't mean he had to be happy about it. She'd have kicked up a fuss if she'd been left out, plus it wasn't Fabs's fault that things were awkward between them since she'd walked out of his life a year ago. He hadn't seen her since.

He cast a critical eye over himself, somehow a stranger in new slim-fitting dark grey trousers, a thin summer shirt and leather loafers. He'd worn socks, then taken them off because it was a hot and humid August day. Now he was wondering if he was trying too hard. To what, look cool? To look younger than his thirty-three years? To look less like a primary school teacher and more like the sexy student he'd once been – had he ever been that next to Fabs?

He looked away from his reflection. He was being too hard on himself. He really was looking forward to a night out with his old friends, it was just his nerves were getting the better of him.

His phone lit up. The Uber was outside; he'd have to do. Pocketing his phone, he grabbed his keys and left the house.

The trouble with his ex being part of his friendship group was that while they'd both been invited to things over the past year, he'd found himself making an excuse if he knew she was going, leaving the way clear for her. Not that he thought Zoe would be bothered if he did show up; she'd seemed to have moved on from their relationship effortlessly, but then again she was the one who'd fallen out of love and had abruptly left him. That was if she'd ever truly been in love with him in the first place.

His thoughts spiralled throughout the taxi journey from his house in Bishopston to the harbourside. By the time he was dropped off a short walk away from the bar, his heart was hammering and his palms sweating. The plan was to do a reverse pub crawl, yet the itinerary was a far more sophisticated evening than they'd ever had at the age of eighteen. Instead of starting off in upmarket Clifton and working their way down to a club in the centre, they would make their way up via a cocktail bar or two, have dinner at The Ivy and end the night with a party at Barnaby's Clifton townhouse, while his wife and daughter were away.

Rhys stalled just before he reached No. 1 Harbourside, a bar they'd frequented as students and the only real nod to their university days. He didn't want to have to face big, confusing feelings, to be reminded of the past and a time when he was happy and carefree. Not joining them would be the easy option, yet he'd come this far.

A group of lads jostled past, their drunken voices cutting over the smaller groups of giggling women dressed in tiny skirts and barely-there tops.

Rhys continued walking, following the flow of people heading beneath the covered walkway lined with bars and restaurants. The sun glimmered on the water and everywhere was packed. The view to Pero's Bridge with its horn-shaped sculptures and beyond to the floating harbour was a familiar sight. He tried to tell himself that it would be like old times, except it wasn't. Everything was different; *he* was different.

The familiar faces of his university friends gathered round a couple of tables in the bar took him back to being twenty and loving life. Fabs stuck out for being tall, dark and easily the most handsome of the group. When girls had flocked to him in those first few weeks of university, the rest of them had all benefitted by pulling the ones who weren't lucky enough to attract his attention. Although only a few months older than Rhys, Fabs had been more worldly-wise, sophisticated, charming and wealthy – not that he'd ever intentionally flaunted it – but his tastes had been far more refined than the average student's. He and Rhys were nothing alike and yet they'd clicked and had become best mates, managing to maintain their friendship even when Fabs had moved to London.

Fabs immediately eased Rhys's worry by enveloping him in a thumping hug and then other friends were greeting him too: rugby player turned personal trainer Freddie, who'd been in the same halls in the first year; lawyer Barnaby, who still lived in Bristol; and another guy, Gareth, who he didn't know as well but had been part of many a drunken night out as students.

Unsurprisingly, Zoe was hanging back. *Avoiding me*, Rhys thought. He glimpsed her standing at another table in her low-cut red dress, the only woman in a sea of men. She'd left him for a quality assurance manager job in a large construction company in Birmingham, which, from talk among their friends, had skyrocketed her career. He should be pleased for her, but the way she'd gone about undoing their life still hurt. He acknowledged her with a polite nod and she returned a tight smile. He didn't owe her any more than that.

As a student, he'd happily ridden the wave of youth, relishing the freedom of escaping a small Welsh town and living it up in a city. At least that was how he remembered it. Overthinking things had increased with age, to his detriment – precisely how he'd wound himself up into a ball of anxiety about tonight, when he should enjoy being out with friends he rarely saw and not let Zoe bother him.

Drinks were consumed down on the harbourside before they moved to a cocktail bar on Park Street. By the time they'd walked to the White Lion in Clifton and settled on one side of the expansive terrace with views of the Clifton Suspension Bridge and the River Avon meandering through the Avon Gorge below, Rhys's remaining uneasiness had been erased by beer, friends and plenty of reminiscing.

'It's been too long since I've been in Bristol!' Fabs threw his arms across Rhys's and Barnaby's shoulders. 'I miss you guys. Perhaps we should make this a yearly get-together.'

'And not let so much time pass between seeing each other,' Barnaby added. 'I'm in.'

'Me too.' Rhys clamped his hand on Fabs's shoulder. 'Might be harder to plan once you're married and living back in Sardinia, though.'

'I'm sure Mirabel will be happy to come back to the UK as often as we can.'

'Yes, for you two to see *her* friends and family,' Barnaby stressed.

'I'll be able to escape for a couple of days; she's laid-back like that.'

It was true, Fabs and Mirabel seemed to be the perfect match: both with striking looks, which made for an enviably beautiful couple, but they also worked effortlessly as a partnership and were friends as well as lovers. Mirabel was as successful in her career as a talent agent as Fabs was as a sales manager in the finance industry. He'd needed someone who knew her own mind and equalled him in confidence and independence.

Until a year ago, Rhys had been content with his career choice and having his own house that he'd grafted for; however, he couldn't really say he was happy. There'd been moments of happiness, but sharing his life with someone and having a happy, loving relationship seemed out of his grasp. A bout of depression after Zoe had left had been the catalyst for making a change. It took all of his effort to be upbeat for his classroom of children – something that felt impossible to maintain outside of work, which was why taking a sabbatical had been necessary. Going to Sardinia for his best friend's wedding would be the perfect way to start off in a positive way.

He didn't have time to mull over things any further, not when Fabs bought another round of drinks and he and Barnaby rejoined some of the others at a table. Rhys sipped his lager and was content to listen, enjoying the gentler heat as the sun slid to the horizon, the river below a silvery ribbon as it snaked through the tree-clad gorge.

Freddie returned from the bar and chose the empty seat next to Rhys. His eyes shifted between him and his pint and he looked downright nervous, which was strange, when he was usually so ballsy, loud and a good laugh – he always had been. When they were students, he'd effortlessly stolen all the attention, even alongside Fabs, in a way that endeared people to him.

Freddie swigged his beer and cleared his throat. 'Not really had a chance to talk to you yet this evening.' He set his pint down, rolled up his T-shirt sleeves and clasped his hands around his biceps, which were toned from his daily workouts in the gym as a PT. Apart from Fabs and Zoe, Rhys knew Freddie better than anyone, which was why his frown and obvious discomfort was out of character. Freddie looked down. 'But I, um... I didn't want you to hear it from anyone else, but me and Zoe, we're, um, together.'

Rhys's heart stilled.

'Together. As in you're going out with each other?' he managed to utter. 'Since when?'

'Just a few months.'

'A few months!' Rhys's grip tightened on his bottle of lager. 'And you're only telling me now?' No wonder Zoe had kept her distance. 'How did you even get together?'

'We don't live far from each other now, so we met up for

drinks a few times. Things progressed.' He shrugged. 'I know it's a bit weird as she's your ex and all, but it's been a year since you guys split. We all good?'

That was it? That was going to be the extent of the conversation? We're together, have been for a while, hope you're okay with it. Rhys wanted to rage and yell and tell him in no uncertain terms that of course it wasn't all right that his *friend* and his ex were together, but instead he found himself saying lamely, 'Yeah, of course. Why wouldn't we be?'

Freddie patted his shoulder. 'That's a relief; I've been shitting myself all evening, getting the nerve to tell you. You want another drink?'

At Rhys's shake of the head, Freddie gave him another friendly thump on the shoulder and strode off towards the outside bar.

The friends surrounding Rhys became a blur, the conversations loud and muddled. He only caught snatches of words as his mind raced, Freddie's blow having hit him harder than an actual punch to the gut. He needed to get away to clear his head and sort through the tangle of emotions.

The terrace was still bathed in sunshine and people were everywhere, making the most of the hot, dry August evening. Clutching his lager bottle, Rhys wound his way towards the inside bar.

'Rhyster!' Gareth said as they nearly collided into each other in the doorway. He flashed Rhys a grin and with his arms did Smithy's 'Gavlar' movement from *Gavin and Stacey*. 'Feels like old times tonight – fucking ace!'

'Yeah,' he said, trying to push past.

Gareth gripped his shoulder. Beer sloshed around his nearly empty pint glass. 'You realise I'm only across the bridge in Cardiff.' Gareth's eyelids were droopy, his heavily Welshaccented words slurred. The few times they'd gone out together at uni he'd always been a heavy drinker, and slightly obnoxious with it. Perhaps little had changed, although Rhys didn't know him well enough for that to be a fair judgement. 'Isn't your family in Wales?' Gareth continued.

'Yeah, Mam and Dad are in Caerphilly.'

'We should go out. You, me, Barnaby. Freddie and Zoe too since she's moved in with him – Worcester's not too far. Maybe we could do a whole weekend.'

Rhys's insides clenched. 'He just told me they were together, but he didn't say anything about them living together.'

Gareth raised his eyebrows. 'Yup. I'm surprised as fuck it took them this long to get together.'

Rhys frowned. 'What do you mean?'

'Wasn't it common knowledge they had a thing for each other at uni?' Gareth said. 'They were the definition of friends with benefits.'

The chatter from outside faded away as Rhys focused on Gareth; his heart beat faster and sweat beaded his top lip as the words played over.

'Me and Zoe were together at uni,' Rhys said slowly. 'During most of our first and second year before she did her year abroad.'

'Were you? I did not realise that.' Gareth slapped him on the shoulder. 'Maybe I got it wrong then.' He lifted his nearly empty pint glass. 'Need another drink.'

He shot off, making a beeline for the crowded outside bar before Rhys could answer.

Rhys stepped into the pub and drained his lager. It left a bitter taste on his tongue. What did Gareth know? They'd had separate social circles while at university and had been on different courses and in different halls of residence, although they'd known each other through Fabs, which meant he would have known Zoe then as well. What if there was truth to what he'd said? Rhys and Zoe hadn't survived her going abroad although they'd remained friends, and by the time she returned to Bristol for her final year of her degree, Rhys had changed his mind about pursuing a career in law and had started a teacher training course with a placement teaching English in Tuscany.

Rhys put his empty bottle on a table and navigated his way through the bar to the toilets. He shut himself in a cubicle. Eight years after he'd graduated and they'd gone their separate ways, he and Zoe had reconnected romantically and had stayed together for more than three years, with her eventually moving in with him back in Bristol. He'd never once had an inkling that she'd been unfaithful to him during that time, but when they'd been at university?

The thump thump of pop music played over the speaker in the men's toilets. Rhys put the toilet lid down and sat with his head in his hands. Those anxious thoughts that had kept him company on the taxi ride once again returned with horrible clarity. Only a few weeks before Zoe had announced she was leaving him for a new job in another city, Rhys had been looking at engagement rings. They'd lived together and he'd loved her, yet sometimes he'd questioned if they were right for each other when they seemed to want different things. Gareth might just have proved that Rhys's gut instinct had been right, not that it made him feel any better.

3

Rhys's fear about revisiting the past and spending time with his friends and Zoe had come true, albeit in a way he hadn't anticipated.

They moved on from the pub terrace to The Ivy, a restaurant housed in an impressive Georgian building in chic Clifton Village, where Freddie and Zoe sat next to each other, their easy intimacy making Rhys wonder how their relationship hadn't been obvious before.

When they reached Barnaby's house, it was much harder to avoid them and even more obvious how Zoe and Freddie radiated towards each other. It shouldn't matter when he and Zoe were no longer an item, but she'd broken his heart, had seemingly cheated on him when they'd first been together at uni and was now with one of his friends. Had everyone else known? Rhys tried to force down his resentment as a beer was handed to him and the music was turned up.

Almost everyone was gathered on the ground floor of the Georgian townhouse, where the front living room seamlessly transitioned into the kitchen, and the patio doors were thrown open onto the terraced garden. Barnaby had done incredibly well for himself with a house that had to be worth seven figures, its sash windows, striped floorboards and dado rails working beautifully with the modern touches. They must have spent a fortune on builders to renovate it, managing to get the place liveable in a fraction of the time it had taken Rhys to finish his three-bed Victorian terrace. He shouldn't compare himself to Barnaby, not when it would only make him feel even worse about himself.

So Rhys went through the motions of pretending he was having a good time – easy enough to do with copious amounts of alcohol. He drifted between people, chatting absent-mindedly while nursing a beer, making a concerted effort to chat with Fabs's London friends, who didn't know anything about him and his past relationships.

But despite his intentions to not let the truth about Freddie and Zoe get the better of him, Rhys kept catching sight of them. He couldn't tear his eyes away, noticing the way Zoe would laugh at something Freddie said and how she'd throw her head back in a full throaty chuckle. His eyes were drawn to the milky skin of her throat and down to her cleavage, which was pushed up in that little red dress. And the way her hand brushed Freddie's arm – his solid, muscled, gym-honed arm.

A fire burned in his core, intent on flaring up and joining forces with that little jabbing voice in his head that made him want to spit and shout and scream, to release all those feelings of hurt and worthlessness that had been building in the year since Zoe had left. What he needed was closure, which Zoe being with someone else should have given him, but not when she'd moved on with *his friend*. Seeing them so comfortable and perfect together made him question everything, particularly their student years and the lies she must have spun. The fact that

Freddie – one of his closest friends – had been complicit felt like a huge betrayal.

A juddering thought slammed into him: had Fabs known about Freddie and Zoe back then too? Tuning out of the conversation about London politics, Rhys swivelled, feeling dizzy as he searched for Fabs, but there was no sign of him and it was difficult to make out who was chatting together in the fairy-light-lit garden.

He did spot Zoe extracting herself from beneath Freddie's arm and heading towards the kitchen. With his sights on Freddie, Rhys made his move. Gripping the neck of his beer bottle, and fuelled by alcohol and adrenaline, he closed the distance between them.

Freddie noticed him too late to move away and Rhys nearly stumbled into him.

'Are you two going to Sardinia together?' he blurted out, inwardly grimacing that he sounded like a petulant child.

Freddie looked at him warily. 'Yeah, that's why I wanted to give you a heads-up earlier.'

'Out of the goodness of your heart, I suppose,' Rhys said, unable to stop the sarcasm in his voice.

'Well, yeah. What the hell's with the tone, mate?' Freddie shuffled uncomfortably. 'I know this is a bit of a weird situation, what with you being Zoe's ex and all, but—'

'A bit of a weird situation?' Rhys spat back. 'You know I was in love with her.'

The second the words were out of his mouth he regretted them because of the pitying look Freddie gave him. Freddie was everything he wasn't: bolder, fitter, bigger, funnier, more confident. The list went on and on. Of course Zoe would wind up with someone like him.

Acutely aware of everyone else in the room, and realising

that the music wasn't quite loud enough to overpower the conversation, Rhys tried to control his anger. Out of the corner of his eye, he spied Zoe hanging back in the kitchen, watching. He lowered his voice and tried to backtrack. 'It's fine to be with her now, but when we were together at uni? Gareth told me.'

Freddie's eyes widened. 'We fooled around a bit.' He shrugged as if it was nothing. 'I honestly didn't think you two were that serious...'

Rhys saw red. Freddie was spewing lies. All nineteen-year-old Rhys had talked about when he'd first been with Zoe was how wonderful she was. Freddie would have been an idiot to not have known how hard Rhys had fallen for her. And yet he'd happily 'fooled around' with her, while she'd obviously cared so little for him that she'd slept with one of his mates behind his back.

Rhys slammed his bottle on the marble mantlepiece and launched himself at Freddie. Rage thrummed through him as he put his full weight into the punch. His fist connected with Freddie's cheek with a satisfying smack, splitting his lip and sending blood spraying. Pain ricocheted up Rhys's arm and his knuckles burned as he stumbled back.

There were shouts of 'what the hell!' as he charged back towards Freddie, still with a desperate desire to smash his fist over and over into his smugly handsome face.

Zoe was screaming at him to stop. Someone grabbed his arms and wrestled him away. Zoe flashed him a look of loathing before rushing over to Freddie, who was cradling one side of his face.

Rhys struggled against the firm hands holding him back. Hot tears blurred his vision, while rage still smouldered in his heart.

Friends rushed around Freddie and Zoe, casting looks of disappointment and downright disbelief.

'Rhys. Rhys!'

It was Fabs who was gripping his shoulders as he herded him out of the room. In the quiet of the hallway, Rhys caught the worry on his friend's face, mixed with a touch of pity. Rhys's heart dropped. Not only had he made a fool of himself, but he'd made a scene at his best friend's stag do by allowing those lingering feelings for Zoe to get the better of him.

'I'm okay. I'm calm.' He dropped his gaze from Fabs's and wrenched himself away from his grip. 'Did you know, though? About them being together when we were at uni?'

Fabs sighed and beckoned him into the room on the opposite side of the hallway. Rhys reluctantly followed and stood his ground in the middle of Barnaby's book-lined study.

Fabs perched on the armchair next to the fireplace. 'I had my suspicions. I'm sorry, Rhys. Obviously they were both invited to the wedding, but until Freddie said they'd only need one room, I hadn't realised they were together. I wanted to tell you, but Freddie asked me not to. He said he wanted to tell you himself; I just didn't realise he was going to wait until tonight.' He folded his arms. 'I should have said something. I knew how much you liked her.'

'And now I know how little she thought about me.' His head swam with regret as much as drunkenness. 'I'm sorry for causing a scene.'

'You don't have to apologise for that.' Fabs adjusted his Rolex and stood up, looking at him firmly. 'Zoe and Freddie are friends, but you're my best friend, Rhys. If anyone's to blame, it's them for telling you about their relationship at the worst possible time. I absolutely should have said something, about them being together now, and my suspicions about them when we were at uni.'

Rhys grunted. 'It wouldn't have made a difference. I was

besotted with Zoe at nineteen. I'd have probably hated you for telling me something I would have refused to believe.'

'Well, for what it's worth, I'm sorry for not speaking up.' Fabs clapped his hand on his shoulder. 'You okay?'

Rhys nodded despite feeling as if his emotions had been dissected. 'I'm gonna go home. Not sure I want to face everyone right now.'

* * *

Rhys never liked getting back to an empty house, but as he staggered in that night, chased by a feeling of shame and leftover rage, he hated it. The whole situation was a mess and he was annoyed with himself for the way he'd handled it, making a spectacle of himself while coming across as the bad guy because of his reaction.

He stood in the dark, quiet hallway. He'd love to get a dog, but knew it wouldn't be fair when he was out five days a week working a long school day. What was the point if he had to get someone else to take them for a walk and keep them company? His sabbatical was only temporary and in a year's time he'd be back to the grind. Not that he felt that way about his job necessarily, it was just how he felt about everything right now, going through the motions of life listlessly, like he was drifting with no clear direction, no idea of what he wanted or how he really felt. That was why he needed some time out. Being snappy and stressed with his classroom of kids wasn't fair on them and had left him with so much guilt he'd decided drastic action was needed.

But tonight, drowning his sorrows had definitely not been a good idea, and the truth about Freddie and Zoe had knocked him sideways. Why had Zoe rekindled their relationship years later, only to wind up with Freddie? He should be relieved that he was no longer with her – he'd put in all the effort, and for what? For her to have played him for years; for her to have lied to him from the very start. She and Freddie had just proved that he was better off without her. Why then did he feel incapable of finding or deserving love?

4

On an overcast day in mid-September, four weeks after the hen weekend, Lola put her out-of-office on and shut down her laptop. Less than an hour later, she was on her way to Heathrow. She loved her job, but bar the hen weekend in Cornwall and a fleeting visit to her parents over Easter, she hadn't taken time off all year. Surrounded by music and interesting people on a daily basis, the distraction of work had been positive, and she'd jumped at every opportunity to get away from London. The thought of a ten-day holiday to Sardinia, culminating in Mirabel's wedding, was incredibly appealing.

Lola knew how much planning had gone into the wedding, because it was pretty much all Mirabel had talked about for the last year. Not that she blamed her. If she was getting hitched to a kind and wonderful man like Fabs, then she wouldn't stop talking about it either. Although she'd also seen Mirabel's stress levels increasing over the last few months. The hen do had been the last time she'd actually seen her relax before they'd returned to London and Mirabel had frantically wrapped things up at work and handed over to her successor, ending a whole chapter of her life, something which had added yet more worry, anticipation and nervousness to an already emotional time.

Jittery nerves started fooling about in Lola's stomach the moment the plane touched down with the lightest of bumps on the tarmac at Olbia Costa Smeralda Airport. Even with Deni next to her, it didn't stop the worry gnawing away that she was about to spend a large chunk of time with a whole load of Fabs and Mirabel's friends and family that she didn't know.

There was excitement too – Deni's own excitement was off the scale. For a workaholic, she was fully embracing this time away in Sardinia and, until her equally workaholic husband joined them for the wedding, Lola was enjoying having her friend to herself.

'I've needed this so badly,' Deni said when they were in a taxi heading up the Costa Smeralda coast towards the guest villa, which was located across the bay from where Fabs's family lived in luxurious Porto Rotondo, with its celebrity mansions and stylish marina. 'I think you do too.'

'Need what?'

'Some downtime, to recharge. Destress. You were quieter than usual on the hen weekend. Is everything okay?'

'Just tired, that's all. And in desperate need of a holiday.'

They fell silent, Deni obviously understanding that Lola didn't want to be pushed on the subject. Both of them were content to gaze out of the window at the island zipping by. Lola caught glimpses of the sea and the glinting white of yachts through the gaps along the bush-lined road.

The message she'd received from Jarek on the hen weekend had knocked her sideways. She'd blocked the number but had remained on tenterhooks every time a message had popped on to her phone since. She hadn't told anyone about it, not Deni, not even Mirabel. She knew pretending that he wasn't still trying to mess with her head was futile, and she hoped that he'd get fed up if she didn't reply. If she didn't react. Perhaps that was his intention, to still make her think and worry about him months after they'd separated.

With Mirabel and her family staying with Fabs at his parents' house, it was just the Brits in Villa Capparis, which came with its own chef, waiting staff and a skipper for the speedboat that was moored on the private dock.

Lola had seen her fair share of exclusive locations and enviable homes as part of her job at Rhythm – a hugely successful record label where she was a PR manager for a roster of pop stars and bands. Photo shoots often took place in iconic London buildings or stately homes, and there were parties at VIP clubs or multi-million-pound pads, but as they drove through the gates of Villa Capparis, she was stunned by the beauty of the sprawling single-storey villa nestled within a tree-filled garden that burst with the colour and fragrance of myrtle, helichrysum and purple bougainvillea. The reality of what Mirabel was marrying into became apparent.

With its high ceilings and clean lines, hidden reading nooks and a colour palette of cream and yellow with the cooler touches of white and blue, Lola loved everything about the villa. The whole place had an indoor/outdoor feel, with views of the colourful garden from every direction to the sea beyond, each outdoor seating space either shaded by a reed-thatched pergola or enclosed within the textured pale-salmon stone walls.

Yet despite her delight about where they were staying, by the time everyone had been shown to their rooms to freshen up, Lola was a bundle of nerves. She met new people every day at work and was a pro at making small talk when so much of her job involved organising events, liaising with radio and TV producers and negotiating publicity opportunities, but she was grateful for Deni and Sarah as they all met back in the central living area, her friends bolstering her even if they didn't realise it.

Fabs and Mirabel introduced everyone, although Lola was certain she wouldn't remember their names until they all got to know one another. The biggest friendship group was Fabs's university mates: four blokes in their early thirties, along with a pretty, dark-haired, pale-skinned woman. It didn't take long for one of the guys to make a beeline for her. Introducing himself in a strong Welsh accent as Gareth, he did all the talking and came across as confident but slightly cocky, and Lola was relieved when she received a message from Polly and she could use it as an excuse to retreat to her room.

Polly was missing out, and Lola really felt for her. She'd sent numerous messages about how miffed she was to be at home looking after the kids and juggling work, her latest stating in no uncertain terms:

> Don't you dare send pics of how incredibly gorgeous the place is. I'll see it next week for myself, but OMG that feels like forever. Jealous as hell! Love you all though x

Smiling, Lola thumbed a quick reply – without any photos attached – then turned her attention to her room, where the cool, summer-living vibe of the rest of the villa continued, with white walls, seascape artwork and blue and white bedlinen. She opened the patio door onto a private terrace edged by a stone wall covered in pink flowers, breathed in the citrusy scent of bergamot, then set about unpacking.

Twenty minutes later, once everything had been put away, a knock on the door made her turn.

'Hey,' Mirabel said, strolling in. 'I'll be heading back to the house with Fabs in a bit to help prepare for tonight. You got time for a walk?'

'Of course.'

They stepped onto the terrace and linked arms. The garden was bathed in sunshine and the trees cast long shadows across the lawn. Through the slender trunks of the pine trees, she spied the clearest, brightest blue water she'd ever seen.

'This place is insane,' Lola said at the jaw-dropping surroundings.

'And it's just one of the properties they own, not to mention the winery.'

'You and Fabs will inherit quite a portfolio one day.'

'He's always been wealthy,' Mirabel said softly as they cut across the spongy lawn towards the wooded edge of the garden. 'We were comfortable when I was growing up – probably even well off, but how Fabs grew up is a whole different world. Their attitude to money is too. To not have to worry about how you're going to afford something is an absolute privilege.'

They reached the furthest part of the garden and Mirabel took a well-worn path that wound beneath the trees. The sandy, pine-needle-strewn ground dampened their footsteps, and only their conversation about Fabs and his family disturbed the birdsong and the lap of the waves on the stony shore just metres away.

The beach, a narrow crescent of sand and fine shingle with a private jetty at one end where the villa's speedboat was moored, was empty and could only be accessed from the villa or by boat. A pine forest screened another couple of villas further down the shore, so they had the spot to themselves.

Following Mirabel's lead, Lola kicked off her sandals and picked her way through the shallows, the water as warm as a hot tub. They perched on a smooth sun-blasted rock and let their feet dangle in the clear water.

'I have no words.' Lola gazed across the shimmering water to the bay opposite, where the island curved round in an inlet and other villas and hotels studded the gentle slopes of a hillside.

'All of the places they rent out are incredible, but this one's special. I like the privacy and peace. Lots of space for everyone to have time to themselves. And given what happened on the stag do, it's probably just as well everyone can escape if they want to.' Mirabel placed her hand on Lola's arm, her pink manicured nails gleaming in the sunshine. 'And at least you'll have a room to yourself until Polly arrives. I hope you don't mind sharing with her for a couple of days?'

'Of course not. It's just a shame she can't come out for the whole time; although with two kids I understand she can't just swan off to Sardinia on her own.'

'However much she'd like to.'

'Deni's living her best life.' Lola smiled and stretched out her legs. She watched the water ripple around her toes. 'She's such a workaholic. Honestly, the deadlines she's had recently and the stress – makes me glad I pursued the PR side of the music industry rather than having to deal with contracts and negotiations. It's good to see her relaxed for once.' She glanced sideways at Mirabel. 'You seem a little stressed, though. How are you feeling?'

Mirabel rested her hands on the rock and leaned back. 'Overwhelmed.'

'It's to be expected though, isn't it? A big wedding in another country; there are so many of us out here to entertain before the big day. It's a lot. I was feeling nervous on the journey over, so I can only imagine how you're feeling.'

'What are you nervous about?' Mirabel squeezed her hand. 'It's not like you.'

'It's just me being silly. Everything feels more of an effort since Jarek.' His name was bitter on her tongue. She hated talking about him, loathed even thinking about him, but his influence still wove through her life. He'd dented her confidence so much that she found herself getting wound up about things that never used to bother her. 'But my worry is nothing. Yours is understandable, but I'm sure it won't last. Hopefully, things will settle down after today. With everyone arriving and the welcome party tonight, there's a lot going on. Hold on to the thought that in eight days you'll be marrying Fabs and becoming Mrs Mirabel Serra in a dream wedding on Sardinia! It's pretty special.'

'Yes, it is.' Mirabel sighed. 'My thinking was why on earth would we get married in the UK when Sardinia was an option. It's where Fabs's family's from, it's where we're going to settle and hopefully start a family.' She shrugged.

'I feel there's a but coming.'

Mirabel shot her a resigned look that was matched by another tired sigh. 'My mum's not happy not being in control and, admittedly, I'm not either. I thought it was a gift to begin with. It took the pressure off my parents having to spend money on a wedding they absolutely can't afford, but everything's run away from me. Being busy in London with work while planning a wedding in another country has been exhausting and I've found myself allowing Giada more and more leeway. You already know this – I've been gassing on to you endlessly about all the things we've been juggling. We set a budget and were firm about it, but I've discovered from Fabs that his mamma's gone way above it, insisting that she's paying for anything that went beyond our limit, but of course it now feels as if I have to do things her way because she and Lorenzo are forking out for so much. Knowing my mum and dad are feeling shit about it is stressing me out. And of course we're all staying at theirs. With so many days to go until the wedding, it doesn't bode well that tempers won't ignite.'

'Wowsers.' Lola leaned back and looked at her friend.

Mirabel gave an empty laugh. 'Do you think I'm mad for feeling like this? When I should be insanely grateful to have such generous parents-in-law-to-be? And, to be fair, they've taken a lot of the work out of my hands.'

'No, I don't think you're mad. And isn't it a known thing that moving house, getting married and having children are the three most stressful things anyone can do? You're doing two of them – getting married, plus winding up your life in the UK to move to Italy. That's huge. Even if these are actually good things, I don't think it would be normal to *not* feel overwhelmed.'

'I do wonder if we're making a mistake having a big showy wedding; perhaps we should have eloped, just the two of us.'

Lola fixed her with a no-nonsense look. 'I've seen the photos of where you're getting married; yes, it might be a big wedding, but it's in a beautiful and understated place. Whatever you think about your mother-in-law taking over, it was yours and Fabs's choice to strip things back to what's important somewhere that's not actually glitzy at all. I promise, your personality and influence is all over this wedding.'

Il Giardino, the location for the nuptials, was a destination in itself and had solely been chosen by Fabs and Mirabel. A spacious creative retreat and hotel with a myriad of bars, restaurants and outdoor dining, it was a far cry from the seductive white-sand beaches and secret coves along the coast. Instead, it was nestled in the forested foothills of the majestic Supramonte mountain range. Lola had spent many an evening after work poring over photos and working out the details with Mirabel.

'You're right of course.' Mirabel knocked her shoulder against Lola's. 'And I know getting married here is the stuff of dreams.'

'And Fabs is your dream man too.'

'A few of his friends are rather eligible bachelors, you know. You can forget about arsehole ex-boyfriends when there are a whole host of gorgeous Italians.'

Lola shot her a look.

Mirabel held up her hands. 'I know, I know! You don't have to remind me about what happened at the last wedding. That's still not going to stop the girls from eyeing up potential matches for you.'

'Gives them something to do, I suppose.' Lola laughed it off, but inwardly she groaned. The last thing she wanted was her friends meddling again and trying to set her up with someone, particularly when one of Fabs's friends had already tried chatting her up.

'You have to be open to trusting someone again.' Mirabel tugged Lola close. 'Not every bloke is a controlling, narcissistic bastard.'

Lola gulped down a wave of sadness as she gazed across the bay to the hill opposite, where the terracotta and white of the buildings broke up the green. 'What if I'm never ready? What if I continue to go for men who are unsuitable and at worst awful people? What the hell does that say about me for falling for someone like that? For not seeing the truth.'

'It says way more about them than it does about you.'

'Yeah maybe, but it still suggests that I'm too trusting, which is why I don't feel I'll ever wholly be able to give my heart to someone again.'

'But you did see through his behaviour and you got out, that's what you should focus on.' She drifted her hand towards the view in front of them, the sizeable diamond on her engagement ring glinting in the sunshine. 'Moving on, even if it's just physically with someone, can only be a good thing.'

'Which is what I attempted to do with Dax at the wedding in May, but you know what a disaster that was.'

'Well, perhaps you'll have more luck here.' She grinned and tucked a tendril of chestnut hair behind her ear. 'Just don't let him or those experiences stop you from having fun.'

'You mean the girls having fun at my expense.'

'I really don't mean that.' She squeezed Lola's arm tighter. 'I know what you've been through, they don't fully understand and unless you open up to them, they never will. But we're here on Sardinia, one of the most beautiful places in the world in my opinion, so try to forget about the past. Use the time to heal and have some fun – no strings attached. Enjoy the here and now.' She gestured in front of them. 'I mean, just look at this place.'

Lola smiled as she gazed out at the calm water, a glistening blue merging to turquoise further out where a line of white speedboats were tethered in pairs to red buoys. The sun's warmth caressed her shoulders and as she wiggled her toes beneath the water, she felt refreshed and hopeful.

'I guess you're right.'

'Of course I'm right!'

'And apart from being here for your wedding, I need a holiday.' Lola repeated the sentiment she'd shared with Deni in the taxi earlier.

'Those jangling nerves are first-day ones,' Mirabel said. 'I'm sure it's the same for everyone, because I feel that way too. We'll meet each other properly this evening and all will be good, I promise.'

5

Rhys reasoned that having Freddie and Zoe parade themselves and their love for each other in his face for the next ten days would result in one of two things: either they'd end up having another fight or he'd loathe the sight of them so much that any reminder of what he once had with Zoe would be quashed. Freddie and Zoe were welcome to each other, but it was hard to ignore how a friend could have behaved that way. While he was desperate to put the whole mortifying situation behind him, he still wanted to punch Freddie again – but perhaps less publicly. Actually, no good would come of violence, least of all for him. His hand had throbbed for days after the stag do, the discomfort equal to the regret he'd felt.

What irked him most was their timing. They could have told him months ago, they could have warned him – his other friends could have too. They could have been honest about their sordid history and that Zoe had cheated on him, but then what would have happened? Would he not have gone on the stag do? Or come to Sardinia? Fabs was his best mate; there was no way he'd have let him down, so what difference would it really have made if he had been pre-warned?

Those troubling thoughts had kept him company throughout the journey and on their arrival in Sardinia. It had been a whirlwind of new people at the villa and he was grateful to have a room of his own to escape to. The names and faces of Mirabel's friends were still a muddle, but they'd each made an impression, particularly Mirabel's best friend Lola, who was strikingly beautiful – she'd definitely caught Gareth's eye; he'd made a play for her the moment everyone had started mingling. The friend she'd arrived with was older, then there was the other friend – Sarah, he thought she was called – who was loud, funny and happy to steal all the attention.

After refreshments on the terrace, they were transferred across the bay in the villa's speedboat to Fabs's family's sprawling home, Villa Sereno, which lived up to its name with an idyllic setting overlooking the Tyrrhenian Sea.

Having spent two summers in Sardinia with Fabs while they'd been at university, learning a smattering of Italian and getting to know Fabs's family and friends, Rhys was grateful for that connection now. Those relationships enabled him to avoid his own friends as he caught up with Fabs's eldest sister Lia and her husband. He couldn't help but notice that Mirabel's friend Lola, with her blonde hair and eye-catching dress, had attracted not just Gareth's attention, but Valentino's too. He was one of Fabs's childhood friends and had moved away from Sardinia to pursue a modelling career in Rome.

After Lia was drawn into a conversation with someone else, Rhys's panic about being on his own was short-lived when Fabs slid an arm across his shoulders and popped a fresh bottle of beer in his hand. 'Sorry I didn't get a chance to spend much time with you earlier.' He swept his hand towards the friends and family mingling on the terrace. 'How you holding up?'

Rhys tried not to roll his eyes. 'Don't worry; I'm not going to do anything stupid.'

'That's not what I meant. And what happened on my stag do was because you'd had no warning. It was a shock.' He led him away from the terrace towards the lawn, where the swimming pool glowed aquamarine in the fading light. 'I keep thinking I should have told them not to come—'

'They're your friends. They have as much right to be here as I do. It's my shit to deal with, Fabs.'

'I'm just sorry they upset you the way they have.'

'Hey, *you* don't need to apologise.' He swigged his beer and stared across the pool to the shadowed bushes edging the garden and the dark sea beyond. 'They sure as hell haven't.'

Fabs pursed his lips and gave a chuffed agreement. He folded his arms across his chest. He was only a little taller than Rhys, yet he filled the space more – not because of his defined muscles, but his presence. He was someone everyone noticed when he walked into a room.

'You can always stay here with us, if it'll help?' Fabs finally said.

Rhys swigged his beer. 'Running away isn't the answer.'

'I know, but if it gets too much, it's an option.'

Rhys nodded a thank you and fought back a wave of upset, not just at his friend's thoughtfulness, but at being singled out as the one who needed looking out for. He appreciated Fabs's kindness, but hated how he was being seen as the vulnerable friend.

'By the way, Mamma's been looking for you,' Fabs said with a smile. 'She was busy organising the caterers when you arrived.'

They strolled back across the lawn. Fabs's parents, Giada and Lorenzo, were epic hosts and had an effortless way of enter-

The Island of Hopes and Dreams 43

taining their guests. Rhys knew from experience that they'd be in their element with a house full of people.

Giada caught sight of them and clipped across the paving in her heels. She'd barely changed in the fifteen years since Rhys had first met her, and on the cusp of her seventies, she was still beautiful. She looked chic in an elegant belted black dress with gold accessories and had the same sleek bobbed hairstyle, her silver hair framing olive skin and chocolate eyes.

'Rhys, I have missed you!' Giada took hold of his face and lightly kissed him on each cheek. 'Why have you not come to visit us? Fabrizio say he invite you. You must come!'

'I'm here now.' He smiled warmly but that didn't stop the rush of regret for not coming back sooner when Fabs had asked him on more than one occasion.

Giada was as warm and sociable as his mum was reserved and quiet. Spending time with Fabs's family had taken some getting used to because their lifestyle was so different to how he'd grown up, and it wasn't just because they had money, but because they thrived on company and entertaining. In Rhys's own family, it had only been the arrival of grandchildren that had injected a much-needed dose of fun into his parents' lives and made them more sociable and outgoing. His two older brothers lived the sort of busy, warm and fulfilling lives with their partners that Rhys craved.

Giada leaned in conspiratorially. 'Ah, but I want you to myself for a bit. Feed you up. Look after you.' She looked at him pointedly. 'I hear what happened at the bachelor party. I do not know this Freddie well, but tsk.' She brushed away a non-existent speck from the sleeve of her dress. 'We have no drama here, *sì*?'

'You don't need to worry about that.' His cheeks flushed hot at the intensity of her gaze. 'I will be keeping my head down and out of trouble.'

'But you must also have fun!' She steered him towards the table on the terrace which was laid out with an array of mouth-watering cheeses, pork charcuterie, bread and salads. 'You seem sad. From the little Fabrizio say, I understand maybe why. I want you to be happy like you used to be when you were here. Full of life, making everyone laugh. We loved having you stay.'

He never thought of himself that way, so he should have been pleased, but her words cut deep because she had sensed his underlying sorrow.

Giada was whisked away by her husband to be introduced to someone, and Rhys found himself on his own. He helped himself to a plate of food and lingered at the edge of the terrace. He was avoiding Freddie and Zoe as much as they were avoiding him; Fabs and Mirabel were busy flitting between people; he didn't particularly want to talk to Gareth, while Barnaby seemed to be having no problem confidently chatting to anyone. He knew he should make an effort to talk to Mirabel's friends, but they were laughing with Valentino and another Italian and Rhys didn't want to interrupt. Instead, he retreated inside to the living room and pretended to study an impressionist painting of trees by a contemporary Italian artist while he ate his food.

Rhys felt out of his depth, while the guilt of punching Freddie at the stag do still swirled around his head. He would love to be able to relive that evening and behave in a completely different way. Instead of admitting to Freddie how much he'd once loved Zoe, he wished he'd been cool about them being together, to have told Freddie calmly what a dick he'd been to have messed about with Zoe behind his back rather than having acted on his rage. Even people who weren't there knew about it.

Of course, the story of the stag do had been relayed to Mirabel and would have filtered through to her friends. His track record with women was abysmal. Zoe might have been his ex-girlfriend but she had also been a friend. Freddie too. That was what hurt the most.

Slipping outside, he discarded his empty plate and skirted the terrace, where conversations competed in English and Italian. A sudden waft of jasmine reminded him of the carefree summers he'd had here with Fabs, sleeping and swimming and enjoying leisurely lunches, then heading out for an evening of drinking and pulling women – an activity that had been ridiculously easy to do alongside Fabs.

The wooden walkway that led to the jetty was reached through the gate at the end of the garden. The house had no beach, but the rocky shore could be crossed via the walkway and he and Fabs had spent hours there sunbathing and diving into the water or sitting on the end of the jetty with their legs dangling in the sea, sharing a bottle of wine while chatting, laughing and making plans. He missed those days when they'd both been single and were young enough for life to not have worn them down.

Worn me *down*, he thought. Fabs was doing just fine.

He reached the end of the jetty and sat down. The water sloshed back and forth against the wooden uprights, just touching the soles of his shoes. He ran his fingers across the rough wood boards and listened to the distant laughter and chatter drifting into the night. The feeling of uncertainty, worry and worthlessness had been instigated by Zoe walking out, and the truth about her relationship with Freddie had brought all that negativity flooding back. That was pretty sobering when he'd tried so hard to get over her and the purpose of his sabbatical was a fresh start. Now, stuck on Sardinia with Zoe for the next ten days, was he really going to allow her to continue to dictate his feelings?

6

There was a lightness to Lola's step as she followed the path that skirted the lawn, her attention on the vast sea that was shrouded in darkness beyond the bushes, trees and solar lights that edged the garden. A bank of clouds clustering on the horizon blocked out the moonlight, and once Lola had passed the garden gate, there was little light apart from a faint silver-grey catching the rippling sea.

The wooden walkway was narrow, cutting across the rocks and jutting over the water into the darkness. It should have felt eerie, but Lola was relieved to finally be away from the constant attention. Her sandals were soft and silent against the scuffed wooden boards and she was glad she'd swapped her heels for them at the last minute.

The clouds were drifting, the wind curling in off the sea a welcome respite to the heat inside the villa; even outside on the terrace, it had been a riot of noise and colour, with flaming torches, heaps of food and people everywhere. It was good to breathe easy and take a moment for herself.

Lola stopped. Now the clouds had shifted, a figure was

visible sitting at the end of the jetty, a silhouette against the moonlit sky.

The figure turned and muttered 'shit', his hand flying to his chest.

'Oh sorry, I didn't see you there.' Lola began to retreat.

'You needed to escape too?' The man's deep voice, with a hint of a Welsh accent, carried towards her.

'Something like that.' Lola turned back. 'Actually, escape is the perfect word. I just needed a bit of time to myself.'

'I can leave you if you want to be on your own.'

'No need. Company's fine if you don't mind me joining you. I just had to get away from my friends.' Lola strolled the short distance to the end of the jetty and sat down next to him. 'That sounds bloody awful, doesn't it. They have a tendency to meddle in things – good-naturedly – but my non-existent love life is their focus and I'm so done with that.' She silently cursed at having revealed more than she'd meant to. 'Sorry, you didn't need to know all that, particularly when we haven't met properly – I know we were all introduced earlier, but it was hard to remember everyone's name. I'm Lola.'

'Rhys.' He stuck his hand out and she shook it.

'Ah, you're a teacher, right? And one of Fabs's friends from university?'

'Yes, we met on the first day and hit it off despite coming from very different backgrounds.' Rhys motioned towards the villa behind them.

'Yeah, I know, it's hard to believe some people are lucky enough to live like this.'

'And to grow up here.'

'Sheesh.' Lola sighed. 'Beats my family's two-bed cottage in Devon.'

'Snap. Although ours was a three-bed terrace in Caerphilly.'

Lola laughed. 'Don't you go showing off with your posh three bedrooms, now.'

Rhys smiled and it lit up his face. She couldn't make out the colour of his eyes in the dark, but he was attractive, in a subtle kind of way. She hadn't really noticed him earlier, because he'd been quiet, fading into the shadows next to Fabs, who was arrestingly handsome and confident. And of course there was Gareth, who'd made it blatantly clear he fancied her. There was another British guy who'd been in-your-face loud and had stolen her attention for all the wrong reasons. A couple of Fabs's Italian friends were typically dark and handsome, and she'd noticed, particularly Valentino, who had been far from shy in his full-on approach. But Rhys was quiet and reserved. He had dark hair, an attractive amount of facial hair and a tall slender build. He wasn't a muscle-bound gym-nut like her usual choice. Friend rather than boyfriend material.

'You grew up in Devon then?' Rhys asked.

'Yes, just me and my mum and dad in a cluttered cottage with loads of land. Dad grew his own veg and Mum was creative – she used to upcycle everything, paint badly but passionately and make all my clothes till I was a teenager and rebelled.'

'Ha! It kinda sounds idyllic,' Rhys said with amused uncertainty.

'I suppose it was in many ways.' Lola flicked away the hair that was stuck to her forehead and tilted her face upwards in the hope of catching a breeze. 'I had a lot of freedom to roam. We were walking distance from the sea and a drive away from Bude. I loved being down on the beach and spent long days exploring. Even so, I couldn't wait to get away.'

'And you moved to?'

'London.'

'You couldn't really get much different!'

'That was the point.' Lola pulled the material of her dress away from the sticky heat of her back. 'What about you moving away from Wales to, I presume, Bristol?'

'I couldn't wait to have some independence. I'm the youngest of three and longed to have my own space and the freedom to do what I wanted. Not that I ever craved city living, but I wanted excitement and that student lifestyle.' He sighed as if remembering those good times. He glanced at her. 'I presume that's how you know Mirabel, then, from London?'

'Yeah, we work together.'

'You're in the music biz too?'

Lola nodded. 'A PR manager at the same record label.'

'Until Mirabel permanently moves out here.'

'Don't remind me.' Lola wrinkled her nose. 'I'm trying to forget she's leaving. I'm going to miss her so much.'

'It's an exciting time for her and Fabs.'

'It certainly is.' Lola stared at the dark shimmering sea, the only light coming from the moon and the lights glinting across the bay where the island curved.

Mirabel was starting a whole new chapter, on an adventure with the love of her life, and what a place to live. Lola had barely seen any of it yet, but Sardinia promised a laid-back lifestyle of white-sand beaches and sun-kissed living. She wasn't jealous – well, no more than any normal person would be – but she did feel as if she was losing out on more than her friend moving away. Perhaps it shone a light on Lola's own life. She'd never experienced the kind of loving and supportive relationship Mirabel had with Fabs; she'd never been in love with someone she'd considered to be her best friend. What Mirabel had found was what Lola had missed out on – being loved for who she was.

The silence dragged. The heat was oppressive, but it was a little fresher by the water. The only sound was the slap of the sea against the jetty and the distant music from the party dancing on the night air. Laughter cut through the stillness.

Rhys cleared his throat. 'What you said before about your friends meddling, it's happened before?'

'Oh yes, with disastrous consequences.' She rested back on her hands, leaning on the sand-scuffed boards, and appraised him. 'You mean you haven't heard the story about what I got up to at the wedding I went to earlier this year that I will *never* live down?'

'No, can't say I have.'

'Well, that's refreshing.'

'Are you going to tell me?'

Lola laughed. 'Oh, you actually want to know!'

'Um, yes. You can't tease me about a story you're never going to live down, then not give me the juicy details.'

'It's pretty gross, so don't say I didn't warn you.'

'Now you've managed to intrigue me even more.'

Lola crossed her legs and leaned her elbows on her knees. Salt spray dampened her skin. 'My friends, who are all determined to find me a guy, sort of set me up with another poor sod of a singleton at this wedding and we spent most of the day together because we were the only two without plus-ones. We chatted, we drank – a lot – and flirted. Our friends encouraged both the drinking and flirting and it was safe to say we both fancied each other. So, um, later that night, way after the first dance but before the bride and groom were waved off, we took ourselves to a quiet spot outside and made out.'

'Okay.' In the moonlight, Lola caught Rhys's frown. 'Sounds like an unsurprising outcome.'

'Yeah, it was all good up till that point. What you have to remember is that I was *very* drunk and I'd done a lot of travelling to get to the wedding, so it was a mortifying combination of travel sickness and drinking too much after eating food that was way too rich. Because I was sick on him right after kissing him.' Lola put her face in her hands. 'Actually, kissing him was what made me sick.'

'Oh, wow, that is bad.'

'It got worse.'

'What on earth could be worse than that?'

'I'm glad you're finding this amusing.' She pursed her lips, but her own rising giggles made her realise that it was funny as well as mortifying. 'Me being sick made him sick and he puked on my shoes. Let me tell you, diamanté heels with the contents of a three-course dinner all over them is not a good look. Neither is a pale grey suit and white shirt after I'd been drinking red wine. We had the look of horror movie characters nailed. He was annoyed, like out-of-his mind incensed – he'd invited me up to his room to, um, continue somewhere a little more private when I puked. If you're not aware of what the biggest turn-off is, then someone inviting you to "come up to my room for a bit of nookie" followed by being sick on them is it.'

Rhys reined back a laugh. 'And he was really sick because you were sick?'

'Yup, we could have been stuck in a hellish loop of being sick for eternity, but he staggered off, turning the air blue in between retching – I really hope I'm not making you queasy.'

'Nope, I'm good – as long as talking about it isn't going to make you puke all over me?' He leaned away and grinned.

'No risk of that, I promise.' She found herself smiling. 'I've paced myself drinking-wise and the drive from the airport wasn't too long.'

'Well, that's a relief.' He folded his hands in his lap and leaned forward. 'So he stormed off covered in sick. What did you do?'

The Island of Hopes and Dreams

'The key thing to remember is I'd been drinking. A lot. I didn't feel great and I had sick on my new shoes, which was making me feel even queasier, so I went for a wade in the lake.'

'You did what?'

'At the time it made sense – it was the quickest way to save my shoes and my dignity...'

'Except?'

'Except I misplaced my footing—'

'Because you were drunk.'

'Exactly, and when my friends found me, I was arse-first in the water laughing so hard I was crying. My shoes were ruined, my dress was covered in muddy lake water and mascara was running down my face because I'd forgotten to wear waterproof stuff. Who knew I was going to end up crying at a wedding?'

'So that's why your friends won't ever let you live it down.'

'And of course everyone heard the guy's version too, which honestly didn't paint me in a good light at all. Yet despite the nightmare end to the last wedding – at least for me – my friends are still determined to hook me up with someone again.'

'Perhaps they're hoping for a happier outcome this time.'

'I think they're hoping for gossip.'

'And being the centre of attention and talked about is the last thing you want,' Rhys said slowly.

'Bingo,' Lola said. 'I get it. They're all married and trying to live out their single fantasies through me. But other people thinking they know best when it comes to my love life is the last thing I want.'

'Is he here?'

'What, the guy I puked on?' At Rhys's nod, Lola shook her head. 'Fortunately not because he's in a different friendship group to Mirabel. I think I might have put him off going to a wedding for life. I'm pretty certain if he ever laid eyes on me again he'd be sick.'

'At least you made an impression.'

'That's one way to put it!' Lola snorted. 'So that's partly why my friends meddling is frustrating and pissing me off, except I don't want to say anything and make a big deal about it.'

'Which is why you took yourself away from the situation and came out here.'

'Ka-ching. Although this is only the first evening; I can't keep reacting this way.'

'I understand that. Trying to hide your true feelings for fear of upsetting others is exhausting.'

'Ah! I've admitted my sad, embarrassing story. Time to share your reason for escaping.'

Rhys brushed the grains of sand on the wooden boards into the water sloshing against the jetty.

'As you know, Fabs is one of my closest friends and there are a few of us here who all met at uni and stayed great friends ever since. An ex is here too, which wouldn't be too much of a problem if she wasn't here with another of my friends—'

'Oh shit!' Lola swivelled to face him. 'I know who you are! At least I heard the story from the stag do. *You* were involved in the punch-up.'

'I was the one doing the punching.'

He didn't seem the type: a mild-mannered teacher. 'I don't know all the ins and outs, but I'm guessing you had a good reason.'

'Is there ever a good reason to punch someone?' Rhys clenched his jaw. 'I've never done anything like that before, but I was incensed. And drunk—'

'That's never a good combination, as you well know from my vomiting incident.'

The Island of Hopes and Dreams 55

'No, it wasn't and maybe I shouldn't have reacted the way I did because it showed me as the bad guy. I can't say I was happy about Freddie being with Zoe – my ex – but it was the fact I found out she'd cheated on me with him when we'd been together at university that threw me. I flipped.'

'And now you're all here together with you feeling shit about the way you reacted and them parading their relationship in front of your face.' He was in an impossible situation and Lola really felt for him.

'And we're all staying in the same villa together. I know it's a seriously big villa, so it's not as if we're going to be on top of each other all the time – so to speak,' he grimaced, 'but there's no getting away from them. Fabs suggested I could stay with them here, but it's just the family. It wouldn't feel right.'

'And why the hell should you be the one to be treated any differently when you haven't done anything wrong.'

'Except the punch.'

Lola waved her hand. 'I'd have done the same. In fact, there's an ex of mine I'd quite happily do that to…' She trailed off as the thought of Jarek and how he'd treated her came crashing into her head. She didn't need to go spinning off on that; dwelling on his behaviour and how easily she'd been taken in by his lies. She needed to turn her focus to living in the moment and enjoy the experience of being on Sardinia. Focusing on what she had and taking her life into her own hands was what she'd promised herself since leaving him. So why couldn't she do that now? An idea was beginning to form. 'Do you know what we should do.' She slapped her hand on her maxi-dress-covered thigh. 'Team up.'

Rhys's eyebrows furrowed. 'Team up how? I can't erase Freddie and Zoe being here, although maybe I can have a word with your friends, suggest they give you some space, but I'm not sure if that'll help.'

'Team up in the sense of being together. *Pretending* to be together. A fake relationship. Like they do in romance novels and romcoms. We pretend we've hooked up tonight.' Lola turned to face him, the idea growing, along with the possibility that it might actually work to help them both. 'It would show your ex that you don't give a shit that she's here with one of your friends, that you've moved on from her, while it'll get my friends off my back and stop them trying to set me up with whichever Italian takes their fancy. I don't want to make a fool of myself again.'

Rhys nodded slowly, and she could tell he was thinking it through.

'And what do we mean exactly by hook up?'

'We kissed.' Lola shrugged. 'But an epically good kiss, mind, because of course that is how it would be if it had happened for real.' She laughed, although inside she was squirming, wondering if he was thinking she was mad to be suggesting something this crazy. Perhaps he'd laugh in her face and head back to the party to his cheating friend and his ex – he might think that preferable to spending time with a deranged woman.

'That might work,' he said slowly, making her insides less squirmy. 'Although it'd be more convincing if we disappeared for the rest of the night.'

'Make everyone wonder.' Lola grinned. 'I like it!'

'They might notice we're both gone and put two and two together—'

'Which will get the rumour mill going. We're genius at this.'

'So, um, shall we get a taxi back to the villa?'

'For a nightcap and a pretend snog.' Lola stuck out her hand. 'We have a deal.'

Rhys took her hand and shook it firmly. They grinned at each other.

He wasn't a dark and brooding Italian, but he had soulful eyes and was easy to talk to. It would be no hardship to pretend stuff had happened so they could control the narrative. She wanted to be left alone to soak up the sights and experience Sardinia, not think about men or mistakes. Rhys seemed to be on the same page, so they might just have fun, playing the game their way. Perhaps she'd even gain a new friend.

7

Rhys could see why Lola and Mirabel were friends. They had the same sparkling personality and there was something intriguing about them both. The first time he'd met Mirabel, he'd understood why Fabs had fallen for her so hard. As for Lola, she was likeable, upbeat and confident, but her beauty put her way out of his league. Zoe was pretty, but Lola was beautiful in an understated way. Zoe always tried too hard. Okay, perhaps he was being bitter because of the way two of his supposed friends had behaved behind his back. This pact with Lola would give him a barrier to hide behind, plus it would be no hardship to spend time with her; Lola's openness was refreshing and he'd felt at ease chatting to her. He liked talking one on one. He often felt lost and unheard when in social situations. Pretending that something had happened between him and Lola, though, might put them firmly in the limelight, but at least the attention would be turned away from him being alone and heartbroken.

Leaving without saying goodbye and '*grazie*' to Giada and Lorenzo felt brazen, but Lola was right that the two of them disappearing would get the rumour mill going.

He'd called a taxi before they'd left the jetty, then they'd snuck out through the garden, skirting the long way round to avoid the groups of friends spilling onto the lawn in front of the terrace. Lola had nipped inside to grab her bag, then they were in the taxi and zooming the short distance down the coast to Villa Capparis and back to the air con. Hopefully it would be an easy story to sell, that they'd become swept up in the romanticism of the evening and the location, because it was stunning, not just Fabs's family home, but the island itself, a jewel in the Mediterranean.

'It's weird being the only ones here,' Rhys said as they strolled into the empty central living area with its patio doors that opened directly onto the garden.

'I could get used to it.' Lola went over to the bar and rummaged for glasses. She pulled out a bottle of wine from the fridge. 'You like white?'

'I'll have whatever you're having.'

Lola opened the bottle and joined him on one of the cream sofas. She poured two generous glasses of wine and handed him one.

'To our love pact,' she said as they clinked the glasses together. 'Let's give your ex and your bastard friend something to talk about.'

They sipped the wine, and the silence stretched between them. This was what he'd been fearful of earlier – being stuck with someone he didn't know and uncertain what to say. Although they'd spent a good chunk of the evening together and the conversation had flowed. Until now.

But Lola managed to save them from an awkward silence. 'You make stuff out of wood, right? Mirabel said you're pretty nifty. Made them a wooden salad bowl and servers for a wedding present.'

'She told you?'

'She showed me photos.' Lola raised her eyebrows. 'They were stunning. And considering some of their wedding gifts have been eye-wateringly expensive and monstrously flashy, it speaks volumes that your gift is one of Mirabel's favourites.'

She was good at this, chatting easily when they didn't really know each other.

'It's something I love doing, and I wanted to give them a gift that meant something which they would appreciate.'

'You nailed that brief.'

'Woodworking is just a hobby, though.'

'You're talented enough to make a business out of it if you wanted to. You've not thought about it?'

Rhys sipped his wine. 'I've been busy renovating my house. Hand-built my kitchen and bookshelves in the living room. I wouldn't have time to do work for someone else, not with teaching. It's something I do for myself and find relaxing, but I'm currently taking a sabbatical so plan to spend a lot more time on woodworking projects. I spent this summer building a workshop at the bottom of my garden. The idea of turning what I love into a job worries me that it would change the way I feel about it.'

'Slightly different, I know, but music is my passion and I've turned my love for it into a career.' She slipped off her sandals and tucked her bare feet beneath her on the sofa. 'And the same with any job, there are times that aren't so great and I can't hand on heart say I love every minute, but to be surrounded by music every day, listening to new artists, promoting the ones lucky enough to be signed and helping to shape future music – I can't stress enough how lucky I am to earn my living doing something I love. It fuels me if that makes sense?'

'You've turned your dream into reality.' Rhys nodded. 'That's something to be envied.'

'Did you always want to be a teacher?'

'No, not at all. I studied law but swiftly realised it wasn't a line of work I wanted to do for the rest of my life. I volunteered at this craft club for disadvantaged children—' He stopped short and swigged his wine to swallow his sudden discomfort. He was rarely this open or shared so much, but what the hell, there was something about Lola that made him decide to keep talking. 'Something just clicked. I know how corny it sounds, but working with and supporting those kids who got so much out of something so simple all because they didn't have the opportunity to be creative at home – it changed my whole outlook. I decided teaching the next generation was more in keeping with what I wanted to do and my values. I saw first-hand the impact I could have on someone's life. It gave me purpose too.'

He glanced at Lola to find her studying him with an openness and warmth that made him feel seen.

'That's quite a U-turn but incredible that it led you to a career that has such an impact on others. Working in the music industry pales in comparison when you're guiding children to a bright future.'

'You make me sound far worthier than I am.'

Lola playfully slapped his arm. 'You're underselling yourself.'

Rhys shrugged and decided to steer the conversation in a different direction. 'Obviously you work in the music industry, but are you a musician as well?'

'I play piano and guitar, and in school I had violin and singing lessons, but it's listening to music that's my first love. I never desired to be on stage. I'm not a good enough singer or musician to have pursued it as a career, but it's a thrill to be in this line of work.'

'You come across as someone who would excel and be happy on stage.'

Lola laughed and he was struck by just how beautiful she was. 'I'm not as much of a show-off as you may think.'

'Oh, I didn't mean you were a show-off' – he was mortified – 'you just exude confidence.'

'Says the person who stands in front of a classroom of kids on a daily basis – now that to me takes guts and a shedload of confidence.'

'I'm in my comfort zone teaching children. Swap them with adults and, trust me, I'd clam up.'

'Woodwork seems like it's quite a solitary occupation. I'm sensing a theme going on here?' She teased him with a sly smile.

'You got me there.' Rhys returned a grin. He swirled the wine around his glass and relaxed back into the deep sofa. 'What did you get them? For a wedding present, I mean?'

'What can you get a couple who have everything and who asked for nothing?' She smiled warmly. 'If I was as practical and skilled as you, then something along the lines of your gift would have been perfect, but I'm not blessed in that way creatively. What I do know is music and I know Mirabel. I also know how much Fabs loves her, so I put together their perfect playlist and framed the song list. I commissioned an artist friend to make it look good.'

'That's as thoughtful as it gets, Lola.'

Their eyes met and she blushed. 'Mirabel's my best friend.' She shrugged, brushing off the compliment as if it was nothing. She smoothed out the creases in her dress and sat forward. 'I wonder what time everyone will get back? Perhaps we should make ourselves scarce before they return.' She drained the rest of her wine. 'Let's leave the glasses – we can be cagey about it, but there's no harm in letting rumours work in our favour.'

Rhys followed her lead, finishing his wine and leaving his empty glass next to hers on the coffee table.

Lola mussed up the sofa cushions. 'Let them wonder,' she said with a wink. 'Actually, one last thing.' She scooped up her phone from the coffee table, opened up the camera and switched it to selfie mode.

With her arm flung across his shoulder and her head resting in the crook of his neck, he put his arm around her waist. She smelt delicious, a fresh mandarin scent, and her eyes were cornflower blue – he hadn't noticed in the darkness of the jetty.

'Don't look so worried!' She tugged him closer. 'Smile!'

He tried to focus on her rather than himself. He'd been faking being okay for a while to get through the day, but her vivaciousness made him let go of his inhibitions and not concentrate on what he looked like.

As she snapped a handful of photos, Rhys tried not to let his worry show. He wasn't drunk enough and not 100 per cent convinced they were doing the right thing, but he was swept up by her enthusiasm and her magnetic smile.

'There we go. Proof.'

She clicked on the last photo she'd taken and he was struck by how convincing they looked, cosy and happy like they were enjoying each other's company, which he realised they had. At least he had.

They swapped numbers and she sent him the selfie.

'Right,' she said, tucking her phone into her bag. 'I'm going to head to bed before everyone gets back. I'll see you in the morning when we can have some fun.' She spun round on her heel. 'A different kind of fun than we had this evening!' She grinned. 'Night, Rhys.'

'Night, Lola.'

He watched her until she disappeared. Leaving the empty wine glasses on the table as Lola suggested – even though he was itching to clear up after himself – he headed to his room, which was on the opposite side of the villa to hers. Although he'd been put at the other end of the hallway to Freddie and Zoe, they were still too close for his liking and he clenched his fists as he walked past their room. He needed to worry less and care more about the things that mattered, not about a past he couldn't change. He should really take Giada's advice and live a little, have fun. He was in Sardinia, a place that held only happy memories, so he should make more of them. Spending the end of the evening talking to Lola was a good start.

After getting a wash, cleaning his teeth and changing into boxers and a T-shirt, he slipped into bed. He clicked on the photo Lola had sent him. While her eyes danced with mischievousness, all he could see of himself was that his smile didn't reach his eyes – he looked weary, a shadow next to Lola. Would anyone actually believe that a woman as stunning as Lola would wind up with him? Maybe, if they thought they'd both been drunk and stuff had happened without them intending it to. Perhaps he'd let Lola lead in the morning, in case she'd changed her mind.

The idea that the only way he'd feel less alone was to pretend to be with someone punched a hole in his heart. He fisted the sheet and breathed deeply, trying to tell himself to think less negatively about the situation, his go-to reaction. Lola's company had been easy and he'd felt more relaxed chatting to her than he had with anyone for a long time. Perhaps the next few days were looking up. Companionship and her friendship would be welcome. That side of things wouldn't be hard to fake.

8

'Where on earth did you get to last night?' Before Lola reached the table on the terrace that had been laid out for breakfast, Deni steered her into the garden. 'Anything you'd care to share?'

Lola hadn't yet seen Rhys this morning. She had wanted to gauge what he thought about their pretence before being cornered by her friends, but Deni was far too observant.

'I got talking to Rhys and we came back here early and chatted some more,' Lola said smoothly. 'We may have kissed a bit.'

There, it was done, their love pact sealed. And 'may have' was a suggestion of what might have happened rather than an outright lie.

'Rhys?' Deni frowned. 'Fabs's friend, the quiet one?'

'Yep, him.' Lola felt her cheeks flush, although it was through worry about being caught in a fib rather than any embarrassment. Rhys wasn't who had caught her eye last night and Deni undoubtedly knew that if her continuing frown was anything to go by.

'I didn't realise you'd even talked to him.'

'I went out for some air and we got chatting. Yes he's quiet, but he's actually really easy to talk to and interesting.' Now that wasn't a lie.

'And one thing led to another?' Disbelief wrapped around Deni's words matched by a raised eyebrow.

'We were both rather drunk...'

Deni grinned. 'I take it there was no vomiting to put a stop to things this time?'

'A lady never tells.' Lola battered her eyelashes and twirled away back across the sunny lawn. 'But no, nothing untoward.'

There, she'd seeded enough suggestion without denying or confirming anything for Deni to start gossiping, which she knew she would do with relish. She wondered how Rhys would spin things to his friends. She guessed she'd find out soon enough as she and Deni headed back towards the villa and the breakfast table.

A little awkwardness around each other would be expected if everyone believed they'd hooked up. Although the perfect thing about feigning things between them was that she wasn't at all worried about seeing him again. She'd thoroughly enjoyed his company and adored his openness as much as it had been refreshing to chat frankly with him. Pretending stuff had happened between them would make it easy to spend time together, put an end to her friends' matchmaking and keep at bay any potential suitors.

The moment Deni clocked Rhys already sitting at the table with Barnaby and Gareth, she cast a look his way and asked if he'd had a good night, finishing off with an unsubtle wink. Rhys's freckled cheeks flushed crimson. He met Lola's eyes as she sat down opposite and flushed even more, managing to perfectly play into their ruse.

Over the next twenty minutes, people drifted to the table,

and freshly toasted breakfast paninis with spicy calabrese salami, pecorino and cooling red peppers were put in front of them. Lola paid particular attention to Freddie and Zoe, noting how they sat as far away from Rhys as possible, whispering together, with Zoe constantly touching Freddie. Annoyance tugged at her heart on Rhys's behalf at the uncomfortable situation they'd put him in.

It wasn't only Deni who'd noticed their absence the night before; Gareth seemed a little put out and avoided looking at her throughout breakfast. She imagined with Gareth's confidence and flirty nature he was rather annoyed that his friend had managed to pull her. She hoped that Rhys was feeling buoyed by their love pact.

At least with a table full of big characters, there was little time for regret. The conversation was hijacked by Sarah and Gareth, both as confidently loud as each other. Freddie and Deni weren't shy either. Zoe was definitely the quieter half of the couple, but perhaps that had something to do with her ex and her current boyfriend sitting at the same table. Lola wondered if she'd noticed her and Rhys's absence last night, but with Deni's comments in front of two of Rhys's friends, she was certain Zoe would hear about it soon enough. *Good*, she thought as she bit into her panini and focused on the itinerary that had been handed around.

Today they were being taken to one of the most famous beaches on the Costa Smeralda before having dinner back at their villas. There was an overnight trip to the west side of the island the day after, plus meals out and evening get-togethers planned. There were opportunities to explore or relax, whatever they fancied. It was a gift to spend time with her friends on a beautiful island, because life would be different when she headed home. She'd return to London and the job she loved, but there would be a Mirabel-sized hole in her life.

She snatched a look at Rhys sipping his coffee while Barnaby and Freddie were relaying a tale about a disastrous trip to Snowdonia. Despite feeling as if she was balancing on a tightrope when it came to her worries while having to keep up the charade of seeming to be okay, she was determined to enjoy this time away from real life.

* * *

Cala Brandinchi was busy even in September, its narrow strip of white sand dotted with colourful towels and umbrellas. As they strolled towards the centre of the beach, Lola's focus was less on the influx of people and more on the expanse of shallow sea that seemed to stretch to the horizon, rippling turquoise and coral.

When they reached the rows of umbrellas and sun loungers towards the centre of the beach, Deni made a point of plonking herself on a lounger one along from Rhys's while raising her eyebrows and motioning for Lola to sit on the free one next to him. Despite wanting to roll her eyes at her friend's lack of subtlety, it made her smile, and actually she had no problem camping out next to Rhys. She sensed his relief when Freddie and Zoe chose a spot at the furthest end of the group.

When Barnaby, on Rhys's other side, strolled to the water and Deni lay back with her earphones in, Lola shifted on her lounger to face Rhys.

She raised an eyebrow. 'You doing okay?'

'Yeah, it's been a good day so far.' He ran a hand through his hair, while his eyes remained fixed on her face rather than her bikini-clad body. 'Barnaby is mighty impressed that I managed to pull you.'

'See, I said us disappearing would kick-start gossip.'

Rhys leaned closer. 'After breakfast, Gareth said "you and Lola?" and raised his eyebrows. I'm not sure if I should feel hurt that he thinks I'm punching above my weight or smug that he seemed to believe something had happened.'

His cheeks turned an adorable pink at those last words. In the shaft of sunlight between their umbrellas, his eyes were the colour of the sky. He wasn't gym-buff like Freddie or Gareth, but he was trim, his tall frame toned and carrying more defined muscle than she'd been expecting, particularly his arms and shoulders.

'Has it worked, getting your friends off your back?'

Lola wrinkled her nose. 'To some extent, yes, but Deni is like a dog with a bone now and will be ensuring we have as much time together as possible. She's the reason why we're sitting next to each other now. Not that I mind at all,' she said quickly. 'I was just trying to play it cool, you know, teasing out that awkwardness of the night before, helping to stoke the flames about what anyone thinks happened.'

'We let them wonder, eh?'

'Why not have fun with it.' Lola snuggled back on the sun lounger. She trailed her fingers through the warm grains of sand between them. 'At least Gareth's attention is off me now.'

Rhys nodded, but looked as if he was debating whether to say something.

'Because I don't want that sort of attention,' she pressed on. 'Flirting's all well and good, but I'm not up for it right now. All I want is time for myself, with my friends, while getting to know new people – like you' – she flashed him a smile – 'without the complication of who fancies who or friends trying to hook me up with whichever bloke they think is the hottest. Our pretence is perfect for removing all of that while we hopefully become friends.'

'I like that sentiment a lot.'

Lola rested back again and stretched out. She was only half in the shade, and her tanned skin glistened in the sun. Even with so many people littering the beach, the dazzling water lapping the sand just a few steps away was utter bliss. She should close her eyes and soak up the warmth and the rhythmic sound of the sea bubbling back and forth, but instead she turned to Rhys.

'I know you said last night that you're comfortable teaching kids and only think of your woodwork as a hobby, but do you actually like being a teacher?'

'I used to love it. Actually, that's unfair, I still do love parts of it – working with the kids is the best – but I'm worn out. Personal stuff has taken its toll. That's why I'm taking a sabbatical. I need to, oh, I don't know, recharge, get re-motivated. Do something for myself, otherwise I'm doing the kids a disservice.'

'What year do you teach?'

'Currently, year five, so nine- and ten-year-olds who are astute and pick up on moods. It's not something I'm comfortable hiding when it's exhausting to constantly put on a brave face, to try to pretend I'm okay and hold it together.' He glanced at her. 'I've had some mental health struggles this past year.'

'I'm so sorry. That must have been really tough.' Lola nodded. 'I understand about trying to hold it together because I feel like I need to perform when I'm around my friends, particularly those who know me well. It's easier with my job to be sociable and upbeat around strangers – I have to do that whether I'm in the mood or not, going to music biz events because I've got an artist invited and I'm the visible PR person for the label.'

'Sounds intense and a hell of a lot harder than teaching a classroom of kids.'

'Oh, I don't know about that. The idea of standing up in front of thirty kids and trying to control them, let alone teach them anything, would terrify me.' One of the bar staff arrived with her Aperol spritz and she sipped it, thinking how decadent it was to be drinking a cocktail on a weekday afternoon on a Sardinian beach. 'Apart from the woodworking stuff, what else are you planning on doing on your sabbatical?'

'I'm starting off by travelling round Europe. Getting away is my priority—'

A shadow falling over Lola stopped Rhys short. She looked up to find Deni towering over her, grinning at them both. 'Okay if I steal Lola away for a bit?'

Lola turned back to Rhys and met his smiling nod. She winked at him and allowed Deni to pull her to her feet.

'We're going for a swim and you're coming with us.' Deni hooked her arm in Lola's. Sarah joined them as they left the shade of the sun loungers. As they strolled into the gentle surf, Deni nodded her head back towards Rhys. 'You two really do only have eyes for each other!'

'You and Rhys?' Sarah said with raised eyebrows. 'Really? I had money on you winding up with Valentino. Sheesh, is he hot!'

Lola bit back a retort, annoyed that Sarah, as well as one of Rhys's friends, had questioned the likelihood of them winding up together. But then he wasn't her type, at least looks-wise, although he was easy to talk to and a decent bloke, which was the reason she'd made their love pact in the first place.

'Yup, me and Rhys,' she said with confidence, before quickening her pace through the warm shallows.

The water caressed her ankles, while her feet sank into the silky sand. She turned back to see her friends wading after her. Beyond them, Rhys was still sitting in the shade of the umbrella.

She gave him a wave and continued on with Deni and Sarah to Mirabel, Fabs and a couple of his friends. The sea only got a little deeper, but it was refreshing as she dipped beneath it, nothing but blue sky, cerulean water and pale sand dotted with beach-goers surrounding her.

Once the tips of her fingers began to wrinkle, Lola waded back to the beach and sat in the warm shallows to let her hair dry in the sun. Watching Deni, Sarah and Mirabel bobbing about made her heart ache in a way that left her conflicted. Happiness radiated off Mirabel, her smile matched by Deni's. It was good to see Deni enjoying herself when she lived and breathed work. Lola only wished Polly could have been here too. Although she knew ten days was far too long for her to leave her children, she still missed her. Her friends were moving on with their lives and Lola was uncertain where that left her. She was happy with her career and enjoyed living in London for the most part, but something was missing, and it wasn't a man. That was not the answer.

Rhys sitting next to her in the shallows shut down her thoughts.

'You don't want to join them?' she asked.

'I might a little later. When it's cooler.'

She followed his gaze to where Freddie and Zoe were and realised his true reason for not going in.

They sat close enough so their shoulders just brushed. Enough to look comfortable together, as if intimacy wasn't a problem. They gazed out in a companiable silence that was as surprising as it was comfortable.

Freddie and Zoe were making a great show of splashing about together, frequently wrapping their arms around each other. Lola had only met Rhys the day before and knew even less about Freddie and Zoe, but first impressions had told her enough. Not that she completely trusted her gut; she'd been burned before, thinking Jarek was the bee's knees. But Rhys, there was a vulnerability about him and an underlying sadness that suggested how much he was hurting.

She rested her hands back in the damp sand and stretched out her legs, relishing the sensation of the warm water bubbling against her bare skin and the whisper of a breeze taking the edge off the September heat.

Lola couldn't hide her smile when Rhys started lathering on yet more sunscreen. Even though the UK was heading into autumn, summer days would continue on Sardinia for a little longer.

Summertime made Lola happy. Her skin would glisten with sunscreen and she could live in flip-flops with tousled hair. Summer meant long blissful days and hot nights, the fresh scent of cut grass and smoky barbecues, packed pub gardens and delicious fruit cocktails. She'd always been more content in the summer months, even during the times when her life had turned to shit. While growing up, she'd lived for long days on the beach and had loved returning home in the evening exhausted, with salty patterns decorating her sun-kissed skin. The downside to her move to London was missing living by the sea and that outdoor way of life.

As Rhys closed the sunscreen lid and pointed to his pink-tinged shoulders, Lola was certain he felt differently about summer. 'How? Just how are you sitting in this heat not breaking a sweat or getting burnt?'

'I'm a natural beach babe,' she said smoothly.

Rhys hmphed. 'I just get freckles and bitten by mosquitos. I'm definitely not cut out for this time of year. Makes me pale and interesting though, right?'

'Most definitely!'

Rhys leaned back and gazed ahead at the sea. 'I loved staying here when I was younger, but it was not my natural environment. Fabs only needed one day in the sun and he'd wake the next morning looking like a tanned god. I'd emerge a patchwork of insipid white and flaming red. Not a good look. But then I did grow up in Wales, not Sardinia.'

'I lived for the summer and still do, but it's different in London than on the coast. Devon summers seemed so short. It could be really wild the rest of the year with the waves battering the coast. Rather different to somewhere like this.'

'Well, we can make the most of it for the next few days, although with one stipulation.' He scrambled to his feet, held out his hand and pulled her up. 'Right now, we head back into the shade. Trust me, the lobster look is not a good one!'

9

Rhys couldn't have enjoyed Lola's company more if he'd tried. A weight had been lifted and he felt buoyed by her, and the easy way they'd connected made it hard to believe they'd only met twenty-four hours before.

Rhys knew Gareth was pissed off, even if he was trying to hide his annoyance. Not that he had any claim to Lola, and by all accounts he'd wasted no time in chatting up one of Fabs's sister's single friends. Barnaby seemed genuinely pleased for him, but then Barnaby had always been the easy-going, supportive friend.

Lola was more than just a distraction from Freddie and Zoe. Talking to her was effortless, yet he was doubtful that they'd have spent as much time together if it hadn't been for the pact. She had a natural beauty and an assured confidence that was captivating. And yet, despite that, she'd hinted at her own insecurities and struggles.

After a day on the beach, dinner on the terrace was upbeat, with mounds of rich linguine with bottarga and clams brought out by Chef Carlo, served with copious amounts of local wine.

With Mirabel spending the evening with her parents, it was good to have Fabs's company.

Among the big personalities around the table, Lola commanded attention, not because she craved it or was a larger-than-life character, but because her friends – and his, to be fair – were drawn to her. If they hadn't stumbled across each other, she'd have been someone he'd have admired from afar, wishing he could get to know her better, while never plucking up the courage to talk to her.

As if sensing him watching, Lola's eyes slid to his. Instead of looking away because he was embarrassed at having been caught, he played into their pretence and held her gaze. Her blue eyes glinted in the candlelight and her cheeks matched the blush colour of the rosé in her glass. The smile she gave him was warm and conspiratorial and he revelled in the feeling of inclusion it evoked.

Deni didn't miss a trick, flashing him a knowing smile. He glanced away, his cheeks heating.

'Everyone seems to be enjoying themselves.' Fabs topped up their glasses of wine and passed the bottle along the table.

'It's not exactly hard to.' Rhys gestured towards the shadowed garden. Beyond it, the moon reflected on the sea, broken up by the ebony tree trunks. 'I thought you were supposed to be going out with Mirabel and her parents this evening? Not that I'm complaining you're here,' he quickly added.

'There were words. Mirabel's mum is annoyed that Mirabel has been spending so much time with my mamma rather than with her.' Fabs smoothed his fingers over his beard. 'It got tense and Mirabel thought it best if she spent time with them alone.'

'And you're okay with that?'

'Honestly, I'm okay with whatever makes Mirabel happy. It's been a lot, leaving her job combined with all the wedding prep.

You know what Mamma's like – she's used to being in charge and managing people. Not that she's managed Mirabel, but it's been hard for her being in London when the wedding's taking place here.'

Rhys spiralled linguine onto his fork and nodded. 'Lola mentioned something.'

'Ah yes, I heard about what you got up to last night.' Fabs leaned back and assessed him, his expression open, not incredulous like Gareth's had been earlier.

'Yep,' Rhys said smoothly, while trying to hide his discomfort about lying to his friend.

'You and Lola.' Fabs shook his head. 'My best mate and Mirabel's best friend. You couldn't make up how perfect it is.'

Except we are making it up, Rhys thought. He held his tongue though, because despite his unease, the arrangement was perfect. There was no reason anyone would find out they'd been pretending, because once they went home their ruse would simply be put down to a summer fling that had fizzled out. There would be no awkward break-up, no regret or embarrassment if they ever saw each other again. Their pact was perfect on every level. So Rhys went with it, allowing Fabs to believe that romance had blossomed between him and Lola.

'After the shit-head of her ex-boyfriend, she honestly couldn't do better than you.' Fabs clapped a hand on his shoulder. 'I don't know the whole story, only the bits Mirabel's said, but that's why you're good for her. Good for each other,' he said pointedly. 'Lola could definitely do with someone like you in her life.'

A friend, Rhys told himself. *Lola needed a friend.* Yes, she had Mirabel and the others, but she was overwhelmed by their attention. What Rhys could offer was uncomplicated: someone who would listen, who wouldn't interfere or have an opinion about her ex or who she should or shouldn't be with. But most importantly, he realised as Fabs was pulled into a conversation with the rest of the table, Lola's friendship was exactly what he needed.

* * *

Over dinner, Lola watched Rhys and Fabs chatting – the suave Italian next to the unassuming Welshman. Even long distance, the depth of their friendship was apparent and she was glad Rhys had a friend like that. They seemed to be able to pick up from wherever they'd left off. There was no reason why she and Mirabel couldn't do that too.

She took a large gulp of wine. Thinking beyond this week was a bad idea.

'Staring at lover boy?' Deni whispered as she leaned in close.

With a start, Lola realised she had been staring at Rhys. Actually, Rhys *and* Fabs, to be fair, but she'd been thinking about her friend rather than fantasising about Rhys.

'Not that I blame you,' Deni continued. 'This place just screams romance and should be shared with someone who can push all your buttons, if you know what I mean. If I wasn't married, I'd have hooked up with someone too.' She laughed.

'At least Mark can share the romance with you next week.'

'Yeah.' Deni gave such a drawn-out sigh it reminded Lola of the conversation during the hen weekend about their hopes and dreams.

'Have you two talked yet?' Lola swirled the rosé wine around her glass.

'We will do, but we need to find the time to focus on our relationship. Mark works bloody hard but manages a healthy balance. Coming here's made me realise it's not okay to so rarely take a break.' Deni clasped her hands together on the table and twisted her wedding and engagement rings. 'And what the hell are we playing at not spending time with each other beyond an hour before bed or squeezing in a weekend brunch out where we spend half the time on our phones replying to work stuff? I go to the gym, while he plays squash. We're shit at downtime and I'm even shitter at putting the health of my marriage over my goddamn career. Having too much time on my hands has made me evaluate things,' she said wearily. 'It's also made me realise how much I miss him.'

The emotion pouring off Lola's tough-as-nails friend was surprising and moving.

'Sardinia is the perfect place to tell him all of this.'

'Yes it is. And hell will I prove it to him when he gets out here,' she said with a dirty laugh.

Lola spluttered. 'I did not need to know that!'

Deni put a hand on her arm. 'I'm a lot older than you, Lola, perhaps not wiser, and I know you're single right now... well, single-ish.' She knocked her shoulder against Lola's. 'But the next serious relationship you have, promise me you'll make time to not only look after yourself but nurture your relationship too. Follow in Mirabel's footsteps, not mine.'

10

'Oh. My. God. Pinch me, someone! This is the most incredible holiday ever!' Sarah announced after breakfast the next morning. 'To not have needed to organise anything beyond flights and what to pack, I bloody love it! Even though I hate being away from my kids, but now they're older, boy oh boy am I grateful for this.'

Deni linked arms with Sarah as they strolled back towards their rooms to pack an overnight bag. 'And your hubby's getting to spend time with them while you get some much needed R&R. It's a win-win in my book.'

Lola choked back a laugh. 'Although you definitely have the biggest win.'

'Oh, I think so too.' Sarah pulled Lola close so the three of them were walking side by side. 'That's why I'm gutted for Polly. Did you see her message in our chat? Sickness bugs are the worst and to have both kids come down with something at the same time. Ugh.'

'She must be crossing everything that she doesn't catch it,' Deni said.

Lola tightened her hold on Sarah. 'We'll just have to make it extra special when she does get here. Positive thinking, everyone!'

'But right now we get to have a night in Bosa and explore more of the island.' Deni smirked. 'A night away, Lola.'

Lola refrained from rolling her eyes at the not-so-subtle meaning behind Deni's words. 'Every night is a night away.'

Deni batted her free hand in Lola's direction. 'You know what I mean.'

Of course she understood what she meant; that had been her intention. She'd played along, casually flirting with Rhys at the end of last night and then again over breakfast. She'd found herself wanting to talk to him and steal moments together, the pretence surprisingly effortless.

* * *

They would need days, weeks even, to fully explore Sardinia. Lola hadn't appreciated the size of the island until they were being driven across it along roads that weren't for the faint-hearted, to Bosa, a picturesque town of multicoloured houses on the west coast. Not that she could wholeheartedly enjoy the experience when she was feeling distinctly nauseous, having forgotten to take a travel sickness tablet, so she spent much of the two-hour journey with her head resting on Deni's shoulder.

Not only was Hotel Melis owned by close friends of Fabs's family, but it had a different vibe to the laid-back luxury of Villa Capparis. Painted a dirty salmon colour, the townhouse hotel was decorated with wrought-iron balconies that had just enough space for a small table and chairs. Bosa was still touristy, but away from the Costa Smeralda, it felt different being in the heart of a bustling town with cobbled streets and the sunshine slanting between colourful buildings, while the river Temo glistened as it ribboned its way to the sea.

The swish hotel lobby, with its chequered black and white marbled floor and luxurious seating area, was teeming with people, mostly Mirabel and Fabs's families who'd arrived earlier. As Lola strode towards Mirabel with Sarah and Deni, it was immediately apparent that something was going on. Despite the amount of people crammed into the lobby, the hushed muttering took a back seat to the sharp words cracking between Mirabel's mum, Felicity, and Giada.

Deni stopped short of the check-in desk and Lola paused too, tugging on Sarah's sleeve to ensure she didn't continue walking into a situation that had obviously been brewing for a while.

'It is too much,' Felicity hissed at Giada. Her cheeks were flushed and she looked as angry as Lola had ever seen her. 'I suggested weeks ago that Michael and I host a dinner at yours and *pay* for it and you said no, you'd take care of everything, and yet here we are being hosted by *friends of yours*.'

'Which we pay for!' Giada's nostrils flared.

'It's not just about the money!' Felicity shot back. 'It's about us being involved in the decisions and the shape of our daughter's wedding!'

'To our son!'

'Oh boy,' Deni whispered, 'this is all kicking off.'

Lola didn't know what to do to ease the tension, feeling as helpless as Mirabel looked. Dismay showed on Mirabel's dad's face as he shifted from foot to foot. Fabs's dad Lorenzo seemed to be edging backwards, while Fabs's sisters were trying to wrangle their children away from the commotion. Fabs and his two brothers-in-law were nowhere to be seen.

'I just wanted something to be from us,' Felicity pressed on. 'To do something for *our* daughter and son-in-law-to-be. Something special and memorable when all they'll remember is what you did for them.'

'Mum, that's not true—'

'After everything we do, you are ungrateful because of it!' Giada cut Mirabel off, while a sharp flash of her kohled eyes was aimed at Felicity.

Mirabel stared open-mouthed as they circled each other like vultures in the middle of the hotel lobby. Everyone else looked on, transfixed by the argument playing out so publicly.

Giada was impeccably dressed in a form-fitting cream and navy dress with tasteful gold jewellery, effortlessly holding her nerve against a flushed and flustered Felicity in a casual blouse and chinos combo.

Mirabel, looking slight and delicate, stepped between the warring matriarchs.

'Mum,' she said tightly. 'Let's take this somewhere else.'

'I'm finished.' Felicity shrugged off her daughter's hand. 'I just wanted to say my piece, considering I haven't had a say in anything else.'

'Mum...' Mirabel looked on the verge of tears as she stalked after her, only pausing to shake her head at Giada, who clucked her tongue in what sounded very much like a dismissal.

Giada scooped up her handbag, flashed a glare around the lobby that a Roman emperor would have been proud of, then stormed off in the opposite direction.

'Shit,' Deni said as the tense quiet of the lobby returned to a hushed mumble. 'The next couple of days should be interesting.'

Lola tightened her grip on her bag. 'Poor Mirabel witnessing that.'

'And where the hell's Fabs when you need him?' Sarah said.

'He's probably wherever his mamma has stormed off to. I'm sure he'll hear her side of it soon enough.' Lola swung her bag over her shoulder. 'Come on, let's check in and make sure Mirabel's all right.' She made towards the check-in desk.

Deni grabbing her arm made her pause. 'By the way, you don't have to thank me now, but I talked to Mirabel and did a bit of room swapping so you're sharing with Rhys rather than me.'

Lola's heart stilled.

Deni frowned. 'I hope that's okay?'

'Of course it's okay,' Lola said with feigned confidence despite the sinking feeling that any attempt to challenge what Deni had done would likely unravel her and Rhys's pretence.

'Gareth has been doing a bit of rearranging as well – quite a lot of hooking up happened those first couple of nights!' She leaned in conspiratorially. 'I figured it was only fair you and Rhys got the benefit too.'

11

While Mirabel spent the afternoon with her parents, Fabs took the rest of them a short way along the coast to Cane Malu, a tidal pool that had been gouged and shaped within the pale volcanic rock over thousands of years by stormy seas and rough winds.

The rock reminded Lola of a huge pumice stone pitted with holes, its rounded sides smoothing down to the pool of rippling turquoise and sea-green water. Fabs had told them that when the wind whipped up and the waves crashed over, it was impossible to dive in, but that wasn't the case today. Freddie and Gareth wasted no time in stripping off and diving neatly into the water with barely a splash, sending delicate ripples shooting across the surface.

Lola settled herself with the others on a flattish part of the rock facing the sea. Fabs was across the other side with his friends, offering them advice, which they chose to ignore, although they did heed his warning about sea urchins so kept their beach shoes on. Lola couldn't help but smile at their camaraderie; it reminded her of the good-natured teasing of her own friends.

She glanced at Rhys, perched on the rock next to her, still in his shorts and T-shirt, his lips tight and expression unreadable behind his sunglasses. His arms were wrapped around his knees, which were drawn up to his chest. She wondered if he was longing to join them, but was holding back, perhaps because of the confidence Freddie and Gareth exuded. When Sarah and Zoe wandered round to join them – Zoe clad in a bikini that showed off her trim figure and Sarah in her low-cut swimming costume which covered, in her own words, her 'mum tum' – Lola knew there was no chance that Rhys would pluck up the courage to join in.

So she kept him company, resting back on the rough, sun-baked rock and soaking up the other-worldly lunar-like landscape. The sky was streaked with clouds so they got a respite from the sun every few minutes and the breeze swirling off the sea tempered the heat. Freddie and Gareth took it in turns to dive into the water, each of them trying to best each other with increasingly impressive flips. It would have been even more special without the constant testosterone-fuelled showing off.

Zoe only had eyes for Freddie. Rhys kept glancing their way, and Lola cringed every time Zoe trailed her fingers across Freddie's toned stomach or planted a sensual kiss on his lips.

'What actually happened with you and Zoe then?' Lola decided to ask the difficult question and get it out of the way.

'Nothing "happened".' Rhys sighed. 'That was the problem – we just bumbled along. At the time, her walking out was completely out of the blue, but looking back there were plenty of signs. She would always suggest we do something like go away for a weekend or for meals out, but I just didn't have the money when I was ploughing it all into my house—'

'Didn't you live together?'

'For the last year we did. She rented when she first moved

back to Bristol, but spent so much time at mine that it made sense for her to move in. Maybe that was part of the problem too – that I always thought of it as my house. I'll be the first to admit I was a bit of a homebody back then, working on the house constantly. It's not that we never went out, we just didn't do anything particularly exciting or spend money on stuff. At least I didn't. The truth is, she got bored, I did nothing to entice her to stay and then when she got a job opportunity too good to turn down, she went for it.'

'Without discussing it with you?'

'Uh-huh.' Rhys nodded. 'The first I knew about it was the day she said she was leaving. She'd made up her mind and was pretty blunt that we had no future.'

Lola mulled over his words. 'Did you see a future?'

'I had till that point.' He tightened his hold where he gripped his arms. 'I've spent the past year trying to move on, because in hindsight I accept we weren't right for each other. It's difficult when home reminds me of her—'

There was an almighty splash as Gareth barrelled into the pool, spraying them with a fine watery mist.

'Watch it!' Deni called from where she was sunning herself on a towel further along the rock.

'Come join us!' Sarah said, swimming her way.

Deni put down her book and peeled off her dress to reveal a stylish black and white swimsuit. She glanced Lola and Rhys's way, raised her eyebrows and leapt into the pool to a chorus of cheers.

Lola wondered what Deni's clients would make of that image: their lawyer's arms and legs akimbo dive-bombing into a pool without a care in the world. She wondered what her husband would make of it too and wished he was here to witness Deni focusing on something other than work.

Lola cast her eyes across the pool to Zoe, who was resting back against Freddie, her slender legs crossed. Lola pursed her lips and nodded in Zoe's direction. 'Did she help you out with the house?'

Rhys shook his head. 'She only moved in after I'd finished doing it up...'

From the way he trailed off, he obviously understood that he'd been used; Lola didn't need to spell it out for him. Zoe had been with him when it suited her and moved on when it hadn't. That wasn't love. Love was when someone stuck with you through the good and bad times, supported you unconditionally, were as much a friend as a lover, allowed you to breathe and grow, rather than supress or cage you, and didn't run away when things got difficult or monotonous. But then what the hell did she know about love when she'd never truly experienced it, only seen it from afar?

Perhaps Rhys was too quiet, sensitive and reticent for someone like Zoe, but on the flip side maybe she never gave him a chance; it didn't sound as if they'd talked, at least not properly. They hadn't delved beneath the surface enough to understand each other. When Lola had delved beneath the surface with Jarek, she hadn't liked what she'd found one bit. Although with Rhys and Zoe, it might have been as simple as them wanting different things. Rhys had the responsibility of a house and a mortgage, whereas Zoe sounded as if she'd been clinging on to the fun and freedom of their student days – actually, she seemed to still be doing that, Freddie too. Maybe they were perfect for each other, while Rhys had been the wrong man for her.

Zoe had been the wrong woman for him; that sounded a hell of a lot better.

'What happened to put you off men and relationships?' Rhys's question broke her train of thought.

Lola watched Gareth pick his way across the rock in his beach shoes. He was confident in his ability to dive into the pool like a pro and in his looks. His ridged chest gave Freddie a run for his money in the muscle stakes, except he was taller and leaner without Freddie's bulk. No wonder Rhys was sitting on the rock with his T-shirt still on. Not that he should compete with his friends, but he wasn't as in-your-face confident as them, which was one of the things she liked most about him. Lola knew she was stalling over whether to open up to Rhys; they'd talked frankly already, but confiding in him about Jarek felt meaningful. Then again, he'd just worn his heart on his sleeve over Zoe.

'I haven't gone off men,' Lola said slowly. 'It's more about not wanting to end up in an unhealthy relationship again. My ex-boyfriend wasn't a good person.' The words caught in her throat and that constant knot of tension in her chest grew.

She glanced around. Deni was in the pool with Sarah; no one was in earshot, it was just her and Rhys and there was something about the way he was looking at her, patiently waiting for her to speak rather than pushing for her to open up, that made her want to.

She traced her fingers across the pockmarks, ridges and grooves of the rock and concentrated on the warmth of the sun on her face. Rhys's gentle breathing was soothing and Sarah's throaty chuckle drifting from the pool grounded her. Talking about him wouldn't hurt her; trying to contain her feelings and deal with the aftermath by herself had done no good.

Lola loosed a breath. 'Everyone loved Jarek. Everyone apart from Mirabel; that should have been the biggest warning sign, but I ignored it because I was in love.' Lola scratched a fingernail across the rock, back and forth, back and forth, as an image of Jarek when they'd first met invaded: handsome in a way that had made her stop in her tracks, in a well-cut suit, his tie loosened and the top couple of shirt buttons undone. He'd smelled delicious, a seductive spiced scent, and he'd wooed her with wit, charm and intelligence as much as a sexiness that had left her breathless and made her so sure that sleeping with him at the end of their second date was the right thing to do.

Lola cleared her throat. 'He was someone who on paper was too good to be true, but then so is Fabs, so I know it's possible for someone to be good-looking, kind, thoughtful, wealthy, have a stellar career, be the whole damn package.'

'But Jarek wasn't like Fabs?'

'No, and Mirabel knew it. She saw through his perfect veneer, or at least got a sense that he was hiding the real him. Not that she knows quite how right she was.'

'Did he hurt you?' Rhys's voice guttered, the warmth of his arm brushing against hers anchoring her to the present when she was at risk of spiralling off into fear at the memories.

'Not physically, no.' Her voice sounded small against the splashing from the pool and their friends' laughter. The intensity of the ever-growing knot in her chest reminded her why even talking about Jarek was a bad idea, when she'd do anything to erase him from her life, both the memory and the destructive feelings. With the distance of time, it was hard to believe how she could have been so easily drawn in, except he'd fed off her fear and delighted in the control. That was who he was. She'd eventually realised, but by then it had been too late to get out unscathed. But she had escaped; that was the thought she needed to hold on to. And in Rhys's comforting presence she wanted to rid herself of the burden of secrecy.

'He was mentally and emotionally abusive,' she said quietly, echoing Rhys's stance by wrapping her arms around her knees. 'The bruises are all hidden, which is why he got away with it. I've tried to cover up the parts of me he destroyed – in many ways, I'm pretending to be who I was before I met him. Someone confident and carefree, sociable and fun-loving. I have to work hard to behave in the way I used to. He shredded my confidence and made me question my decisions, my feelings, how I felt about my job, my friends, my family, about myself, until everything revolved around him.'

Lola took a deep breath of the salty air. Someone took a running dive not far from them, and the cool spray of water was delicious on her hot skin. Her arms were wrapped so tightly around her legs, she felt as if she was suffocating, the memories dragging her under into the cool, quiet depths of the glinting pool before her.

Rhys was silent. He reached his hand across and gently prised her fingers apart so he could slide his into hers. The gesture said more than words and comforted her too.

'He was charming until he'd hooked me in completely. I told him I loved him and he said it back. He chipped away at my self-esteem so slowly that I didn't notice until I found myself spending all my time with him. If I suggested us going out with my friends there'd be a reason not to and suddenly my life was consumed by him and I hardly saw anyone outside of work.'

'Did they notice?'

'Mirabel did, but that was because she hadn't warmed to him from the beginning, but Deni and other friends just believed I was loved up and in the honeymoon phase. But everything ended up revolving around him. I stayed at his place, because he preferred it to mine. We went to the places he wanted to go to and we started to do things together, never with friends of mine. I remember Deni inviting us to a dinner party and he didn't want to go and begged me not to either, so I made some lame excuse. Then he ignored me all evening. Apart from work colleagues, he didn't really have friends – another red flag I missed. The only respite I had was when he travelled to New York for a week or two for work. His family lived in the US so we never saw them, something I didn't think much of because I'm not close to my parents. Jarek wasn't keen on visiting my parents, then talked me out of going to see them even by myself.' Lola dragged in another breath of warm salty air. 'When we talked about my parents, he'd focus on the things that were wrong and unhealthy between my parents and me. He tried to alienate us like he did with my friends. He knew what to say for the most impact and he was deft at moulding me into the person he wanted me to be, one who I didn't recognise. He charmed me into loving him, then destroyed my spirit in order to control me.'

It felt absurd talking about the two years of her life he'd stolen, when she'd felt small and helpless, in a landscape that still made her feel small but somehow powerful. The wild beauty surrounding them was dangerous yet freeing. It mirrored her own journey because she had escaped and was physically free of Jarek, yet she was still wounded and tortured by the memories of how he'd treated her, particularly when he was still trying to edge his way into her life. Despite having got out, she still felt like a broken version of her former self.

Neither she nor Rhys should allow the damaging influence of their ex-partners to shape their lives the way the sea had carved out the Cane Malu pool. Except the pool was curved and smoothed from the sea's caress while Lola was full of jagged edges that kept snagging and getting rebroken, reminding her of the pain and fear that still had a hold on her.

'How did you get out?' Rhys asked softly.

'I had the opportunity to travel to Dubai as part of the team for a huge New Year's Eve bash with Starlight. I'd already said no to things because of him; his constant pressure for me to conform to what he wanted was impacting my work and I just snapped. So I didn't tell him and went. I changed the locks on my apartment and only let him know where I was going and that we were over when I was on the plane. You must think that makes me sound like Zoe?'

'Not even close.'

Rhys's fingers were warm and tight between her own. She turned to him as tears threatened to spill. 'When you're constantly told you're worthless or nothing without someone, you eventually begin to believe it.'

'But you're not, Lola.' Rhys pulled her close. 'You're everything without him. That's what you need to believe.'

12

'We should have insisted on separate rooms, Lola,' Rhys said under his breath as he unlocked the door to their room after a delicious dinner, which had thankfully been uneventful despite the continuing tension between the two sets of parents. *Their room.* The thought juddered into his head. They'd let the rumours fly and neither of them had said no to sharing when Deni had reorganised the sleeping arrangements. Pretending they'd been intimate was one thing; sharing a room for a night was another matter. 'I'm up for still pretending, but I didn't think we'd be taking it this far.'

Lola studied him before pushing past and opening the door. 'I'm fine with this as long as you are?' Her smile was so reassuring, he found himself nodding and following her in. 'And, to be honest, I don't like the snarky way Zoe looks at you. Freddie looks guilty when he's around you and at least has the decency to not pack on the PDA, but *her*. She didn't want to be with you, she's hooked up with one of your friends and yet is still intent on rubbing it in your face. That's a bitchy thing to do, so I'm more than happy for us to show her that you're enjoying yourself.'

'But pretending doesn't change the way I feel.' Rhys closed the door.

During their heart-to-heart at Cane Malu that afternoon, they'd opened up to each other in a way that had been refreshing and enlightening. The hurt and sorrow that had emanated from Lola as she'd talked about her experience with Jarek had shocked him, that there were people in the world who could be so cruel. What he'd struggled with the most was how anyone could have treated someone as vivacious, kind and loving as Lola so badly, and all for what? To make themselves feel bigger, stronger and in control, all because they were a terrible person?

'You're really not over her?' Lola asked gently.

'I'm not in love with her, that's for certain, but seeing her again like this, with him... I don't know.' He shrugged and wandered over to the French doors that opened onto a small balcony with a view towards the stone buildings opposite. Lola's concern moved him as much as the way she'd cried in his arms when he'd hugged her tight on the edge of the pool earlier had. Then she'd brushed it off with laughter, switching on that fun-loving side that he now realised took some effort to maintain. He turned back to her. 'It's made me realise how much her walking out of my life impacted me. I've felt like a failure for a long time and being here with them has highlighted that.'

Lola paced over and placed her hand on his arm. 'Hey, it's okay to be upset about a relationship failing.'

'I desperately want to be over her, but I think it's more about not having this constant feeling of anger and hurt when I see her.'

'She's not exactly making it easy for you. And it's extra complicated when she's part of your friendship group.' She smiled up at him. 'I know it's easy for me to say but try to not let her get to you or spoil your time here.' She let her hand drop. 'I want a shower before bed. Do you mind if I go first?'

'Go for it.'

She scooped up one of the rolled-up towels from the bed.

'Hey, Lola.' He waited until she turned to face him, her blue eyes wide, long lashes framing them. She looked stunning when she wore make-up and got dressed up, but she was naturally beautiful, appealingly so, but she wasn't as confident as she projected. There was a vulnerability she covered well. 'Thank you.'

'For what?'

'For the pep talk, for helping make the time here bearable – for making it actually enjoyable.'

'You've helped me too. And thank you for listening this afternoon and not judging, and for, I don't know, just letting me talk.'

Had her cheeks gone a little pink? Maybe.

She turned away and delved into her overnight bag, while he stepped outside onto the tiny balcony. The buildings opposite were only a stone's throw away, warm light spilling into the night from a couple of windows. A moped zoomed past on the cobbled street below and Italian chatter came from the restaurant further down. Louder voices drifted towards him from the adjacent room. Two very familiar voices that made his heart sink and blood pound in his ears.

He backed into the bedroom, heart thumping. He clenched his fists, furious with himself for still having such a visceral reaction to her; *to them*.

'You okay?' With a washbag in her hand and a towel slung over her arm, Lola looked at him quizzically.

'Freddie and Zoe,' he said under his breath, jabbing a finger in the direction their voices had come from.

'They're in the next room?' Lola raised an eyebrow.

The Island of Hopes and Dreams 97

'Yup.'

A sly smile crept across her face. 'Well, let's rattle the walls then. Show her what she's missing.'

Before he realised what she meant, she'd dropped the towel and washbag on the armchair and launched herself on the bed. Then she said 'Coming to join me?' so loudly and seductively that he very nearly did, only faltering when she grinned manically and clapped a hand over her mouth to stop giggles from escaping. He couldn't tear his eyes away as she flipped on to her back, making the mattress groan. In another fluid move, she pressed her bare feet against the headboard and thudded it against the wall.

'Athletics throughout my teens and being the fastest cross-country runner at my school means my legs have fabulous stamina.'

Fabulous legs full stop, Rhys thought.

He watched, transfixed, as her feet pounded against the headboard, while her shorts rode up her shapely legs – or was it down at this angle? – lying on her back. Going for it. On. The. Bed.

Rhys swallowed and shifted uncomfortably from one foot to the other. Actually, he was incredibly comfortable watching her, wishing he wasn't a spectator but that he was participating, that *he* was the reason the headboard was thudding so forcefully.

He considered retreating to the bathroom just to put some distance between them, because, hell, was she doing things to him. Until now, he'd admired her beauty, been swept up by her easy-going nature, but he hadn't entertained the idea that there was anything more than a fledgling friendship between them. She was attractive, smart, funny and independent, but she was also not interested in having a relationship. They were helping each other out, nothing more. But seeing her like this, he couldn't help but think about her in a different light.

Lola was as interesting as he was normal; boring even. Perhaps he shouldn't be so hard on himself, but wasn't that the truth? Leading a predictable life, never really taking himself out of his comfort zone, doing what was expected. No wonder Zoe had left him and was shacked up with Freddie. Being this fearless and fun just to make him feel better while attempting to make Zoe wonder what she was missing out on was nice of Lola. Yet Zoe wasn't missing out on anything because this was fake and he knew exactly what she'd be doing for real in the next room. *With his so-called friend.* Lola was just being kind even if it was turning him on. She didn't want him – she didn't want anyone. Pretending suited her just fine. It had suited him too. But not any longer.

Being thrown together like this had allowed them to actually get to know one another without worrying about giving off liking each other vibes.

And he did like her. He liked talking to her and opening up in a way he rarely did. He appreciated her beauty, but it hadn't affected him in the way appreciating her was doing right now.

Her legs were still rhythmically pounding and, *oh my god*, he thought, was she beckoning to him? His heart dropped into his stomach with the realisation she really was trying to get his attention – yep, that hand signal was definitely suggesting he join her. He stumbled towards the bed, suddenly feeling hot and bothered and in desperate need of the air con. Or a cold shower.

With a wicked grin, she grabbed his hand and pulled him onto the bed. He twisted round so he was lying next to her.

'Let's give them a big finish,' she whispered. 'Because, by the way, I'm super ticklish – I will scream the place down.' She winked and his heart raced even faster as he understood her meaning.

She didn't give him a choice, kicking things off by attacking him with tickles. Not that he was particularly ticklish, but a laugh escaped him. Her eyes blazed with mischief as she focused on his armpits. His fingers swept up her sides, skimming her ribs. Only the thin material of her top separated his fingertips from her skin and the intimacy left him with all kinds of conflicting emotions. She'd been telling the truth about being seriously ticklish. She squirmed beneath his feather-light touch, squealing with a mix of pleasure and pain as he tickled her until they were both lying on their backs panting, laughter fading.

'Now I definitely need a shower!' Her laughter filled the room again. She launched herself off the bed, scooped up her towel and washbag and dived into the en suite.

The doors to the balcony were wide open and he assumed, after he'd so easily heard Freddie and Zoe's conversation from the next room, that it would have been impossible for them to not have heard *that* display.

Oh God, had they taken it too far? Was it pathetic that he wanted to get back at Zoe in this way? Although, in truth, he hadn't been thinking much – if at all – about Zoe when he'd joined Lola on the bed.

Rhys lay back and gazed around at the simply furnished room with its cream walls and glass wall lights. What had started off as a bit of fun and a way to help each other out had turned into so much more. He really wanted to talk to Fabs about his mixed-up feelings over Lola, but he wouldn't because it would sound pathetic when his friend had his life together in every way.

The shower stopped and, a couple of minutes later, Lola

stepped into the room with just a towel wrapped around her middle.

Rhys shot off the bed, grabbed his towel and strode towards the en suite, avoiding looking at her. He needed to cool down.

'I can sleep on the chair,' he said, gesturing towards it, his mouth dry. 'Or on the floor.'

'Don't be silly,' Lola said with a shake of her head. 'The bed's plenty big enough for us both.'

13

The bed was big enough, but that didn't stop Rhys from being acutely aware of Lola lying next to him. She'd fallen asleep quickly, her breathing now slow and gentle, keeping him company in the darkness. He figured her ease at sharing a bed was because she hadn't been thinking about him in the way he was thinking about her now.

A cool shower had helped to some extent, but as he lay coffin-still staring up at the ceiling, Lola remained firmly fixed in his head. The tickling had all been a bit of fun, but the memory was driving him insane in a way that he'd be fantasising about it for a long time to come: the feel of her smooth skin as she'd squirmed beneath his touch, his fingers tracing her collarbone and sides, making her wriggle and cry out. There was no way they'd not heard from the next room. Hell, with the balcony doors wide open the whole hotel and anyone on the street below had probably heard. He flushed hot. His senses tortured him: the sound of her hushed breathing, the scent of her mandarin body lotion and the warmth of her next to him. Would it be wrong to shuffle close, to put his face to her skin, to breathe her in?

Certain that it would be impossible to fall asleep while his thoughts eddied, his heart pounded and every part of him throbbed with desire, he got out of bed. He padded the short distance to the balcony doors and slipped out, closing them quietly behind him.

'You couldn't sleep either?'

His heart ricocheted against his ribs at the sound of Zoe's voice.

He turned towards the adjacent balcony and met her eyes. She was sitting on one of the wrought-iron chairs with a glass in her hand and her bare feet resting on the railing.

'Nope.'

She grunted and glanced away. 'I'm surprised you're not knackered after your earlier performance,' she said with an underlying tone he couldn't quite decipher.

Performance. Did she believe it had been real or known they'd been pretending and had intended for her to hear? Either way, she was looking uncomfortable, which was making him feel as guilty as his and Lola's earlier 'performance' had heartened him. He hadn't laughed that hard for ages.

'It's surprising really,' she continued, 'given you were always so worried about what other people would think, to make that much noise. Unless of course you've changed drastically, which I'm guessing not.' The look she cast him could have flayed a person top to toe. 'So I assume it was all for my benefit.'

'I think you're getting me confused with someone who actually cares about you still, which I don't,' he said coolly, despite his stomach twisting with guilt and disappointment that she'd managed to get the upper hand. Him still having rumbling feelings for her was why he was in this mess.

'You keep telling yourself that.' She crossed one ankle over the other and studied him with a smirk. 'At least I don't have to fake anything with Freddie.'

He knew he should take a deep breath, go back inside and not let her get under his skin. 'And I see you haven't changed a bit either, still being casually cruel and not caring if you hurt me.'

'I thought you said you didn't care about me any more? If that's the case, why be bothered what I say? Unless of course you're aware it's the truth.'

'Are you happy with him?'

Zoe fixed him with a glare. 'I had to wait two years before we even moved in together and that was because *I* suggested it. How long would I have had to wait for anything more?'

His heart dropped into his stomach, remembering how close he'd come to asking her to marry him. 'You're honestly telling me you'd have said yes if I'd proposed? You gave me no indication that was what you wanted and the fact you left so abruptly only makes me think it was actually the last thing you desired.'

'At least Freddie is decisive and knows what he wants.'

Rhys snorted and leaned his hands on the railing so he wouldn't have to look at her. Despite being outside, it was claustrophobic with the houses opposite looming close, but at least the touch of cooler air was helping to temper his rage.

'You never did understand me,' Zoe said.

'No, I didn't,' Rhys swung back. The balcony light cast shadows across her face, but she looked tight-lipped, angry, bitter, and all for what? 'I didn't understand you then and I sure as hell don't understand you now.'

'Well, that makes two of us. When we were at uni you were fun and up for a laugh. You took risks – what the hell happened?'

'And yet you still slept around behind my back.'

'You're too straight-laced for your own good. Try living a little, Rhys. It's the only way you'll end up keeping a woman like Lola. Everyone can see she's way out of your league. Probably just wants to have a bit of holiday fun. Although maybe you have learnt a thing or two if you can make her scream like that.' She downed the rest of her drink, thumped it on the table and stood up.

'I only wanted you to be happy and truthful,' Rhys said softly. 'I wish you'd left me well before you did instead of leading me on. Make sure you don't do the same to Freddie when you get bored of him.'

He turned on his heel and strode back inside, closing the door as quietly as he could manage when he wanted to slam, smash and rage.

How had he ever loved her? Had she been that good an actor or was she skilled at playing games to get what she wanted? He couldn't comprehend how he'd once thought of her as a friend, a lover, a partner, someone he had envisaged spending his life with. He didn't recognise the person she'd become – actually, she'd always been like this, she'd just hidden it well and played him for a fool for too long. Freddie was welcome to her.

Rhys knew he was better off alone, rather than being trapped in a toxic relationship. Zoe was in the past and he would no longer wallow in the what ifs or live with regret. It was time to move on for good.

14

Something had changed. Lola couldn't quite put her finger on it, but Rhys was subdued the next morning. Even the glances in their direction from Zoe and Freddie over breakfast did nothing to lift her niggling worry that she'd made Rhys uncomfortable last night. Although she'd struggled recently to be confident in big social situations, she knew Rhys wasn't an extrovert. That was who she was – at least who she used to be.

Rhys was far chattier, funnier and more open when there were only a couple of people around. She could see him shutting down when he was in a large group, suddenly going quiet. Perhaps she had pushed things too far last night. She imagined it through his eyes and grimaced at how idiotic she must have looked banging her feet against the headboard to pretend that they were having... Ugh, she didn't even want to think about that. She'd come to care about Rhys as a friend, a feeling he seemed to reciprocate. She hoped she hadn't messed up their friendship, not when they'd bared their souls to each other.

Lola wasn't alone in her worry because Mirabel looked pensive over breakfast, as if she had stuff playing on her mind too, which wouldn't be surprising after the tension between the two mothers yesterday.

Much to everyone's relief, the day had been planned out with the friendship groups sticking together. Rhys was heading on a boat tour along the coast with Fabs and his friends, while Lola would be joining Mirabel and her friends and family for a stroll through Bosa for a spot of shopping, lunch and sightseeing. If there was any awkwardness between her and Rhys, they wouldn't have to deal with it until they returned to Villa Capparis later that evening, although she didn't envy him having to spend the day with Freddie and Zoe.

By mid-morning Lola was exploring the medieval heart of Bosa. The narrow cobbled streets made her want to hold her breath when a car squeezed by. She'd only got as far as having a handful of driving lessons in her early twenties and had never got round to taking a test, but her anxiety soared at the idea of navigating a car through streets that had only been intended for a horse and cart. Some buildings were so close together that Lola imagined people could reach across to each other from the opposite balcony. In the really narrow streets, leafy green plants decorated the doorsteps instead of colourful flowers, probably because the sun rarely reached the cobbles with the houses so close together. With potted palms outside doors and trailing foliage cascading from balconies, the backstreets were an oasis of green amid stone walls, some crumbling in patches. Lola was enjoying strolling through the town, getting a sense of the real Sardinia away from its picture-perfect beaches.

One of the reasons for coming to Bosa – besides Giada wanting to show off more of her beloved island – was for Mirabel to choose her wedding jewellery, and Lola was pleased that Giada had sensibly allowed Felicity to take charge. The excitement for the upcoming wedding ramped up the moment the friends stepped inside the jewellers to find a treasure trove of earrings, rings, bracelets and necklaces. Filigrana Vadilonga specialised in traditional Sardinian filigree: delicately textured small spirals reminiscent of embroidered gold that gave each piece of jewellery a unique and eye-catching look.

The love and pride on Felicity's face was heart-warming as they browsed the display cases, all of them pitching in with ideas about what Mirabel should go for.

'How about a heart-shaped one?' Deni suggested as they wandered round the compact shop.

Lola's eye was drawn to the ones without any jewels: a threaded gold pendant sun and a tiny round filigree pendant designed with four concentric circles.

Sarah spun round. 'This four-thousand-euro choker is so me, don't you think?' She gestured to a display cabinet containing a statement necklace made from gold rosettes and delicate teardrop pearls.

Mirabel baulked at the price.

'This is our gift to you,' Felicity insisted as she tucked her arm in her daughter's. 'We want you to choose what you love. Forget about the price. It's something we want to do for you. From us,' she stressed.

'Perhaps not the choker though,' Sarah whispered.

After the hotel lobby stand-off the day before, they understood how important buying the wedding jewellery was for Mirabel's mum.

With all of them coveting something different, Mirabel eventually chose a delicate pearl and yellow-gold pendant with a teardrop blue topaz at its centre and earrings to match that was expensive but not eye-wateringly so.

They left the shop in a flurry of voices, their shopping spree a much-needed reminder that they weren't just on Sardinia for a holiday.

'Only five days to go till your wedding!' Deni said as they stepped onto the street and into blazing sunshine.

* * *

After lunch at a nearby pizzeria, Mirabel's parents headed back to the hotel for a siesta, while the friends climbed the steep stone lanes towards the top of Bosa, where Malaspina Castle overlooked the town from its perch on the hill. Sunshine bathed the lanes and they were all puffing by the time they reached somewhere they could stop and admire the view. A heat haze rippled towards the hills that edged the town. The terracotta-red tiled roofs soaked up the sun, while the colourful pastel stonework of the houses brought warmth to the valley which was enclosed by hills and the sea. The low wall in front of them was packed with pots blooming with flowers and swarming with bees in the September sun. It was the perfect time after the intense heat and crowds of the summer; something that Sarah and Polly always complained about. With school-age children, they missed out on the blissful quiet away from peak season.

They continued on up the hill. 'Your mum seemed happier after going shopping this morning,' Lola said as she tucked her arm in Mirabel's and they followed after the others. 'And all the parents were okay at dinner last night.'

'Only because they were ignoring each other,' Mirabel said. 'I think this place tipped Mum over the edge. It's one thing them staying at the family house and you lot at one of their villas, but this night away has felt unnecessary even if we did combine it with shopping for the wedding. I know Giada wants to show off the island, but it's come across as them flaunting their wealth and connections by putting everyone up here all for *one* night. That wasn't their intention because I understand they're not like that, but for my parents, knowing they're spending this sort of money...' She shook her head and clasped Lola's arm tighter. 'And Mum and Dad really can't afford that jewellery—'

'They can or they wouldn't have and it's something they wanted to do for you when so much else is out of their hands.'

They continued on in silence, their calf muscles aching with the climb, the gentle heat wrapping around them.

'What does Fabs think about the whole situation?' Lola eventually asked.

'Fabs is being Fabs and trying his hardest to keep the peace, but I feel trapped in the middle. This should be a joyous time, but it's just a melting pot of tension.'

They'd trailed behind the others but caught up when they reached the top of the hill. The stone walls of the imposing castle came into view.

Mirabel paused and tilted her head towards the sun, while the others continued across a narrow road and began the climb to the castle.

'I told you it was a bad idea having everyone come out so far in advance. Our parents are already at each other's throats; imagine how awful it'll be by the actual wedding.'

'You're talking about family, but not your friends. If it's any consolation, I've never seen Sarah look so happy, and this time away for Deni has already taught her a thing or two about getting a little more balance in her life. Everyone is having a good time, although none of that matters if you're not.'

'Oh, it's not that I'm not enjoying myself, it's just there's a pressure I can't shift. I'm constantly trying to please everyone. It's exhausting.'

'Come on, you two!' Deni's voice from further up the path

floated down. 'Stop gossiping about Lola's helluva night with Rhys!'

Lola cringed at the confirmation that it hadn't been just Freddie and Zoe they'd managed to put a show on for last night; no wonder Rhys had been out of sorts this morning.

Mirabel smiled knowingly as she pulled Lola close and they started up the last bit of the path.

'Remind me why we climbed this flipping hill?' she muttered as they followed after the others, their pace snail-like.

'For the view and to see the castle.'

'Cocktails by the river might have been preferable.'

'You were the one who seemed keen to walk things off this morning.'

'I was, I am, it's just... Ugh. I'm tired, that's all.' Mirabel's shoulders dropped. 'I needed to get out. Get away.'

Lola nodded. 'Maybe have a word with Fabs about easing back on big days out, keep it simple. Just spending time together at the villa is more than enough.'

'We have a restaurant booked for tomorrow evening, just friends mind, but yeah, no big plans after that until the evening before the wedding. Maybe he can try to rein his mum in.' Mirabel gave her a look that suggested she wasn't at all convinced by that idea. 'Come on, let's go see this castle. At least it will be downhill on the way back.'

'And a cocktail or two waiting for us, I'm sure.'

* * *

The sun was retreating towards the horizon by the time they returned to Hotel Melis. The river, reflecting the golden sunset, glistened amber, while the tightly packed lanes in the old town were lit up with light spilling from windows, and the open doors of restaurants enticed with welcoming warmth and fragrant scents. But with their whirlwind trip to Bosa at an end and the nearly two-and-a-half-hour journey back to Villa Capparis still to go, cocktails on a picturesque terrace had been replaced with a glass of Malvasia wine from the family's vineyard in the hotel bar.

Lola sipped her glass of dessert wine while they waited for the taxis to pick them up. She wondered how wise it was to have everyone waiting together. There was an obvious division with Fabs and Mirabel's families sitting on opposite sides of the bar, while the friendship groups were clustered together. She couldn't tell if Rhys was purposely avoiding her or if he was just too embarrassed to talk to her with everyone there. The idea that her actions had put a wedge between them upset her more than she thought possible.

Downing the remainder of the wine and leaving her rucksack with Deni and Sarah, Lola nipped to the bathroom off the lobby. She slicked on lipstick, ran damp fingers through her hair, pushed open the bathroom door and came face to face with Zoe. Instead of letting her through, Zoe paused in the doorway, her head cocked as if studying her.

'Having fun with Rhys?'

On the surface, it was an innocent enough question, but it was a loaded one. Her tone was edged with bitterness, or perhaps annoyance. The tightness of her lips and a cool steeliness overpowered her delicate features and made Lola hesitate, unsure how to answer. Zoe was like a cat with her claws out.

Annoyance flared within Lola. Someone who had dumped Rhys, who no longer wanted to be with him and had hooked up with a mutual friend of theirs had the audacity to look pissed off that someone else was with her ex.

Lola placed her palm on the door and leaned in close. 'Actually yes, a huge amount of fun, thank you.' She pushed past and didn't look back as the door swung closed.

And she'd been telling the truth; she was having fun with Rhys, just not in the way everyone was assuming. However Rhys felt about it, she hoped to God she'd managed to wipe the smarmy smile off Zoe's face. From what she'd seen and everything Rhys had said, she was convinced he was well shot of his ex; she just hoped he realised it too and learnt to move on properly rather than waste any more time and effort on someone who should remain in the past. That was what she was trying to live up to herself.

15

It was late by the time they got back to Villa Capparis, too late to talk to Rhys when all Lola wanted to do was crash into bed and sleep, tired but happy from plenty of sunshine, walking, talking, eating and drinking. Only the argument between the two matriarchs had dampened the jovial spirit, although Mirabel and the immediate family were the ones who'd suffered as a result. Lola gave Mirabel an extra-big hug as they said goodnight; she couldn't help but worry how she was coping as she and Fabs were ferried across the bay to join their two sets of parents back at the family villa.

The next morning, everyone was left to their own devices, most choosing to lounge about at the villa, reading by the pool or strolling to the beach, only coming together for a light lunch on the terrace. Freddie and Zoe made themselves scarce by going out for the day. Lola was relieved to witness not only Rhys's spirits lift because of their absence, but that he found a way to be at ease with her again. Perhaps she hadn't completely messed up by taking things a bit too far the other night.

Later that evening, the friends joined Mirabel and Fabs further up the coast at a restaurant in Porto Cervo. They were seated all together at a long table, the terrace jutting out of the hillside with a garden and pool directly below and an unparalleled view of the marina, which was packed with white yachts. The fading sun lit the sky citrine and blush, reflecting in the restaurant's windows.

All of the friends were there, including Fabs's Italian friend Valentino from the first night, and Lola was relieved to be sitting between Rhys and Deni. Freddie and Zoe were at the other end of the table opposite Mirabel, while Fabs was at the head, the sea awash with sunset colours behind him.

Lola was glad their pact had thrown her and Rhys together. Although he was quiet, he was also funny and self-deprecating. They'd had a laugh together as well as bared their souls. She'd forgotten how good it felt to be that relaxed with someone, to be open and joyful without a hint of fear. She swallowed back a wave of upset with a mouthful of ricotta gnocchi. She missed the companionship of a partner, to have someone to bounce ideas off and share the ups and downs of life with, and yet she hadn't been in a relationship like that since her mid-twenties. Even then, it had been fleeting. With Rhys, she felt she could be herself and not the person her friends still expected her to be, because that wasn't who she was any longer.

The setting was spectacular, the gnocchi delicious and the citrusy local white wine washed it down beautifully. Mirabel and Fabs seemed far more relaxed without their families around, and Lola was relieved to see a smile on Mirabel's face. They were the epitome of a couple in love. To find a soulmate like that, someone who would look at her in the way Fabs was looking at Mirabel, what were the chances?

She turned back to pick up her wine and met Rhys's eyes.

'They look so happy, don't they?' he said with a resigned sigh.

Was he feeling the same? That after his own heartbreak and disappointment, would he ever find a love as wonderful?

'They really do.'

Maybe she was putting too much pressure on herself to find perfection. Perhaps Fabs and Mirabel were a one-in-a-million couple. Not everyone got so lucky in love. With her track record, she'd settle for someone half decent.

At the other end of the table, Freddie stood up and raised his glass. As everyone's attention turned to him, the conversation around the table petered out, while the clatter of cutlery and chatter from the other diners rumbled on.

'Fabs, Mirabel, I just wanted to say thank you for an incredible few days so far, to you and your families for wining and dining us. I can't think of anywhere more romantic for you to be getting married, which is why it's also the perfect place for making big romantic gestures.' Freddie raised his glass higher and glanced down at Zoe. Her cheeks flushed as she met his eyes. 'So I have a bit of an announcement to make. *We* have an announcement to make.' He cleared his throat. 'Earlier today when Zoe and I went off for a picnic, I proposed and she said yes.'

The silence around the table intensified as if everyone had sucked in a breath and were unable to let it out. Lola tensed and Rhys shifted in his seat. She didn't dare glance at him.

Was that worry on Zoe's face? Had she not wanted Freddie to announce their news in front of everyone? Fuelled by the uncomfortable quiet, Lola seethed on Fabs and Mirabel's behalf. To hijack the lead-up to their friends' wedding and steal the limelight, even for a moment, to announce their own engagement – people just didn't do that, did they? At least not without the bride and groom's permission, and if Mirabel's open-mouthed shock and Fabs's thinly veiled annoyance was anything to go by, then no, permission had not been sought.

Instigated by Mirabel, glasses were slowly raised and calls of congratulations filtered around the table. Glasses clinked, the sound drifting into the darkening evening, mixing with the chatter from elsewhere on the terrace.

It could have been worse, Lola thought, *he could have actually proposed in front of everyone rather than announce their engagement.* But that thought faded the second she clocked Rhys's ashen face. The tightness of his jaw was echoed by his clenched fists. His lips were pursed white as if he was trying to bite back the hurl of abuse he probably wanted to throw at them but couldn't, because he was decent and thoughtful and wouldn't dream of making another scene somewhere so public just four days away from his best mate's wedding.

Conversations had started up again. Lola turned her attention from Rhys back to Zoe. Nope, that wasn't worry plastered over her face, it was smugness. Lola wanted to wipe the smile off her face so badly. The second Zoe met her gaze, Lola made her move.

'Just go with it,' she said under her breath to Rhys as she clasped the side of his stubbled jaw. Manoeuvring herself so they were facing each other, she brought her lips to his and kissed him. He tensed and worry coursed through her that once again she'd pushed things too far, that their ruse would unravel right in front of his newly engaged ex and he'd end up feeling even more mortified. She was about to pull away when suddenly he was kissing her back, tentative but responding, his lips parting, his hand gliding around her waist. They broke apart breathlessly.

Rhys stared at her, his eyes wide as he held her gaze, an unspoken something passing between them. Kissing him had been impulsive and born out of annoyance at Freddie and Zoe's insensitivity, the only way Lola felt able to help him, an alternative to sticking up two fingers in his so-called friends' faces. But what she'd intended to be a quick 'fuck you' moment to Freddie and Zoe had turned into something unexpected. Her heart raced as Rhys closed the gap between them, his lips finding hers again, and it was far from tentative this time, but a lip-smashing, tongue-probingly good kiss that took her by surprise.

When she heard Deni comment 'get a room you two', she was pretty sure everyone at the table was witnessing their very public display.

As if realising it too, Rhys suddenly pulled away. But the look that passed between them spoke volumes. The earlier shock and hurt that she'd witnessed had been replaced with something else entirely. It felt good to be the reason he didn't look quite so sad. It felt good full stop. *He* felt good.

It was one thing to pretend she was into Rhys, another thing to actually feel something. Them 'being together' wasn't real, but that had been a hell of a kiss.

Deni nudged her shoulder and she didn't dare meet her friend's eyes as she tried to cover the thumping in her chest and the confusion in her head with a large gulp of wine.

Perhaps she'd behaved as badly as Freddie and Zoe, although a kiss was nothing compared to an engagement announcement. She drained the rest of her wine and silently told herself it had meant nothing, that she'd only kissed him to help him out, and yet the way he'd reciprocated hadn't felt like nothing. It had felt like...

What had it felt like, Lola? she asked herself sternly. The feelings that kiss had stirred scared her senseless, because it had felt like magic.

16

There was no opportunity for Rhys to talk to Lola about the kiss, not while they were at the restaurant. Did she regret it? She was gulping down her drink and avoiding looking at him, seemingly relieved when Deni started talking to her, stealing her attention firmly away from him.

What he did catch was Zoe looking his way with an expression he couldn't decipher. The moment their eyes met, she switched her focus to Freddie, like Lola had done with Deni. The promise he'd made to himself in Bosa to move on from Zoe for good had been thwarted by their engagement announcement, but it was an emptiness he felt rather than anger. What had Freddie been thinking to choose now?

Suddenly, it all slotted into place: Freddie's announcement, Rhys's own devastation, and the way Lola had turned to him with fire in her eyes to instigate a kiss so public Freddie and Zoe couldn't have failed to notice. It had been a pity kiss; of course that was all it had been, however good it had felt. It was no different to Lola putting on a show for the benefit of Freddie and Zoe when they were in Bosa. She was just being nice, pushing the boundaries of their pretend relationship to make him look good in front of the two people who continuously kept hurting him.

And yet it had felt real. His whole body was on fire, and he was fighting the desire to kiss her again. Those feelings that had been stirred during their night in Bosa had ignited and he didn't think he could push them back in their box or pretend that kiss hadn't meant something.

At least to him it had.

The last hour or so at the restaurant passed by in a blur. He ate his plum gelato without really tasting it, chatted to Barnaby about rugby and joined in another toast to Fabs and Mirabel. As the evening ticked by and the sky darkened to midnight blue, he felt more and more alone. Fear crawled through his chest that somehow he'd messed up with Lola, and his gut reaction to kiss her back had pushed her away. As everyone got up to leave and Lola hooked her arm in Deni's without even glancing his way, it certainly felt as if she was trying to avoid him.

Lola made the journey back to Villa Capparis with Mirabel and their friends, while Rhys found himself climbing in a taxi with Barnaby, Gareth, Freddie, Zoe and Fabs. Not that returning to the villa separately meant anything. He rubbed his hand across his face as if it would somehow erase his worry. The closer they got to the villa, the more unsettled he felt.

The second Rhys got inside, he escaped to the bathroom and splashed cold water on his face. He needed to take hold of the negative feelings that were beginning to choke him and calm the hell down. Leaning on the sink, he stared at his reflection. He'd caught the sun since being here and the freckles across his cheeks were more pronounced. At least he looked less washed out than when he'd first arrived.

He wiped his hands, gave himself a stern look and left the

bathroom to find Gareth hovering in the hallway, a beer clasped in one hand.

'You and Lola, eh?' Gareth slung his free arm across Rhys's shoulders. 'Putting on quite the show for Freddie and Zoe's benefit.' He whistled low. 'You've got a keeper there, and she's smoking hot too. If you want the truth,' he said, lowering his voice, 'Lola looks at you with far more love than the way Zoe looks at Freddie. And to be honest, that was a shitty thing they did announcing their engagement in front of everyone – in front of you. Lola shoving what you two have in their faces was the perfect comeback.'

Except it wasn't real, Rhys thought with dismay. Lola was a good actor – that was all Gareth had seen.

Rhys ran his hand through his hair as they strolled towards the others in the living area. He tried to focus on what Gareth was saying rather than on Lola, who was chatting to Deni, the scooped back of her summer dress revealing an expanse of smooth skin. Her bracelets jangled as she talked animatedly to her friend.

'Parading it right in your face was wrong,' Gareth continued to say. 'I'm not sure Fabs was best pleased. I knew they'd gone off for a romantic picnic, but shit, I didn't think he was going to propose to her. Stupid bastard.'

'You don't think they should get married?'

Gareth shrugged. 'They're both impulsive and headstrong, and Zoe changes her mind about things as often as I change my underwear.'

Rhys raised an eyebrow.

'Which I do frequently,' he stressed. 'Honestly, even when they moved in together, I didn't fully believe they were that serious about each other. I was expecting them to break up, not get engaged. But you and Lola are the real deal.'

'I don't really know what we are.' He shrugged, his earlier confusion returning despite Gareth's surprising words. 'But I like her a lot.'

That was the truth. So what if everyone thought they were more to each other than they really were? He felt different when he was with her; positive and happier, like there was more to life than a constant battle to keep himself upbeat and not spiral into depression. Lola was the reason for that, which was why his current uncertainty over where he stood with her hurt so much.

After a final drink with everyone, Fabs and Mirabel said goodnight. Freddie and Zoe slunk off too, more subdued than they'd been earlier in the evening, perhaps realising too late the mistake they'd made. Rhys didn't feel even a little bit sorry for them.

Lola was sitting with her friends on the terrace and Rhys watched as Gareth joined them with a tray of limoncello cocktails. He was smooth and a charmer, which made Rhys wonder if he had an ulterior motive wanting to sit with them, possibly to talk to Lola.

Rhys turned to Barnaby. 'Gareth's been overly nice about me and Lola and trashing Zoe.' He swirled the wine around the glass. 'That first night we were here, I got the impression he fancied Lola.'

'What, until you swooped in?' Barnaby laughed. 'I'm teasing.' He knocked his shoulder against Rhys's. 'Gareth's not really bothered who he winds up with as long as he eventually gets laid. Which he managed to do in Bosa with the friend of one of Fabs's sisters. I'm surprised you hadn't noticed, but then you do seem to only have eyes for Lola. Which is a good thing, considering what Freddie and Zoe announced tonight. You shouldn't let them bother you one bit.'

Rhys huffed. 'They're not making it easy.'

'Fabs ignored their faux pas. Mirabel wasn't best pleased, but then she's too nice to say anything – although I'm sure if it had been one of her friends making an announcement like that she would have.'

'If it had been her friends, they'd probably have talked to her about it first,' Rhys said with a raised eyebrow. He knew Lola would never upstage her friend, but of course it was something Zoe would do. Freddie too. They'd been thoughtless or conniving or just plain hurtful. Probably all of those things. And Barnaby was right, he shouldn't let them get under his skin any more than they already had. Neither of them deserved his time or thought, and truthfully, he was having a hard job thinking about anything other than Lola.

* * *

Lola hadn't intended to ignore Rhys after their kiss, but she had, and she felt awful. They could have laughed about it together; the perfect way to get back at Freddie and Zoe and end a fabulous evening. Until it *meant* something. Shit, it really had meant something, stirring feelings that had long been buried. And because of that she didn't feel able to laugh it off, so she'd taken the coward's way out and ignored the situation, shoving those difficult, twisty feelings down, then retreated to the familiarity of Deni.

Even now, back at the villa, there was an invisible divide that she didn't know how to cross. Rhys was in the living room talking to Barnaby, while she was on the terrace with her friends and Gareth. Making them cocktails had been an excuse for him to join them because he seemed to be fishing for something, the looks he kept sending her way indiscernible. He definitely wasn't hitting on her; Sarah had revelled in telling them the gossip earlier about the bed swapping that had gone on while they'd been in Bosa.

Apart from Deni's 'get a room' comment when they'd been at the restaurant, she hadn't commented further, but why would she when she'd believed that kiss had been one of many and not Lola and Rhys's first?

Shit, they'd had their first kiss. Lola hadn't expected him to kiss her back, at least not in the way he had, like he meant it. And enjoyed it. And it had been a proper kiss, a toe-curlingly good one. The look of shame or embarrassment she thought he'd given her when he'd pulled away had perhaps just been confusion. Gareth was the exhibitionist, Freddie too to some extent, while Rhys was thoughtful, sensitive, giving, kind, not one for being in the limelight.

Shit, shit, shit, she thought again as she tuned back in to the conversation bouncing between Gareth and Sarah about which famous person each of them resembled.

A message pinged on Lola's phone and she scooped it up as a throaty chuckle erupted from Sarah at Gareth's suggestion that she had a passing resemblance to Sheridan Smith.

'I wish!'

Lola clicked on the message. There was only an image from an unknown number. Everyone around her faded away, their voices becoming distant as she stared at the screen, her heart juddering as she took in the image. She slammed the phone face down in her lap and looked up to find Rhys watching her. He flicked his eyes away. Deni and Sarah were focused on Gareth and, despite being surrounded by friends, she felt utterly alone. She knew the message was from Jarek.

Clutching her phone to her chest, she slipped away, sensing Rhys's eyes on her retreating back as she escaped to her room.

Perching on the end of her bed, she clicked on the photo

again. It looked very much like Sardinia. She fought back the urge to scream. He was still finding ways to mess with her. It was probably a stock image from somewhere to screw with her head, because of course he knew she was here for Mirabel's wedding. It wasn't a secret, not with all of her friends posting countless photos to their socials over the past few days. *He's a controlling narcissistic bastard*, she told herself, *nothing more*. He wanted to unsettle and upset her.

She tried her hardest to force those panicky feelings down and was about to delete the photo and block the number when she froze. The location in the photo wasn't just Sardinia, it was of the riverfront in Bosa, close to where they'd stayed. She hadn't immediately recognised it as the angle was from across the other side of the river. Oh God was he clever. He'd obviously spent time trawling through social media, looking at what her friends had posted to work out where she'd been. He was digging in his claws, twisting and hurting her just like he'd done when they'd been together.

Throwing the phone on the bed, she stood and paced across the room, the fear and upset having morphed into rage. She slammed open the French doors to her garden terrace and breathed in the sweet night air.

A knock on her door made her jump. She sighed as she went back into her room, pulled open the door and came face to face with Rhys.

'Hey, are you okay? You seemed upset.'

'I'm fine,' she snapped, immediately regretting her tone.

Rhys visibly leaned away. 'Sorry, I just thought... If it's about what happened earlier, then—'

'It's got nothing to do with that.' The message had left her rattled, but she didn't want to talk about it, at least not with Rhys right now. 'It was nothing,' she said dismissively.

He did take a step back this time. 'Yeah, well, I thought not. It's fine, I get it, we made a mistake. I'll leave you alone.'

He pushed away from the edge of the door and started down the hallway.

'That's not what I meant,' Lola called after him, but he kept walking.

Lola slammed her bedroom door closed and threw herself face down on the bed. Jarek had his claws in and the one person she'd opened up to while here, she was pushing away. Talking about the message and sharing her worries made it real. But if it had been Deni or Sarah who'd come knocking, would she have reacted the same way? Probably not, because pushing Rhys away felt easier than acknowledging that their kiss had sparked both joy and confusion. But it was more than just how it had made her feel. Being contacted by Jarek reminded her of the risks of letting someone into her heart again. That was what scared her and made her want to run away. The more time she spent with Rhys, the more they'd talked and laughed together, coupled with that earlier kiss, well, he'd managed to chip away at the barrier she'd put up and she didn't know how to deal with that.

17

Lola woke with a raging headache, not because she'd drunk too much the night before, but because she'd cried herself to sleep. She hated how Jarek had so easily got under her skin, and yet she was more upset about the sharp words she'd had with Rhys. He'd only come to check on her and she'd reacted thoughtlessly.

She decided to skip breakfast, because she didn't want to face him. A cowardly reaction, but her swirling emotions were too confusing to deal with.

Of course her friends noticed her absence and Sarah came knocking, finding her still in her room long after breakfast would have been cleared away. She sidled in with a plate of cornetto, a freshly made Italian version of a croissant, and a cappuccino.

'I thought you might be hungry,' she said, setting the plate and cup on the coffee table between the two armchairs that faced the garden. She sat down in one of them and crossed her legs. 'Lovers' tiff last night?' At Lola's blank face, Sarah continued. 'You left abruptly. Rhys followed soon after and came back with his tail between his legs.'

'Oh no, it was nothing like that...' Lola trailed off, but why the hell was she hiding what was going on? Twice now in the last few weeks Jarek had contacted her at the times he knew he'd upset her the most, almost as if he was reminding her that wherever she went, he wouldn't let her forget about him. Why was she trying to deal with this on her own? 'It was just I got a message completely out of the blue—'

Sarah's phone ringing stopped Lola short.

'Hold on; it's Harry. Sorry, I need to take this.' Sarah stood up and answered her phone. 'Everything okay, love?' she asked as she headed into the garden.

Lola sighed but gratefully tucked into the pastries and coffee, slowly feeling more able to face the day as the caffeine began to work its magic. She was even more grateful when Sarah didn't return, but not because she didn't want to talk. The burning feeling of anxiety in her chest would only grow if she didn't have an outlet, but Sarah wasn't it, because she wouldn't be able to keep her mouth shut to Deni, to Gareth – hell, to anyone, friend or stranger – and Lola didn't want a whisper of Jarek to reach Mirabel's ears.

But there was one person she could talk to, who happened to be the one person she needed to apologise to as well.

By late morning when a few of the friends, including Rhys, decided to go to Porto Cervo, Lola jumped at the chance to join them. One of the most exclusive locations along the Costa Smeralda coast, it was a playground for the rich and famous. Huge yachts were tightly packed together along the marina, which was thrumming with people in designer dresses and expensive linen suits. There were plenty of tourists too, gawking at the wealth on display as they posed in front of yachts that must have been worth millions.

After exploring the town, they joined Mirabel at the florists to check all was in hand with the flowers for the wedding, then they ate a late lunch at a restaurant with a peaceful garden terrace that overlooked the marina. With Sarah, Deni, Mirabel, Barnaby and Gareth's company, any awkwardness with Rhys was erased as the friends laughed and chatted together while tucking into salmon carpaccio and red snapper tartare. But the knot of tension returned with the realisation that the longer she left the conversation she needed to have with Rhys, the harder it would be to broach the subject of the kiss. Even the thought sent heat rushing through her body, and it wasn't just heading for her cheeks...

Lola dabbed her mouth with her napkin, drained the remainder of her grapefruit juice and leaned close to Rhys. 'Can we talk?' she asked him.

'Of course,' he said hesitantly.

'I mean privately.'

Rhys had been subdued throughout lunch and that worried Lola as they left the others ordering more drinks and headed out of the restaurant onto the sunny square. Rhys stuffed his hands in his trouser pockets and they strolled in silence. Lola barely took in their surroundings as her head whirred with the different ways she could start the conversation. It was only when they'd walked for a good couple of minutes and reached the wide promenade lined with the gleaming white yachts that she finally plucked up the courage to speak.

'About last night—'

'You don't need to apologise, Lola.' Rhys shrugged. 'You were upset and I came to see if you were okay, but I probably overstepped, you know, in my role of pretend boyfriend' – he gave her a sideways glance – 'or whatever it is we are.'

'No, you behaved like a friend and came to check if I was

okay because you care. I shouldn't have shut you out the way I did or snapped at you. You didn't deserve that.'

They wandered along the promenade that was dotted with exclusive bars and seating areas right by the yachts – a perfect place to people-watch and be seen.

'Is that what you wanted to talk about? What happened at the *end* of last night?'

'Sort of.'

His stress on 'the end of' suggested he was differentiating it from what had happened earlier in the evening. He deserved an explanation about why she'd been short with him, but it was the kiss she really wanted to discuss.

At the end of the marina, they cut up some steps to a path that disappeared beneath the trees and was lined with street vendors selling jewellery. They emerged into the sunshine and Lola found a spot to sit on a sun-baked wall. It was calmer away from the bustle of tourists on the promenade, although there was still the constant chatter from people at the nearby bar, mixed with the rhythmic click of cicadas. Lola tilted her head to the sun, breathed in the scent of honeyed flowers and decided to get the awkward conversation out of the way.

'What I really wanted to talk about was what happened at the restaurant earlier in the evening.'

'Ah, okay.' Rhys braced his palms on the edge of the wall, which gave the impression he was either attempting to anchor himself in anticipation of an uncomfortable conversation or he was readying himself to spring off and run away. 'I wasn't sure you wanted to discuss that.'

'I did, I do.'

Lola's phone pinged. Relieved that she had a momentary distraction, she picked it up. Thinking it would be from Deni wondering where they'd got to, she clicked on it.

Her heart stalled.

> Fancy seeing you here :)

Not from Deni, but an unknown number, different to the one she'd blocked last night. The tone of the message was somehow jovial, yet the underlying meaning sent ice-cold fear racing down her back. She very nearly deleted it straight away, except there was a photo attached and from the thumbnail, something was telling her to look closer, to understand what she was dealing with. So she clicked. And gasped.

A photo of her and Rhys at the end of the promenade they'd just walked along.

Jumping to her feet, she whirled around, searching him out. And, when she saw her ex gazing down at her, she stared in disbelief. Jarek was sitting on the terrace of Zamira Lounge, the lounge bar just above them, his arm casually resting on the black railing, sunglasses pushed up into his dark hair, a sly smile on his face. The blood drained from her, leaving her light-headed. Her heart thumped so hard it threatened to overwhelm.

'Lola? Are you okay?' Rhys was on his feet, worry creasing his forehead.

Breathe, Lola, breathe, she told herself.

From the terrace above, Jarek raised his glass and fixed her with a look that nearly made her knees buckle.

18

'You've gone white.' Rhys's hand was on her arm, firm and real, steering her back to the stone wall.

Lola knew she should focus on Rhys and not let the shock of Jarek throw her off balance, but she was shot through with fear and confusion. If he was willing to follow her all the way to Sardinia, what else was he capable of? That had been why he'd sent her the image of Bosa, not just to let her know that he knew where she was, but because *he'd* been the one to take the photo. Messages were one thing, but to follow her out here, to spy on her, was something else entirely. What was he getting out of continuing to torment her? It was a question she knew the answer to: her reaction. *This* was what he wanted and got off on: her shock and fear, a reaction to him when she'd been the one to end things, to extract herself from his control and reject him. She knew he wouldn't have dealt with it well, but she'd done it to save herself.

She forced her eyes away from Jarek to Rhys, who was frowning, his eyes filled with concern. He was still holding her arm and his touch grounded her, calming her racing heart.

She'd already opened up to Rhys about Jarek and told him more than she'd admitted to anyone. She didn't want to feel this scared or to have to deal with a troubling situation by herself.

'Don't turn around, but the ex I told you about is sitting in the bar just above us.'

Rhys's nostrils flared. 'He's what?'

'He sent me a message yesterday evening that caught me unawares and I dismissed it as nothing, just him trying to get under my skin, but now...' Lola's breath was once again short and sharp.

'That's why you were upset last night,' Rhys breathed out slowly. 'You said he wasn't physically abusive, but is he dangerous?'

'He's definitely unhinged. Who does something like this?'

'Someone who wants to feel in control, to continue dominating you. You should report him when you get home.'

'And say what? That I saw my ex from afar while on holiday – any sane person would put it down to coincidence. You hear stories all the time of people going abroad and bumping into their neighbour or friends. It's not unusual.'

'No, but we know that's not the case and you need to trust your gut. Not talk yourself out of it because you don't think you'll be believed.'

She knew Rhys was right. She'd dismissed Jarek's attempts at communication for too long, but he'd been clever about it, making contact when he knew she'd least want him to and using a new number each time. It had been so infrequently that she'd begin to relax, believing he was finally out of her life, when another message from an unknown number would appear. A handful of times in six months hadn't been overly concerning. But this was on a whole new level.

'How do you want to deal with him?' Rhys's hand on her arm focused her attention.

All the joy of a holiday in Sardinia for her best friend's wedding had, in less than twenty-four hours, been wiped out by the stress, fear and unhappiness she'd battled so hard against towards the end of her relationship with Jarek. An easy decision to walk away from him had been harder to do in practice because of the way he'd worn her down and managed to control her. Yet he still continued to have a hold, his presence making her heart race and palms sweat.

Without saying anything to Rhys for fear of him talking her out of it, Lola strode across the small parking area and up the steps that led to the Promenade du Port. With her focus on Jarek, she weaved her way between the tables on Zamira Lounge's terrace. It wasn't the loss of the relationship and the future she thought they'd have or the person she once believed him to be that she mourned, but the way his behaviour and manipulation had made her doubt the possibility of having a normal, healthy relationship in her future.

Jarek tracked her the whole way, his eyes piercing slits reminiscent of the snake he was. They might as well have been glowing demon-like.

'What the hell are you doing here?' She stopped a short distance from him, close enough for him to hear the terseness in her voice without causing a scene or him being able to touch her.

He gazed up nonchalantly as if him being in Sardinia was the most normal thing in the world. The slight lift of his lips incensed her. He was getting a kick out of this.

'I'm on holiday. You are too?' He held her gaze. 'What are the chances?'

She'd played right into his hands. Getting her attention and making her riled and not in control was what he'd wanted. He'd managed to drag her emotions right back to those terrible weeks leading up to her leaving him, a time she'd fought so hard to put behind her.

All she wanted to do was rage and tear into him, when she knew she should take a deep breath and walk away, because wouldn't he just love the chance to tighten his grip on her, to get an uncensored reaction. He'd never hurt her physically, but she wouldn't put it past him, not when he'd manipulated and controlled her in every other way. She loathed the desire coursing through her to hurt him physically as much as he'd hurt her mentally. She wouldn't give him the satisfaction of letting him see her anger.

She was rarely lost for words, but right now any cutting comeback eluded her. All she had was an ever-growing hatred for someone she'd once loved. How was it possible she'd fallen for him? How had she not seen beyond his charm to the person he really was?

A hand clasped her shoulder. Warm, solid and dependable when her heart was sprinting, her head a muddle and her breathing rapid.

'We have that restaurant reservation,' Rhys said calmly as he gently squeezed her shoulder, a comforting rather than controlling gesture.

Rhys was giving her a way out, showing her she wasn't alone in dealing with her ex. She didn't want to even be thinking about him or be anywhere near him.

With her attention still fixed on Jarek – as if letting him out of her sight for even a second would somehow give him more of an upper hand than he already had – Lola finally breathed a little easier. 'Yes, we should go.'

Rhys moved closer to stand beside her, his arm shifting to encircle her waist.

'I don't believe we've met,' he said smoothly, looking down at Jarek. 'I'm Rhys, Lola's friend.'

Jarek's smile grew as he stood, completely unruffled and held out his hand. 'I'm Ja—'

'I know who you are,' Rhys cut in, his free hand remaining firmly by his side. 'No need to introduce yourself.'

With a blink-and-you'd-miss-it tightening of his lips, Jarek snatched his hand back. 'Who the fuck do you think you are?' There was a promise of violence in his tone that made Lola feel sick as his calculating gaze swept over Rhys. 'You're seriously with him?' He narrowed his eyes and stepped closer. 'I'm sure you do know who I am because I'm certain she's been talking about me lots,' he said with menace. His attention flicked back to Lola. 'As sure as I'll be seeing you around.'

Lola forced herself to hold his gaze, refusing to flinch despite his attention making her skin crawl. Yet she broke eye contact first, desperate to get away. She grabbed Rhys's arm and walked off without another word, certain that Jarek was following their every move.

She wondered where Rhys's assertiveness had come from. He'd confidently taken charge and been what she'd needed in the moment. She was immensely grateful to him for snapping her out of the terror she'd been in.

'Thank you,' she said, clutching his arm tighter. They reached the path beneath the trees that led down to the marina and took the left fork away from Jarek.

'What do you want to do?' Rhys asked.

'I don't know,' she said quietly. 'But get away from here.' Even in Porto Cervo, surrounded by summery-looking people, she desperately wanted to be somewhere she felt he couldn't invade. 'Do you mind if we go back to the villa?'

'Of course not. I'll message Barnaby so they don't wonder where we've gone.'

* * *

Lola didn't say a word during the short drive back to the villa and Rhys didn't try to engage her in conversation, and it wasn't just because he didn't know what to say. Only a couple of days ago, Lola had opened up about how controlling and manipulative her ex had been, but him showing up here had left her shaken. The confidence she'd exuded had been extinguished. What he was struggling with most was not knowing what to say to make her feel safe. If he was feeling unnerved by Jarek going to such lengths to upset her, then he could only imagine how much it had affected Lola. She'd held her nerve while talking to him, but the moment they'd walked away, Rhys had felt her trembling. Violence was never the answer and, until punching Freddie at the stag do, he had never hit anyone in his life. He'd controlled the urge to wipe the smirk off Jarek's face because it would have done more harm than good with a sociopath. The more attention they gave him, the more they'd play into what he wanted and fuel his desire to control and manipulate, but Rhys had never felt such loathing for someone before.

The villa was empty and quiet, a sanctuary that he hoped Jarek either wasn't aware of or wouldn't dare infiltrate. At least Lola would never be alone here.

They reached the central living area that opened onto the garden and Lola sank into the sofa while Rhys went over to the bar. He joined her, their fingers brushing as she took the bottle of Ichnusa lemon from him.

'Thank you,' she said quietly. She took a sip of the light and zingy beer. 'Not just for this, but for being there. For helping me to hold it together.'

'Are you okay?'

'Yes... Actually, no.' Lola shook her head. 'Oh, I don't know. I knew what he was like, yet I still didn't expect *this*.'

Rhys nodded, except he didn't understand. It was hard to get his head around someone behaving this way when the relationship was clearly over. He breathed deeply. The herb-scented air wafting through the open doors seemed out of kilter with the conversation. 'He's seriously come all the way out here just to get under your skin?'

'I know he has.' Lola put her drink on the coffee table and rubbed her fingers over the sides of her forehead. 'There's no such thing as coincidence with him. He's calculating and purposeful. He can swear blind that he's here on holiday, but I know he knew I was here. However careful I am, it's impossible to block him from all the stuff my friends share on their socials. And then there are the messages—'

'Messages? More than the one he sent yesterday evening?'

Lola flicked her attention away from Rhys to the garden.

'He's messaged me a few times, nothing too worrying until the hen do, and then of course last night. I should have said something, I just didn't know how to, and I certainly didn't want anything finding its way back to Mirabel. By acknowledging the message and talking about it – feeling anything, even anger, annoyance. Fear' – she drew in a long breath, her lips pursing – 'it would feel as if he'd got the upper hand and won.' She shifted until she was facing him. 'I want him out of my life. Every message is a reminder of what he put me through, how trapped I felt. He's always found a way to chip at my confidence. By the time I left him, I had zero romantic feelings remaining, but I underestimated the damage he'd done.'

Rhys took her hand and held it tight, his heart splintering at the tears lining her eyes and the way she was still trembling. 'You need to report him to the police, Lola. As soon as you get back, file a report, plus apply for an injunction – Barnaby will help you with that – you'll need to give as much information and evidence as you can, if you still have stuff?'

'I've kept the messages, yes.'

'And I'm witness this time.' He reached for his phone and showed her the photos he'd taken of her talking to Jarek before he'd joined her. 'I promise you're not alone.'

19

Those words, steadying and heartfelt, meant everything and confirmed Lola's thought about Rhys being there for her. As a friend, she trusted him completely, but would it be possible to continue trusting him if he was more than a friend? The idea that she was even considering letting someone close again scared her.

Lola gulped back a sob as all the stress of the last two days bubbled over. The tears fell and not just because of the shock of being confronted by Jarek, but at the realisation that she was no longer on her own dealing with him.

Rhys wrapped his arms around her and pulled her close, whispering that it would all be okay as his fingers threaded her hair. The desire to trust and believe him scared her as much as it soothed, yet she allowed her pent-up emotions to overflow, sobbing against his chest until her tears had dried tight on her cheeks.

* * *

After Lola had cried her heart out, they talked a bit more and Rhys promised to keep what had happened with Jarek between themselves. He probably thought not saying anything was a bad idea, but she'd been adamant that nothing should get back to Mirabel. It might have been wise to give Fabs a heads-up about what was going on, but Lola convinced Rhys not to, because there was no way that Fabs would keep anything from Mirabel.

At least them leaving together early from Porto Cervo didn't need explaining when everyone assumed they'd come back for some alone time before that evening's gathering. *If only*, Lola thought as the villa filled up with friends. Doing something pleasurable with Rhys would have been preferable to having to deal with the fallout from Jarek. He'd hijacked her emotions and diverted her attention away from the conversation she'd meant to have with Rhys about their kiss. Now her thoughts were straying into territory she was uncertain how to navigate, thinking about Rhys in a completely different way. What was real and what was pretend had become entangled.

Lola's first impression of Rhys had been that he was nice-looking in an understated way. He had a James McAvoy vibe about him, whereas she usually went for men who had more of a Chris Hemsworth build. Muscles over personality, perhaps. Although Jarek had seemed to have it all: looks and personality – until he didn't. Six-packs and sexiness didn't mean a thing if someone was cruel. Rhys was handsome in a way that had crept up on her, perhaps because his personality shone through his soulful eyes.

There were even more people at the villa than usual with Fabs's Italian friends joining them for drinks. Although Gareth had backed off with his flirting, Lola was conscious of Valentino's attention in particular, because she'd noticed him looking her way with come-to-bed eyes.

'I didn't think anyone could be more handsome than Fabs, but hell,' Deni said under her breath as she leaned close to Lola, 'he has some damn fine-looking friends. To be that good-looking should be illegal.'

'Missing your husband by any chance?' Lola quipped, knowing her tone was clipped but not caring because she was annoyed with herself for being attracted to Valentino's dark brooding looks when he reminded her of Jarek.

'I do miss him,' Deni said smoothly, her own tone laced with something that edged towards annoyance. 'But he's never looked like that.'

Lola hmphed.

'Not that I ever wanted him to be *that* good-looking.' Deni drew closer to Lola, her tone softer. 'To me, my husband's the most handsome man in the world because I love him – not that I tell him enough. I've never wanted someone so stupidly good-looking I'd spend my whole time worrying that I wasn't good enough for them.'

'Because you think you're out of his league?' Lola subtly gestured towards Valentino. 'Because that's a load of bull made up to make people feel shitty about themselves.'

'I don't believe for a minute anyone's ever said anything like that to you.'

'Not to me, no, but they have about Rhys.'

'Oh.' Deni nodded. 'Because you and he are—'

'What? Not well suited?'

Deni shrugged. 'You don't think that's the case?'

'Of course not.' Lola drained the rest of her wine. 'Saying someone is out of someone's league is as shallow as it gets. It suggests that someone not traditionally beautiful or handsome shouldn't be with someone who is, when there are so many other things to consider in a relationship, like personality – if the person is kind, loving, thoughtful. A good person.'

'Mr Drop Dead Gorgeous over there might be all of those things.'

'Yes, he might be,' Lola said, then thought, *But I already know that Rhys is.*

They fell silent and Deni sipped her drink while they watched everyone. Although Lola avoided looking in Valentino's direction, she could sense him glancing their way. She shifted so her back was to him.

Deni noticed and opened her mouth, then closed it. She laid a hand on her arm. 'I'm sorry if we've been overly pushy about all those sexy blokes who've been tripping over themselves to capture your attention.' Deni laughed, but it was gentle. 'I know I've been living vicariously through you; Sarah and Polly too. Our intentions are good, but perhaps we've been a bit full on.'

This was the conversation Lola should have had with Deni ages ago; she should have been open about the way she was feeling. She should have been able to talk to her friends and tell them in the nicest possible way to back off from trying to set her up with men, but she knew that would have led to deeper conversations, and that was what she'd feared. Not that she'd had any problem opening up to Rhys.

Lola was about to say she knew their teasing had all been in jest when Deni's eyes went wide.

'Heads up,' she said.

And then Valentino was next to them, all six-foot-something of chiselled Italian good looks with distractingly snug trousers that made Lola want to walk swiftly in the other direction, except he was clutching two glasses of white wine and his eyes were fixed on her.

'I noticed your drink was empty.'

Hell was he smooth.

Deni lifted her own nearly empty glass and raised her eyebrows. Lola inwardly sighed but accepted the drink from Valentino.

'Thank you,' she said, not wanting to be rude but also annoyed at his snub of Deni, who, Lola realised with horror, was slowly backing away.

'Just going to grab some food,' Deni said. Her voice was full of amusement, although she looked sympathetic. Perhaps there was a touch of glee. Lola knew she wouldn't go far, not when she'd want to see how this played out.

Lola took a sip of the citrusy wine. Where was Rhys when she needed him?

'We have not had much chance to talk since the first night.' Valentino leaned against the wall. A waft of sultry spiciness encroached on her personal space.

Although his English was almost as good as Fabs's, his accent was richer: deep and seductive. And he knew it.

'Lots of people to talk to, that's why.' She'd make polite small talk, then find an excuse to escape to her friends. Deni was already snuggled up on a sofa with Sarah, both watching her, as she'd anticipated.

Annoyance flared. Despite what Deni had said moments before, she knew they would still prefer her to hook up with a sexy Italian rather than believe she could be into Rhys.

'You are enjoying yourself in Sardinia?' Valentino asked smoothly, while his chocolate eyes bored into her.

She could do this: a polite, uninteresting conversation. She opened her mouth to reply when he added: 'With the Englishman?' A smirk tugged at his full lips.

Fire raged inside her. 'Yes, I have, thank you,' she snapped. 'And he's Welsh, not English.'

'If you want to have more fun than you have with him, you only have to say.' His voice was dripping with suggestion. He was clean-shaven and classically handsome. Valentino might be benign, but there was no way to know without putting her trust in him. But his arrogance incensed her, along with his belief that he'd give her a better time than Rhys because of the way he looked.

The idea of a fling with a sexy Italian should have been tempting, and yet... He put her on edge, whereas around Rhys she'd felt relaxed and safe from the moment she'd sat with him at the end of the dock, their conversation flowing effortlessly.

She scrunched her lips. 'You honestly think I'd have more fun with you?'

He raised an eyebrow and snorted like he could see right through her, that the fun she was having with Rhys wasn't the sort of fun he was suggesting.

But what if she and Rhys could have fun that way? Their kiss. She hadn't stopped thinking about it. Something had ignited and he'd surprised her. He was quiet instead of confident. He didn't dominate, crowd her out or overpower. He allowed her to be her. He listened and understood. He was sensitive and thoughtful. His eyes twinkled when he laughed, and the way the hollow of his neck pulsed and focused her attention on his skin, imagining how it would feel beneath her fingers...

'I am certain you would have more fun with me.' Valentino's voice was deep and seductive.

Lola held his gaze, her annoyance growing at the way he was invading her personal space, his eyes zoning in on her lips and shifting down to her cleavage. 'Yet I'm not sure I would with you.'

'You only have to say if you change your mind.' He leaned closer and kissed her on each cheek while his hands caressed her arms.

'I won't,' Lola said lightly, because despite his looks, he left her cold. But most of all he wasn't Rhys. That alone was enough to make her walk away and not look back.

* * *

Rhys wanted to pace over and claim Lola because his blood was boiling so much, yet he stopped himself because of how inappropriate that was. Claiming Lola was what Valentino was trying to do; sex appeal oozed off him, while his eyes undressed her. Claiming her was what Jarek was still attempting to do. No one should be treated like that. What Rhys wanted to do was protect her, to hold and kiss her. To be with her and there for her. So he watched from afar, letting his friends' conversation wash over him as he clenched his bottle of beer and breathed through his annoyance. She wasn't his, they weren't really together, and he couldn't – wouldn't – interfere.

It had been different earlier with Jarek, to witness her shock as the blood had drained from her face before she'd stormed up to her ex and confronted him. Rhys had feared for her safety then. He'd wanted to help her, to make sure she was okay and could walk away unscathed – at least physically. Emotionally, he knew she was a mess. But he had no right to interfere now, even if he loathed the look Valentino was giving her because it was the way he wanted to look at Lola, with seductive desire and longing. Not that he'd have the nerve to be so blatant, and he sure as hell wasn't a tall, dark, handsome Italian who could effortlessly sweep her off her feet.

Valentino had obviously tried to do that; Rhys didn't need to lip-read to understand his intentions when his body language said it all, but Lola's reaction was clear too as she leaned away, angling her head to avoid that intense gaze. When he'd kissed her on each cheek, she extracted herself from his hold and walked away.

Across the room, Rhys met Valentino's eyes, dark moody pools that narrowed arrow-like at him. Valentino batted his hand, a dismissive gesture as he pushed away from the wall and stalked off into the garden. Rhys should have felt smug, yet he didn't. Lola had obviously shut down Valentino's advances, but she hadn't sought him out either. Now he didn't know what was right: to go and find her or leave her in peace. So he took the easy, least complicated way out and followed Gareth and Barnaby onto the terrace.

Ten minutes later when Lola hadn't returned and he noticed Deni and Sarah leave – presumably to find her – he regretted his cowardice. But by then it was too late. Doing anything now would feel like an afterthought and he hated himself for his indecision.

20

It had been easy for Lola to turn down Valentino, but it wasn't easy to drag herself out of the well of worry she'd fallen back into. She woke early and couldn't get back to sleep. An uneasiness nibbled away. Jarek was on Sardinia. What else would he do? She wished Polly was here sharing the room so she wouldn't be alone. Or that they were back in Bosa and Rhys was lying next to her.

She was worried about that too. Her thoughts kept straddling the line of friendship and the possibility of more. Not that they needed to define their relationship, but she was longing to feel comfortable around him again. They still hadn't talked about their kiss and since their conversation before yesterday's gathering, Lola hadn't seen much of him at all.

Rhys wasn't at breakfast, but not many people were, likely taking the opportunity to have a lie-in after a busy few days.

Lola found a shady spot beneath a pine tree on the villa's beach and read for the rest of the morning, only joining Sarah and Deni for lunch.

Lola had messaged Mirabel earlier that morning to check in

on her after she and Fabs had left unusually early the night before. She'd thought it strange to not have heard anything back, but hadn't been concerned until she got an unexpected call from Fabs when she was on her way to her room.

'Hey there,' she said, 'everything all right?'

'Not really, no. Is Mirabel with you?'

'No. Why?'

Silence, apart from the birdsong floating in through the open bedroom doors.

'What's happened, Fabs?'

'A huge fucking argument, that's what, which I'm trying to resolve with little luck so far.'

'With Mirabel?'

'No, between my mamma and hers. Again.' He sighed. 'Mirabel left half an hour ago and I can't get hold of her. At least she's not answering to me. I thought you might have more luck.'

'I can try calling her now.'

'Thank you. I assume she's gone off somewhere to get away from everyone, but she was really upset. I'm worried. Hell, everyone's out-of-their-minds upset.'

Fabs suggested the places she might have escaped to and by the time they said goodbye, Lola's chest was even tighter with worry. First the shock of Jarek, now concern for her friend.

Perching on the end of her bed, Lola phoned Mirabel. She focused on the vibrant pink of the flowers decorating the wall outside her room as it rang and rang and went to answerphone. At the beep, Lola left a message.

'Hey there, Fabs said you've gone off somewhere and aren't answering his calls. I understand if you need some space, but I just want to make sure you're okay, so let me know, yeah? And if you need a friend or a shoulder to cry on, please ask. I'm here for you, always.'

She ended the call and gazed across the lawn to the turquoise sea, which was bright against the dark trunks of the trees. It was possible for problems to be eased by beautiful surroundings, candlelit dinners and fancy parties, but only temporarily. Those deeply embedded worries could never be outrun unless they were dealt with one way or another. That meant reporting Jarek and taking his threat seriously; for Mirabel it would be finding a balance of what she wanted alongside two sets of parents who felt rather differently about things. Honest, open conversations were needed, that was key to everything, but Lola understood that her friend needed space and time to think.

Lola's phone pinged. The tightness in her chest shifted a little at Mirabel's name.

> I'm okay thanks, it all got a bit too much. I'm in a taxi going to Cala li Cossi and could do with your company, but only you right now please. Xx

Lola thumbed a reply to say she'd be on her way, phoned Fabs back to let him know and went in search of Rhys, finding him on his own in the living room with his head buried in a book.

'Hey, I need your help.' She sat down next to him and relayed the conversation she'd had with Fabs. 'I know where she's going and Fabs left his car here last night, so said I could use it, but I don't drive, so I was hoping you could.'

'Of course.' Rhys put down his book. 'So we're on a rescue mission.'

'Something like that.'

* * *

Once she'd packed a bag with refreshments and they were on their way to the beach Mirabel had fled to, Lola tried to focus on the horizon to combat her travel sickness. Her head swirled with thoughts and so much was left unspoken between her and Rhys. Mirabel's crisis had taken the focus away from Lola's own and she was relieved to have a distraction.

Keeping her head still while she focused on the road, she steadily breathed through the nausea. The hot patch of sun on her arm was tempered by the breeze funnelling through the open window. Rhys was a quiet, comforting presence as he concentrated on driving across the forested interior of the island.

After they'd navigated a couple of hairpin bends with panoramic views of sun-dappled forest, Lola felt the need to talk rather than dwell on her torturous thoughts. 'Did you get a sense that things had got this stressful between the parents?'

'Not really, but then Fabs is a pretty chilled guy. He's definitely been a mediator between his mamma and Mirabel's parents. If Mirabel was stuck in the middle feeling the pressure, it's no wonder she snapped.' He glanced at her. 'Is this usual behaviour for her?'

'Things have stressed her out before, certainly at work, but she's never run away from problems. I'm guessing everything got too much and she took off to decompress.'

'Is it wise us going to find her then?'

'She's told me where she is and wants my company. I'm not sure she wants to be alone, just away from everyone who's causing her stress.'

Rhys raised an eyebrow. 'Fabs included?'

'For the time being, yes.' Lola shrugged and her head swirled. She gulped down a wave of nausea, rested back and closed her eyes.

'You okay?'

'I'll be glad when we get there.' Lola breathed out long and slow. 'Mirabel likes her space, but she's also someone who needs to talk things through. I think this may be a cry for help. She probably felt more comfortable escaping the situation rather than trying to navigate her way through it.'

'So you're going to help get her back on track?'

'Hopefully.'

That was the plan. What else could she do? With the wedding just two days away, supporting her friend was the most important thing, even if it meant putting aside her own concerns for the time being.

After parking in a car park to the west of Costa Paradiso, Lola and Rhys set off along the dirt-sand path that was punctuated by stone steps. Hugging a rocky outcrop to the left, it allowed sweeping views across grey boulders to the sea, which looked enticingly blue and cool in the afternoon sun. Mirabel had pinged her location on the far side of the beach, so that was where they were headed.

'She took a taxi to somewhere an hour and twenty minutes away,' Rhys said as they climbed narrow stone steps beneath overhanging rocks. Once through, the way opened up, with the sandy track meandering between small trees that clung to the hillside. 'She really did want to get away.'

The path wasn't quite wide enough for them to walk side by side, so Lola led. It was the sort of day that she wanted to capture; the heat was gentle, the sea air fresh and sweet and she felt a hell of a lot better than she had done throughout the journey.

They walked on for another couple of minutes in silence before Rhys said, 'I do wonder if having parents who care enough to be so invested in your wedding that they come to blows is a good thing.'

Lola glanced back at him. 'You're saying your parents don't about you?'

'Not exactly.'

Only their footsteps scuffing the compacted dirt path sounded for a moment; a sharp call of a gull wheeling overhead broke the silence.

'I'm being unfair,' Rhys finally said. 'My parents do care about us all, it's just my brothers and their families take up all their time and energy and very little is left for me.'

'Is that because you try not to bother them or because you're the son who doesn't demand their attention?'

Rhys grunted. 'A bit of both.'

They continued on, both quiet again. The path steadily climbed between forest-green bushes, which were broken up by cream-toned rocks.

'Maybe I don't make the effort,' Rhys piped up. 'Actually, I know I don't. Sometimes it's hard seeing my brothers with their families...' He trailed off.

'Because it's what you want, right? A partner to share things with. Perhaps children one day?' Lola said the words carefully because she could sense his conflict and had heard the sorrow in his voice. She wondered if he was thinking of Zoe and the future he'd imagined with her.

They rounded a corner and suddenly the beach was visible. Lola halted, open-mouthed. A thick swathe of sand was sandwiched between the emerald-green sea, and a dark-blue river cut behind the beach and through the gap in the towering pink-trachyte rocks, its multicoloured crags peppered with bushes.

'I've never been here,' Rhys said as they continued along the path that wound down to the beach. 'Although I'm not surprised as it's a rather romantic spot. Perhaps Fabs saved it for Mirabel.'

There were a few people dotted about on the oyster-pale

sand, mostly couples or family groups. Lola shaded her eyes and squinted, searching the beach for Mirabel.

'I think I can see her.' On the far side, a woman was sitting on her own, her red dress bright against the sand. 'I should go and talk to her on my own.'

Rhys nodded and moved off the path, settling himself on a rock next to where the river narrowed to a stream and flowed out to sea. 'I'll be here if you need me.'

21

Lola wished more than anything that she was strolling barefoot across Spiaggia di Cala li Cossi with Mirabel's arm hooked in hers and a beach bag slung over her shoulder with towels and a picnic inside. As it was, her trainers kicked up sand, her crossbody bag contained little more than her purse, phone, lip balm and a bottle of water and she was on her own as she passed groups of happy people making the most of the late September sun.

As Lola neared Mirabel, she couldn't help but notice how forlorn she looked, with her legs crossed and shoulders hunched as she stared towards the pond-flat sea.

'Hey, you doing okay?' Lola said softly as she sat down next to her on the warm sand and they hugged. The sea barely lapped the shore and the voices from the other beach-goers were distant, twirled away on the lightest of breezes.

'This is the beach Fabs took me to the first time I visited his family.' Mirabel drew her knees up to her chest and wrapped her arms around them. 'Everything felt simple back then, even if I was overwhelmed by meeting his family. How wealthy he actu-

The Island of Hopes and Dreams 155

ally was wasn't really apparent till I came here and saw how they lived and where he grew up. None of that mattered back then, whereas now...' She exhaled deeply. Lola allowed her the time to put her thoughts into words. 'Now, everything is different.'

Mirabel's need to escape to somewhere that held happy memories was understandable, yet Lola sensed there was more to it than she was saying.

'What's really going on?' Lola asked gently. 'You running away has everyone worried. I understand how overwhelming the last few days have been, but are things okay between you and Fab—'

'Yes! Nothing's wrong with us. I love him with all my heart, it's just...' She glanced away but not before Lola noticed her tears.

Lola reached for Mirabel's hand.

'I want to marry Fabs more than anything; I want us to start a family. I've got to the point where those things mean as much to me as my career, yet it's the thought of starting over with everything that I'm struggling with: quitting my job, building my own business and client list, leaving my family and starting a whole new life in a country without friends of my own and on an island I've only ever visited. I've always loved being here, but that's with the knowledge that I'll be going home again at the end of a week or two.

'I'm not just marrying Fabs but his whole family, and that's *a lot*. Being referee between his mum and my mum got me thinking, what happens when there are grandchildren involved? I'm still learning Italian and we'd need to bring up our children bilingual. There's so much to think about. And what if this never gets any easier? What if I hate living here and miss my life back home?' She turned to Lola wide-eyed. 'London's my home.' She was trembling, her breathing sharp and her face flushed. It was almost as if she was having a panic attack.

'Oh Mirabel.' Lola slipped an arm across her shoulders. 'Have you shared these thoughts with Fabs?'

'Not in so many words, but I will. I need to.'

Lola hugged her close. 'It's an awful lot to be processing, and emotions are bound to be running high when you're all living together.'

'It's not like we're on top of each other – their place is palatial.'

'But isn't that partly the problem? Your parents aren't wealthy or used to this lavish lifestyle. I mean, we have a chef at our beck and call at the villa. The first night party was a catered affair – it's so far removed from the way your parents live and how you grew up. You said that yourself. Your parents are probably feeling the stress of it all in a different way to Fabs's parents. Different lifestyles, different cultures. It's a lot.'

'I know, you're right and it was my worry all along, yet I ran with it, wanting the most luxurious wedding in the most photogenic location.'

'No one can blame you for that. And this is Fabs's home – one of you was always going to get married away from your home country.'

'Mum's pissed off because she feels the focus should be on the bride and therefore the bride's family, as weddings usually take place in the bride's home town with the bride's parents hosting—'

'Yet here it feels as if Giada has stolen her thunder.'

'Exactly, and I can't do anything about it now, apart from try to put out the flames and make the best of everyone living together when tempers are frayed.'

'No wonder you needed to escape.' Lola gazed towards the

sea. The emerald shallows turned a deep blue further out where rocks emerged from the water like huge stalagmites. 'I kinda felt like that the first evening here, although for a different reason.'

'Ha, yes! And you ran straight into Rhys's arms.'

'Something like that,' Lola said, biting back the desire to tell Mirabel the truth about her and Rhys. Now wasn't the time. She didn't know how she felt about Rhys, how he felt about her or what the hell they were doing to be able to explain it anyway. She held Mirabel's hand in her lap. 'You're torn in every direction and don't have any time with Fabs either. It's no wonder you've reacted like this. A wedding is stressful enough, but to then be starting your married life in a completely different country and leaving every—' Lola stopped talking as Mirabel's face crumpled, her eyes once again damp. 'What I'm attempting to say is try to see the positives, see beyond the stress of the lead-up to what will be the happiest day of your life. You're so incredibly lucky, not just to be getting married to the most gorgeous and lovely guy, but to have parents who care and support you enough to go along with your dream wedding, even if it's not what they'd have chosen, and you have in-laws who would do anything for you – it's not just about money. They adore you because you make Fabs unbelievably happy. You have the chance to start a new exciting life in a place that people can only dream about living, and yes, you have to start from scratch jobwise, but that's exciting too and it's not as if you'll have a financial pressure to go along with it. You're choosing to work because you love what you do, but you don't have to work if you don't want to. There's freedom in that.'

Mirabel pursed her lips and wedged her sunglasses in her hair. Her eyes glistened damp in the sunshine. She drew out a long breath. 'So what you're saying is I shouldn't be complaining because I'm lucky and should hold my tongue and be happy.'

'Okay, you've taken me the wrong way. Maybe I didn't say it right. Everyone's stressed, Fabs is too, although he might not show it, so everyone's reaction is understandable, yours included.'

Mirabel pulled her hand from Lola's and smoothed out the creases of her red dress.

At work and at home, actually in every aspect of Mirabel's life, she was usually so unruffled. She was the dependable friend who had her shit together, and that had a lot to do with having a supportive family, her head screwed on and making wise choices. Plus she had great taste in men – not because of the way they looked, but because beneath their handsomeness they were good people. Mirabel couldn't have asked for a better partner and fiancé in Fabs. If Lola hadn't known him, she would have thought Mirabel had made him up because on paper he was beyond perfection. And in real life he was perfect. So yes, Lola believed Mirabel was lucky, but she also knew that didn't mean her worries weren't real.

'Your upset is valid, Mirabel.' Lola reached out and touched her arm. Mirabel's hands stilled, pressed tight against the material covering her thighs. 'I didn't mean to belittle how you're feeling. I just wanted to give you a balanced perspective because I understand how panicked you're feeling. I've witnessed the stress rolling off you for weeks, increasing the closer we got to coming here. But you've run away today, which has Fabs worried, and me; hell, everyone will be freaking out.' Lola watched the sea sending tiny ripples to the beach, dampening the sand and turning it honey-coloured. Her eyes travelled beyond the rocks scattered in the calm water of the bay, to the horizon, where the azure sea merged in a hazy line with the sky. She understood why Mirabel liked this beach so much – it was enclosed and majestic, beautiful and interesting. Lola turned back to her friend. 'I also know what a panic attack feels like, and what the stress and underlying feeling of being constantly in flight-or-fight mode does to you, not being able to think straight—'

'Because of Jarek?' Mirabel cut in.

'Yes, because of him.' Lola couldn't bring herself to even say his name – again a defence mechanism, as if ignoring him and not talking about him would make him go away, despite what the evidence of the last couple of days had proved.

'You're right,' Mirabel said. 'I'm sorry for snapping.'

'You have nothing to apologise for. I'd be more surprised if you weren't stressed, I just wanted to refocus you on the positives and remind you that your parents and Fabs's love you both and want what's best for you, but they're likely stressed too, which is why it's all come to a head and made you want to get away.'

Mirabel raked her fingers through the sand between them. 'Perhaps deep down I'm wishing I could enjoy myself like you, Deni and Sarah are, without the pressure of being the bride, of having to ensure everyone is happy, while trying to keep the peace between our families.'

'Which is a normal and sensible reaction, wanting to enjoy the time with everyone, Fabs in particular.'

Mirabel huffed. 'When even time for us is scarce.'

'Well, you have an epic honeymoon in New Zealand to look forward to after all the madness is over.'

'That I can't wait for.'

The smile Mirabel gave reached her eyes and made the tightness in Lola's chest loosen.

'And if it's any consolation, everyone's having a wonderful time – maybe not your immediate family right now, but friends definitely are.'

Mirabel flashed her a cheeky grin. 'Everyone can see how

much you've been enjoying yourself – or enjoying a certain someone, I should say. But you have surprised me.'

'Oh?'

'Because Rhys isn't your type.'

'Oh, I don't know about that—'

'You have a type, Lola.' Mirabel cut her off with a shake of her head. 'And you definitely go for looks over personality.'

'I do not. And I don't have a type either.' She attempted to ignore the knowing look Mirabel was giving her, but realised her protestation was an outright lie, something that had become clear over the last week. Okay, fine. Maybe she did have a type, but didn't everyone?

'I'm just saying I'm surprised by you and Rhys because he's not someone I'd ever thought you'd go for. He's good-looking but not in the way you rate.' Her voice softened as she touched Lola's arm. 'It's a good thing and I'm happy for you.'

'I do rate personality,' Lola said, unable to control the edge to her tone. 'It's just I keep getting it wrong.'

Epically so, was what she didn't say. Mirabel knew an awful lot, but she didn't know everything and not as much as Rhys now knew. Not sharing everything had been Lola's way of protecting her friend, because she knew that Mirabel had held back her true feelings about Jarek, not wanting to dampen Lola's spirits when she'd been in love. And she certainly wasn't going to risk talking about him now and adding an extra layer of worry to Mirabel's shoulders when Jarek was on Sardinia. That was something she needed to deal with alone. Actually, not alone – with Rhys.

She glanced back across the beach to where she'd left him perched on a rock bathed in the late afternoon sun. Dependable, kind, thoughtful and supportive Rhys. She hoped he'd remembered to apply his factor 50 this morning.

'What do you want to do?' Lola asked, turning her attention and the conversation back on her friend.

'I don't want to go back, not yet.' Mirabel visibly shuddered. 'The thought of another evening being a mediator and attempting to please everyone, I just can't do it.'

'You need to talk to Fabs though – you can't let him worry that you might want to call the whole thing off.'

'Oh God, that wasn't my intention at all.'

'He needs to know that.'

Mirabel scrunched her nose and dug her fingers deeper into the sand.

'Why don't we get Fabs to come out here,' Lola suggested. 'Rhys drove me; I'll get him to call him.'

'I'll let Mum and Dad know where I am too, so they don't worry, and maybe the four of us can go somewhere this evening – I could do with the easy-going company of our best friends.' She suddenly grinned. 'I'm sorry what I said before about you favouring looks over personality, I know it's not just about that and I honestly didn't mean to make you sound shallow—'

'It's okay, and I know my track record with men has been shocking. Rhys has opened my eyes to that because I've got to know him slowly rather than jumped in feet first.'

'If you say so!' Mirabel said. 'I'd say you moved pretty fast. I never would have put you two together, but somehow it works.'

Lola's smile hid her true feelings because Mirabel had a false idea of her relationship with Rhys. They were friends, nothing more, and yet they were obviously doing a convincing job of pretending they'd fallen for each other.

22

After sitting in the sun for what seemed an age, Rhys had been mightily relieved when Lola had messaged asking him to call Fabs. With his arms and the back of his neck feeling hot and tingly, plus a numb bum from sitting on a hard rock, he was more than happy to phone his friend, then find a shady spot to sit with a drink. Yet by the time Fabs arrived in a taxi over an hour later, Rhys was cursing Mirabel for having retreated so far away.

Fabs may have sounded okay on the phone earlier, but his face was pinched with worry and his broad shoulders were hunched. He walked towards him with the gait of a man who'd had enough.

They hugged and thumped each other's shoulders, although Rhys noticed Fabs held on for a touch longer than normal.

'Where's Mirabel?' Fabs shoved his hands in his pockets.

'Still on the beach with Lola. You want to join them?'

'No, let them talk. There's a pizzeria where we can wait. You must be hungry.'

There was no argument from Rhys about that. They set off

along the sun-blasted road that skirted Costa Paradiso and overlooked the iron-red roofs of stone and honey-coloured houses. Beyond them, the sea foamed against the small clusters of rocks that dotted the northern coastline.

They'd walked halfway to the pizzeria before Fabs said anything. 'I nearly proposed to Mirabel on Cala li Cossi the first time I brought her here. It was her first time in Sardinia, first time meeting my family, and we'd only been together a few months, but even then I knew how much I loved her and that I wanted her to be my wife.'

Rhys glanced at his friend as their feet pounded the tarmac road. 'What stopped you?'

'Worrying about what everyone would think, my parents in particular, jumping into a serious relationship so quickly—'

'Your parents married young, surely they would have understood?'

'They married young because it was the done thing back then; my *nonna* would not have tolerated Mamma living with Papa before they were married. But yes, their views have changed since then.'

'If that wasn't the problem, what was?'

'That Mirabel is British, not Italian.'

'Ah,' Rhys said.

'Of course she won them over, but even though I knew she was the one, I put off proposing. I didn't want my family weighing in, thinking my decision was wrong.' He gestured inland. 'And now everything is blowing up. Everyone has an opinion of what we should have done, what we should or shouldn't be doing, no one happy or satisfied with anything.'

'But not because anyone thinks you and Mirabel shouldn't be getting married. Their interfering is because they all love you so much.'

Fabs snorted. 'It doesn't feel much like love with our parents at each other's throats. Mirabel's been in tears and I've struggled to defuse the situation and no one – *no one* – seems to be listening.'

It was uncharted territory for Fabs to be so troubled. Out of all of Rhys's friends – with the exception of Barnaby – he always seemed to be in total control, confident in his looks, beliefs, ideals and his place in the world. Tension between his family and Mirabel's might have seemed like nothing to other people, but Rhys knew how much the feeling of helplessness would affect Fabs.

Rhys allowed Fabs to set the pace, striding along the quiet, narrow road which was peppered with bushes and lined with single-storey stone houses. His need to walk off his anger and frustration was unsurprising after being the one to hold everything together while attempting to calm the situation.

'I remember my mamma and *nonna* arguing over how to make yogurt cake when I was about ten and thinking how formidable they were, and that I didn't want to get in the middle of them. *No one* wanted to get involved. No one was stupid enough to.' He glanced at Rhys, his cheeks and lips clenched so tight they'd turned white. 'But my mamma and Mirabel's' – he shook his head – 'they could burn a hole in hell with the fire raging between them. Nonna staying has made things worse. This should be a happy time, one of the happiest of my and Mirabel's lives.'

There was nothing Rhys could say. The truth was, Fabs had struggled to defuse the situation that Mirabel had run from, and now he'd scarpered too. Not that Rhys blamed him; he couldn't think of anything worse than being trapped in the middle of that kind of family tension. Perhaps that was why he was content to stay on the periphery of his own family; not only was it a way of avoiding conflict, it was also easier than getting too involved, which would only highlight how alone he was and how far away from having a relationship as loving as his brothers had found.

The pizzeria was tucked away down a lane, housed in a simple cream building with a terracotta-tiled terrace and a handful of wooden tables, a few already occupied.

'So how did you leave things back at the house?' Rhys asked after they'd been shown to a table with a view to the soothing blue sea dancing in the light of the retreating sun.

Fabs finished messaging Mirabel with their location and looked up. 'I told both my mamma and Mirabel's to get their shit together.' He leaned his elbows on the table and clasped his hands together. 'Well, not in so many words, because Mamma wouldn't have tolerated that. But I said what I said because I needed to come to Mirabel. They're grown-ups; we're all soon to be one family. They need to sort things out among themselves. My concern right now is Mirabel,' he growled.

That was the end of that conversation; Rhys knew not to push it any further. So they ordered wine and shared a Neapolitan pizza while they waited for Lola and Mirabel. They chatted like they used to when it was just the two of them putting the world to rights over a beer in their student flat in Bristol. Alone with Fabs, it was easy for Rhys to slip back into an older version of himself, someone who was more open, more upbeat, more willing to try things and say yes – before life had worn him down. Perhaps the change in him had less to do with his best friend and more to do with the woman he'd been spending most of his time with on Sardinia.

Caught up in reminiscing about the past, Rhys lost track of time and it was only when Lola and Mirabel strolled towards them that they cut their conversation short. The evening sun cast a golden light over the women. Fabs's focus was on Mirabel, but

Rhys's eyes were drawn to Lola, who was glowing with happiness. At least that was the impression she gave, walking down that sun-kissed path looking radiant and carefree.

Fabs got to his feet and Mirabel left Lola's side to fold herself into his embrace.

Rhys stood too when Lola reached him, both of them standing awkwardly while averting their attention from their friends' passionate kiss.

'Is everything okay?' Rhys gestured towards Mirabel as Lola sat in the chair next to his.

'Better than it was.' She nodded. 'A long talk and time away from parents was sorely needed. Oh, and seeing Fabs of course.' Lola placed her hand on Rhys's knee. He stilled, his breath hitching as he zoned in on the warmth of her through his jeans. 'But let's steer the conversation away from anything to do with the wedding. That and parents are out of bounds. At least till we get back.'

Rhys didn't allow himself to think ahead to the headache that Fabs and Mirabel would return to. He took Lola's lead in helping to make them forget their worries and why they were in a rustic but cheerful restaurant miles away from family and friends.

They ordered another three pizzas, bottles of Coke and a second bottle of wine and continued a conversation that reminded Rhys of a time that he'd thought he'd lost. He revelled in Lola and Mirabel's close, easy-going friendship that matched his own with Fabs as they talked about their work, their hopes and dreams and everything in between.

Once the pizza had been demolished, plenty of wine had been drunk and the sun was low on the horizon, Fabs and Mirabel started talking quietly between themselves. Rhys turned his attention to Lola, who was sipping her wine and watching her friend, her blue eyes dark in the golden light.

Mirabel being happy and relaxed had rubbed off on Lola, who was relieved her friend was okay. With a glimpse of the sea from their table, the setting was perfect, and the place was unpretentious with surprisingly good food. And as for the company...

He suddenly realised they were on a double date. That was something he and Fabs hadn't done since their uni days and it had only happened once because it had been painfully obvious that both girls had been into Fabs while he was the runner-up prize. Part of him believed he should have a similar feeling of worthlessness that he'd experienced at the age of eighteen; he and Lola were anything but madly in love, and yet... Lola looked at him in a way that made his heart swell. Once they got over their awkwardness and realised Fabs and Mirabel only had eyes for each other, their conversation meandered from topic to topic as they slowly managed to find the easy way they'd had from the start. It felt as if they'd known each other for years and their worries and inhibitions faded away as the sun melted into the horizon in a line of honey-gold.

23

'Let's not go back!' Mirabel announced loudly an hour later with a drunken smile plastered across her face.

Darkness had descended, the bill had been paid and they were about to leave the restaurant.

Rhys held his hands up. 'Might be a wise idea not to cos I've drunk too much to drive.'

He hadn't meant to get drunk, but he'd become so swept up in the energy and exuberance of the evening that he'd forgotten he'd driven there.

'I've only had one glass,' Fabs said. 'I can drive.'

Mirabel stuck her tongue out at him. 'Spoilsport.' She placed her hands on his chest and leaned so close her lips brushed his. 'I *really* don't want to go back tonight and face our parents.' She lowered her voice so it was sultry and suggestive. '*Amore mio*, one night away from everyone, just the two of us.'

Fabs glanced over her head towards them. 'Just the two of us and our friends...'

'I'm sure they're in no rush to go back either.' Mirabel raised an eyebrow and looked pleadingly at Lola.

'I'm happy to go with whatever you two want.'

Rhys couldn't work out Lola's tone, not when her face was a masterclass in neutrality, her eyes fixed on Mirabel.

Mirabel's face, however, was a picture of mischievousness as she whirled back to Fabs with a seductive flutter of her eyelashes. 'Come on, one night away, before the craziness really begins.'

Rhys was certain there was no way Fabs would be able to resist.

Already reaching for his phone, Fabs grinned at his soon-to-be wife. 'Let's see if I can find us somewhere to stay.'

* * *

Even if Fabs was sober enough to drive them back, Lola knew how tightly Mirabel had him twisted around her little finger. Of course he wouldn't be able to resist her blatant desire, not when the alternative was to go back to the warring parents and a shit tonne of headachy stuff to deal with. A night away must have seemed like a dream, and they lucked out when he managed to book a two-bedroom Airbnb with last-minute availability in Costa Paradiso.

When they reached the lane that led to the Airbnb, Mirabel steered Lola away from Rhys and Fabs. 'Are you two okay sharing a room?'

'Of course,' Lola said with far more certainty than she felt. They'd shared a room and a bed once before; why would it be a problem doing so again?

Mirabel leaned closer. 'I know what I said earlier on the beach, it's just I didn't want to assume.'

'Unlike Deni and Sarah.' It was too hard to explain, even though she *was* worried about sharing a room with Rhys again.

The first time had been a bit of fun; they'd known where they'd stood with each other and there'd been no expectations. This time she had no idea what he was thinking, while she was second-guessing each look and every interaction. Not to mention the confusing mix of longing and lust that had coiled through her this evening. Her thoughts were running wild with the what-ifs – what if they took things further than the pretend kiss that had felt anything but pretend? What if she kissed him again – how would he react to that?

The thing that had changed between them was intimacy and expectation, precisely the elements that always changed a friendship into something undefined and more complicated. Their love pact added complexity, because what part was she pretending any longer?

The Airbnb was a simple one-storey building painted white, with just a small kitchen, living room and two bedrooms. They hadn't got any further than the living room before Mirabel was tugging Fabs towards the nearest bedroom. Fabs gave a backwards glance and a brief shrug in their direction, but there was zero resistance from him and their lips were on each other's before they'd even shut the door behind them.

'So,' Lola said, twisting round to look at Rhys, who was standing in the middle of the room looking as awkward as she was.

'I can sleep out here.' Rhys pointed at a two-seater sofa that would leave his legs dangling off the end.

Lola gestured to the closed bedroom door where Fabs and Mirabel had retreated. 'You seriously want to sleep out here while they're in there?' She raised an eyebrow.

Rhys pulled a face. 'Fair point.'

Lola started towards the dimly lit hallway, which she presumed led to the second bedroom.

The Island of Hopes and Dreams 171

'I'm happy to sleep on a chair,' he said as she pushed open a door. 'We might be lucky, and our room has a sofa...'

They both stopped short in the doorway. A double bed was pushed against the wall, with a narrow bedside table on the other side. There was a rail to hang clothes, a window and two doors; one onto a tiny terrace, another to what Lola assumed was an en suite.

'I can sleep on the floor,' Rhys said quietly.

Lola stepped into the room. 'Don't be ridiculous, there's hardly any floor space.'

'At least it looks clean.' Rhys pulled back the bed cover. 'Although perhaps not the romantic bolthole Fabs and Mirabel were hoping for tonight.'

'I honestly don't think they're going to care one bit.'

Rhys closed the door behind him. 'Do you think it's all kicking off back at the house?'

'I'm not sure Mirabel running off then Fabs following is going to have helped, but then it's Fabs and Mirabel's wedding, so I say whatever makes them happy should be the priority.'

Lola sat down on the bed, her heart sinking as the bed springs creaked. The place might be clean, but the bed sounded like it had had a lot of use.

Rhys turned on the bedside lamp and switched off the main light; his shadow dominated one wall as he opened the window.

'It's sort of got a sea view.'

She could tell he was stalling, but then she was feeling as tense as Rhys looked, even more so when he eventually sat down, the space between them a yawning chasm.

The ease with which they'd talked at the restaurant earlier had vanished. They did manage to chat about random stuff, if only to avoid having to actually lie down and attempt to go to sleep, but even that got a hell of a lot more awkward when the hushed noises from the next room became way too loud to ignore.

Lola would have found the way Rhys's cheeks flushed the colour of raspberry gelato utterly adorable if she hadn't been quite so mortified. A headboard thumped into the wall directly behind them, and then the moaning started.

'Who'd have thought a cheap Airbnb with last-minute availability and no air con would have such paper-thin walls,' Lola hissed under her breath as she clamped her hands over her ears. She launched herself from the bed and flung open the door to the patio.

Pretending to have sex with Rhys to get back at his ex had been one thing. To hear her best friend getting amorous with Fabs while she and Rhys were trying to navigate how they were going to share a bed again was something else entirely.

Rhys closed the door behind them and joined her on the white plastic chairs that only just fitted on the narrow patio.

The street light cast an orange glow over the road that ran in front of the house. Beyond was darkness, but she could just make out the expanse of ocean glinting silver where it shifted and caught the moonlight. It was far better than sitting in a small stuffy room listening to Fabs and Mirabel getting it on.

'It's a bit better out here.' Laughter coated Rhys's words as he mirrored her thoughts.

'Yup.' Lola rested her feet on the peeling paint of the railing. 'Just wish we had somewhere comfy to sit and a drink in our hands.'

Rhys huffed in agreement. 'I don't think Fabs and Mirabel cared about any of that tonight.'

'No, they didn't.'

They lapsed into silence, listening to the sound of the sea

The Island of Hopes and Dreams 173

churning against the rocks and the incessant chirrup of cicadas, which drowned out everything else.

'I hope both Fabs's and Mirabel's families work things out because her mum is the loveliest woman in the world – it's where Mirabel gets it from. Her dad's quieter, but the same, just two great, caring people – parents anyone would love to have. Perhaps Mirabel being their only child has heightened things.'

'Because they feel they're losing her?'

Lola nodded. 'Exactly.'

'Believe it or not, Fabs's parents sound very similar. Giada is the best, she welcomed me into their family when I stayed, but I can understand how she might be overwhelming for Mirabel. But she cares and loves her family fiercely.'

'Which is what matters most, although an overbearing mother-in-law might be a bit much for anyone, even someone as easy-going as Mirabel.'

'An overbearing *Italian* mother-in-law.' Rhys raised his eyebrows.

'I hadn't factored that in.' Lola laughed. 'But one who cares and who's present and interested in their son and daughter-in-law's lives is something special. They all want what's best for their children.'

'It's a nice problem to have.'

'Isn't it just.' Lola sighed. 'I should make more effort to see my parents. I love London, but I miss Devon and being by the sea. Mum hates cities and I resent their expectation that I should visit them when they don't make the effort to come see me.'

'Do you miss them though?'

Lola nodded and fought back a wave of sadness that took her by surprise. 'More than I realised. Since Jarek...' Glancing away, she watched a black cat dart across the road and into the bushes. 'He bad-mouthed them and played on my insecurities and resentment and made my relationship with my parents even more strained.'

Rhys leaned forward in his chair, rested his elbows on his knees and looked at her intently. 'You saw through him and got out. He manipulated and played you, but you've not lost your parents, have you?' At her shake of her head, he continued. 'If you miss them, go see them. I'm sure they miss you just as much. Sometimes it's best to swallow pride or those feelings of resentment and make amends to get a relationship back on track.'

'You're right, but it's hard to do in practice.' Lola wound her thumbs around each other and breathed in the salt-tinged air. 'I need to change that, particularly now my parents have retired. There's no excuse. And with Mirabel in Sardinia, there's going to be less reason to hang around in London.'

Rhys ran his fingers through his hair and rested his leg on his knee. 'You're really going to miss her, aren't you?' he said softly.

'She's like a sister. We feel that way about each other; surrogate sisters because we both grew up alone. We clicked the moment we met; instantly more than colleagues, a friendship that's grown closer than best friends. She's family.' She met his eyes, warm and comforting, but there was something else, a steadying presence that sent tingles through her to the parts of her body that longed for him. The caring, thoughtful and introspective side to him was an aphrodisiac. And the way he left her wanting more: to talk all night, to sit in companiable silence with his arms wrapped around her, to eagerly slide into bed together to see where it could lead... It undid her in the best possible way.

Her phone pinging made Lola jump. She felt physically sick with worry as she picked it up, expecting the message to be from Jarek.

'You okay?' Rhys asked.

Lola nodded and breathed easy as she clicked on the

message. 'It's from Deni, checking up because we've not come back.'

Her heart returned to its normal pace as she sent a reply to say they were fine and she'd see her tomorrow. She looked up to find Rhys watching her.

Lola nodded towards the closed door. 'Do you think they're done?'

She couldn't help but smile at the situation they'd found themselves in. Confined to a shadowy, concrete patio to escape having to listen to their mutual best friends having sex. How the hell were they supposed to get to sleep when all she wanted to do was make similar noises with Rhys?

'Mirabel was pretty drunk; she may have passed out by now.'

Passed out satisfied, was what she felt Rhys didn't say.

Her heart fluttered and she was glad the light was too dim for him to notice her cheeks flushing.

Rhys tilted back in his chair and cracked open the patio door. Little more could be heard besides the insects – no thumping headboard or squeaky bedsprings.

Rhys turned back to her with a grin. 'I think we're in the clear.'

'It's actually quite fresh tonight.' Lola wrapped her arms around herself as she followed Rhys back inside. When she'd left the villa earlier that afternoon dressed in a midi skirt and a slim-fitting T-shirt, she hadn't expected to be out all night without even a cardigan, let alone a toothbrush or nightclothes.

She slipped into the en suite and splashed water on her face. Finding a packet of mints in her bag, she chewed one in place of cleaning her teeth. She was about to leave the packet on the side of the sink for Rhys when the thought that he might think she was hinting at him to freshen his breath before kissing her slammed into her head. She tucked them back into her bag and cursed herself for overthinking and not being drunk enough to be at ease sharing a room with Rhys.

Her heart was racing by the time she emerged from the en suite. She didn't really want to sleep in her skirt, but then just knickers and a T-shirt didn't seem appropriate either. Rhys was lying in bed, resting back on the pillows with his arms tucked behind his head. He seemed to still be fully dressed. This was beginning to be a total headache.

Rhys untucked his arms and shifted over as she slid beneath the cover. He was practically pressed against the wall, as if needing to keep as much space between them. Because he didn't want to be in this situation again or because his thoughts were similar to hers?

'At least it's quiet now,' Rhys whispered.

Lola grunted an acknowledgement. It was too quiet because her ears were filled with the thudding of her heart and the sound of Rhys breathing next to her. They were far too awake to be stuck together with so much left undiscussed and she had no clue how she'd be able to sleep.

'I'm sorry for kissing you,' Lola blurted out, deciding that clearing the air was the sensible thing. 'I only did it because I thought it would help; I didn't mean to embarrass you.'

Rhys remained silent, making Lola nervous that bringing up that subject was the wrong thing to do. But then he shifted on the bed, the springs creaking as he turned to look at her.

'You didn't embarrass me.'

'I just thought afterwards you regretted it, because of something you said when you came to my room.'

'You'd been ignoring me all evening; if that wasn't regret, then I don't know what is. Then you snapped at me.'

'I didn't mean to do that, just Jarek—'

'Yeah, I realise now that was what had wound you up. But I didn't understand at the time.'

'So the, um, kiss. You were okay with that?'

Rhys held her gaze, intently enough to make her heart thump.

'I was more than okay with it.' His eyes traced her face, briefly flicking to her lips then back up. 'I enjoyed it a lot, but I wasn't sure you did?'

'Oh, I enjoyed it.' The tightness in her chest began to ease as her smiled grew. 'I enjoyed it a bit too much.'

There was a heartbeat of a pause, then in the dim light, Rhys matched her grin. 'Fancy repeating it?'

24

Rhys was rarely this forward, but he was certain he didn't want to hide his feelings or second-guess things any longer. More than anything, he didn't want to miss out on a chance with Lola. He'd been captivated by her from the moment they'd met on that moon-bathed dock, and he'd wanted more since the first time they'd shared a room. The easy way they'd chatted earlier in the evening had been a reminder of what they'd had before the kiss had confused things, but with an added something: obvious attraction. Now he had the confirmation that she felt the same way.

It was too dark to make out her expression. Perhaps that was why he'd felt brave enough to make the suggestion; he hoped it would be taken in a this-feels-natural way rather than a this-will-ruin-our-friendship kind of way.

Lola clasping the side of his face and tugging him close so they were pressed together shut down any further thought. Her breath caressed his lips and sent his heart skittering; her perfume was sweet and seductive, her lips on his an addiction he knew he wouldn't be able to give up.

The breeze curling in through the window did little to slay the heat rushing through him. His senses were on fire: hot skin and tickling breath, teasing touches and heady laughter, their lips as eager as their hands.

He and Lola were now the ones making a noise. He was acutely aware of each creak of the bed and the breathy moan that escaped Lola when his hand slid upwards to cup her breast. His joy was only outdone by his surprise at just how eager she was: passionate kisses and unrestrained exploration.

Damn, was this good.

The last time they'd been in bed together had all been for show for Freddie and Zoe. Now the sensation of sweeping his fingers across Lola's bare skin was achingly real and he was trying to rein in his own moan, fully aware of the paper-thin walls between the rooms.

Before he knew it, his T-shirt had been discarded, and he was wriggling Lola's top off up and over her head. In the subtle glow from the street light, her breasts were barely contained by a lacy bra. He planted a kiss right between them, extracting another moan from Lola that sent his pulse racing. Lola's breath hitched as he began to tug down her skirt, while her hands caressed his back, dipping lower so they teased inside the waistband of his jeans.

From the other side of the wall, a phone started ringing.

Lola managed to kick away her skirt, then her fingers started work on the buttons of his jeans. Rhys traced his fingers up her smooth thigh, his heart pounding faster with every inch.

A muffled voice started speaking in the next room.

Their lips found each other's again and he was lost in her taste and the feel of her as his hand slid even higher.

Fabs was talking, louder now.

Lola's hands stilled on his bare chest. Rhys's fingers paused just a breath away from where he wanted them to be. She pulled away from their kiss. 'Do you think something's going on?'

Despite Rhys having heard Fabs answering his phone, his attention had solely been on Lola in just a lacy bra and knickers. The subtle glow from the street light caught her curves and he could barely think straight as they remained quiet for a moment, still entwined on the bed.

A thud sounded, as if someone was getting out of bed. Two voices now; Fabs and Mirabel talking.

Rhys's heart sank further as a door opened and footsteps strode along the hallway.

'Shit.' Lola entangled herself from him and scooped up her top from the floor.

A knock on their bedroom door.

'Rhys, Lola?' Fabs's voice was just-woken-up-rough. 'We need to leave, now. Mamma's been taken to hospital.'

* * *

Being interrupted by Fabs at gone midnight to drive back to Villa Sereno was not how Rhys had envisaged the rest of the night going, not after being in bed with a nearly naked Lola.

Fabs was focused on the road, his hands clutching the steering wheel, while Mirabel was quiet in the passenger seat. Rhys and Lola sat in the back in silence as they zoomed along the dark roads past forested countryside shrouded in darkness. The imprint of her lips remained and the delicious smell of her lingered, yet he was unsatisfied and once again felt awkward around her. The heady delight had been shattered by having to stop so abruptly. How far would they have taken things if Fabs hadn't interrupted?

Rhys silently berated himself for such a selfish thought. They were heading back because Giada had been taken ill with a suspected heart attack. Of course they needed to return. Whatever had been happening between him and Lola was less important when his best friend was understandably distraught.

Chaos reigned back at the villa. Everyone was up and lights blazed. They were greeted by a chorus of voices, multiple people weighing in on what had happened – or what they believed had happened – over the last couple of hours. Mirabel rushed to her parents and was swept up in their arms. Both sides of the family had gathered in the living room in pyjamas, nightdresses and dressing gowns. Rhys did wonder if the drama had been embellished, but by the time Fabs decided to drive to the hospital with his eldest sister to find out how his mamma was for himself, it had become clear that she'd woken with chest pain and the moment she'd mentioned feeling faint, an ambulance had been called.

'Look after Mirabel, will you?' Fabs clapped a hand on Rhys's shoulder and planted a kiss on Mirabel's forehead. His *nonna* and aunt shouted a barrage of instructions at him in Italian as he left.

Mirabel's escape from the family tension had been short-lived. Her earlier happiness had been wiped from her face now she was back in the house.

With tears in her eyes, Mirabel grabbed Lola's hand. 'Keep me company.'

'What about Rhys?' Lola glanced towards him. 'We can get a taxi back to—'

'Please stay.' Mirabel's tone was pleading and Rhys knew there was no way Lola would refuse her. Picking up where they'd left off would have to wait for another time, he realised with dismay.

A warm hand landed on his shoulder. 'I make bed for you in

study,' Fabs's ninety-year-old *nonna* said with a sharp nod of her head.

'I'll help you.' Mirabel's mum took hold of him and, before he knew it, he was being swept one way, Lola the other.

The night of what-could-have-been was well and truly over.

25

Lola and Mirabel had never lived together, but they'd been friends for nearly a decade and had crashed at each other's flats on numerous occasions. It was like old times, sitting cross-legged together on the bed – except they were in Fabs's luxurious bedroom, which resembled a suite in a five-star hotel.

Mirabel's eyes were red and puffy, her earlier joyful drunkenness extinguished, much like the promise of Lola's passionate night with Rhys, which she was trying her hardest not to think about.

Lola took hold of Mirabel's hands. Her diamond ring glinted in the lamplight. 'It's all going to be okay.'

'You don't know that.'

'No, but it wouldn't help things if I said "it really has all gone to shit" now, would it?'

Mirabel smiled, except it looked more like a grimace.

'Giada's in the best place right now, so try not to worry about something you have no control over.'

The huge windows framed the velvety black sea that glinted silver in the moonlight. Lola could make out the wooden jetty where she and Rhys had first chatted. It was hard to believe that had only been a week ago.

Lola turned back to Mirabel. 'How long are you planning on living here once you move to Sardinia?'

'For as little time as possible,' Mirabel said, but then shook her head. 'Forget I said that. Considering what's happened to Giada, I don't mean it like that.'

'I get what you mean. Even if you have space here, you and Fabs need a place of your own.'

'We need to find a place that's right for us, that feels homely rather than ostentatious. It'll be easier once we're here and can look at places properly rather than online.'

'You and Fabs don't agree on what you both want?'

'It's not that; he's in no rush, while I'm desperate to have our own space.' She waved her hand towards the bedroom door, which Lola took to mean space away from Fabs's parents.

'She'll be okay,' Lola said again, softly this time. 'It sounds as if everyone acted fast and the paramedics got here quickly. She's in the best place right now.'

'I keep thinking I added to her stress by running away, then getting Fabs to join me, leaving everyone in the lurch.' Mirabel fisted the silk sheet, her face once again scrunching with worry.

'*You* aren't the cause of Giada's heart attack – even if that was what it was. We don't know anything yet, apart from she's okay and they're running some tests.'

'No news is good news, I suppose.'

'Exactly.' Lola squeezed Mirabel's hands. 'It's really late and you're getting married in thirty-six hours, so why don't we try to get some sleep.'

Mirabel bit her lip and glanced at her phone, which was on the bedside table.

'He'll call if anything happens.' Lola scrambled up the bed

and plumped up the pillows. 'Not that you need any beauty sleep, but being tired as well as hungover in the morning isn't going to make you feel better about things.'

Lola slid under the covers on Fabs's side of the bed, although her thoughts turned to Rhys on a sofa bed in the study. With everything that had happened, she'd not had time to consider how far things would have gone between them. Kiss for kiss, stroke for stroke, their passion had matched each other's. He'd captivated her completely, the abrupt stop leaving her desperate for more. But not tonight, she told herself. Not tonight.

Mirabel got into bed next to her with a sigh. 'Thanks for staying.' She gave her a sideways glance. 'I know this isn't how you wanted your night to be, but I do appreciate it. It's not that I can't cope being on my own, it's just everything's got too much and I need my friend.'

'Always.'

'I'm going to miss you.'

Lola nodded and tried to swallow the sudden lump in her throat. 'I'm going to miss you more.'

* * *

While Mirabel fell asleep almost instantly, it took a while for Lola to nod off. Everything was changing; both her life back home and how she was feeling inside. After staring at the mirror-black sea glistening in the moonlight for what seemed an age, she was tempted to message Rhys, but didn't know what to say or what she wanted from him. Eventually, she drifted off to the memory of Rhys gliding his hands up her body, warm and firm, and how surprisingly and wonderfully sexy he was.

Lola woke to Mirabel reading a message from Fabs, which said his mamma was fine and they'd all returned home in the early hours of the morning. While Mirabel shot out of bed to go and find him, Lola showered, found a spare toothbrush, borrowed toothpaste and deodorant and got dressed again in the clothes she'd been wearing the day before.

She picked up her phone and messaged Rhys.

> Are you up?

He replied immediately.

> Yes, just spoken to Fabs. Going to find coffee. Want to join me?

Lola thumbed a quick reply.

> Be down in five.

Lola finished drying her hair and borrowed some of Mirabel's delicious-smelling hair product to scrunch it into waves. Voices drifted up from downstairs, less panicked than when they'd arrived the night before, which boded well. She followed the sounds through the sprawling villa to where most of the family were milling around in the main living area that opened onto the outdoor terrace shaded by olive trees.

She spotted Rhys clasping a cappuccino cup and talking to Fabs's youngest sister. When he caught sight of her, his smile made her insides go squirmy and immediately filled her with the memory of bare skin and sensual kisses.

'Morning,' he said as he reached her.

'How soon do you think we can get out of here?' Lola whispered, nodding towards the gathered family.

He leaned in close, wafting a zingy cologne her way. 'It does very much feel like we're in the middle of a domestic.' His breath was a mix of coffee and mint. 'Mirabel's okay though?'

Lola nodded. 'Just about. Fabs?'

'Shattered but mightily relieved his mamma didn't have a heart attack.' His arm brushed against her shoulder. 'How about you?'

'Tired, relieved, needing coffee and eager to change my clothes. You?'

'Ditto.' The way he grinned at her made her heart flip, and she realised her eagerness to get back to the villa was less about getting away from the family drama and more about having time alone with Rhys. Not that there would be much chance of that with Polly, Deni's husband Mark, and Jenny from the hen weekend and her husband arriving today.

Lola was about to say more when Fabs clamped his hands on their shoulders and steered them towards the terrace with its view across the pool to the jetty and the sea beyond. 'Have breakfast with us before you head back.'

'That answers your question,' Rhys whispered once they'd sat down and Fabs had joined Mirabel on the other side of the table.

Lola didn't know what breakfast with the family was usually like, but there was a subdued air this morning, although no raised voices or arguing.

A refreshing breakfast of fruit, yogurt and a honey-sweetened wholemeal bread was brought out by the chef, and Lola was grateful when a coffee was placed in front of her. Mirabel's parents, Felicity and Michael, were sitting across from her, their tiredness apparent in the yawn Mirabel's dad failed to hide.

Giada and Lorenzo were the last to join them, Giada looking pale but otherwise her usual pristine self. Lola wouldn't have believed she'd been in hospital for most of the night if she hadn't known.

Giada remained standing at the head of the table. 'I feel foolish.' She spread her hands wide. 'To disturb your sleep and all for nothing.'

Next to her, Fabs splayed his hands on the table. 'It wasn't nothing, Mamma.'

'I'm with Fabs on that,' Felicity said, gently adjusting the spoon and fork on her napkin. 'You had the symptoms of a heart attack. That should never be ignored.' She glanced at her husband. 'If we'd ignored Michael's symptoms we'd never have known he'd had a mini heart attack.'

Mirabel's head shot up from her plate. 'What heart attack?'

'*Mini* heart attack,' her dad said pointedly. He flashed a warning look at his wife before turning back to Mirabel. 'I had a little health blip at the beginning of the year. We didn't want to worry you when you had so much going on with work, the wedding and planning the move.'

'Something like that is *exactly* what you need to tell me.' Although anger flared across Mirabel's face, it was layered with concern. Fabs reached for her hand. 'You start withholding things, then it's only going to make me worry even more.'

'I understand your parents not telling you,' Giada said slowly, her eyes sliding along the table to Mirabel's parents, who were sitting straight-backed, their hands clasped. 'It is what we do as a mother, as a father, to protect our children, even if we do not always make the best choices. Or behave the way we should.'

Lola noticed quite a lot of shuffling in seats, particularly from Mirabel's and Fabs's closest family.

'I did not have a heart attack, but bad – how you say in English? – acid...'

'Acid reflux,' Fabs said.

'*Sì*. Acid reflux. Heartburn. I had heartburn. We eat much, we drink, we argue, we have many late nights. We are all stressed. That is why I feel the way I did. It is clear I need to slow down, to take it easier, to be kind to myself. To everyone.' She looked around the table again, her eyes pausing on Felicity and Michael, then Mirabel. She clutched Fabs's shoulder. 'Tomorrow is Fabrizio and Mirabel's wedding. We have much to celebrate, but perhaps we take it a little quiet today.'

'I'll second that!' Michael raised his coffee cup and laughter trickled around the table.

With a flourish of her hand, Giada sat down. 'Now, we eat.'

* * *

Giada's thoughtful words and Felicity and Michael's honesty over breakfast seemed to put an end to the animosity and power play between the parents.

Revived by coffee and food, Lola and Rhys were ferried across the bay to Villa Capparis, but any chance of spending time alone was snatched away the second they stepped inside. Their friends pounced on them with a million questions about their overnight disappearance, and they were forced to catch them up about Mirabel running away and Giada's health scare.

Eventually, Lola escaped to her room to get changed – although with Polly's imminent arrival, it would soon be hers no longer. The huge bed had been separated into two singles with chocolates left on the pillows. Lola should have felt elated at shortly seeing her friend, at Giada being fine and Mirabel less stressed, yet niggling uncertainty was still burrowing into her. Swept up in Mirabel's drama and off her feet by Rhys, Lola's own concerns had briefly been forgotten about. Now her thoughts returned to the one person she didn't want to think about. When life felt as if it was back on track, that would be when *he* would strike. She didn't want to consider how closely he was keeping an eye on her. At least here she was surrounded by people; it would be back in London when she'd be at her most vulnerable.

A knock on the door dragged her away from her spiralling thoughts. Sarah was standing in the doorway holding a bunch of flowers.

'These just arrived for you.' She raised an eyebrow and handed them to her.

The flowers were striking, but not in a good way. Yellow and mauve were Lola's least favourite colours and she knew before she'd even opened the attached card who they were from.

> A night away with your new bloke, eh? What was his name again? Rhys, that's it. Rhys Strickland, lives in Bristol, teaches kids. He's seriously your rebound choice? I do hope you were thinking about me the whole time. Forever yours, J

'Do you have a secret admirer or are they from Rhys?'

Sarah's words barely computed as Lola stared at the black-printed words. It was if he'd known her thought process.

Sarah plucked the card from her hand. Her chatter abruptly stopped as she read, then reread the card. Her head snapped back up to look at her. 'What the hell, Lola?'

26

'Lola, talk to me.'

Lola dropped the flowers on the bed and looked up at Sarah, whose face was pinched into a frown.

Sarah pointed at the discarded flowers. 'They're from Jarek?'

Lola nodded.

'This note is weird. Plain creepy.' Still clutching the card, she shook her head. 'I have so many questions.'

'It's a long story.'

Sarah shoved the flowers to the other side of the bed, sat down and patted the space beside her. 'Then catch me up.'

So Lola did, starting with the truth about her relationship with Jarek and what he'd really been like, along with the times he'd contacted her, from the hen do in Cornwall to the messages he'd sent while she'd been here, all the way to seeing him in Porto Cervo.

Sarah looked at her in open-mouthed disbelief. 'So he's here on Sardinia spying on you? Does anyone else know?'

'Just Rhys. I didn't say anything because I didn't want to worry Mirabel.'

'Oh Lola, I get that, but you could have talked to me, to Deni. We're here for you.'

Fighting back tears, Lola bit her lip. Dealing with Jarek on her own was what she'd been doing the whole time. Perhaps she'd been naïve to think he'd allow her to humiliate him. The idea that he still believed she belonged to him terrified her.

'I know you are,' Lola finally said, squeezing Sarah's hand. 'Thank you.'

'What do you want to do?' Sarah gestured at the flowers as if they were the problem rather than symbolic of the hold her ex still had over her.

Lola opened her mouth to reply, but before she could, an excited shout sounded from the hallway.

'They're here!' Deni dashed past the open door in a flash of white linen trousers and a patterned blouse, looking more dressed up than she had the whole time she'd been here, as if she wanted to impress her husband.

'I don't know,' Lola said in reply to Sarah's question. She gestured at the flowers. 'Get rid of these for starters.'

'It wasn't really the flowers I was talking about.'

Lola stood up, smoothed the creases from her dress and shrugged. 'I'm not sure what I can do until I get home.' She breathed long and hard. 'For now, please keep it to yourself.'

'Lola, you can't ignore this.' Sarah's frown deepened. 'This is out of order, not to mention more than a bit alarming.' She lowered her voice as someone else walked past the open door. 'He's stalking you.'

'What do you want me to do? Call the police? Try to explain my ex has sent me a couple of texts and some flowers?'

'And cornered you while you were out.' Sarah frowned. 'I had no idea what a creep he was. He knows where you are and what you're doing.'

'Please, don't say anything. Mirabel does not need to know. Rhys is fully aware of Jarek and what he's like; now you are too.'

'I'm telling Deni. She's a force to be reckoned with, and if he even thinks about doing anything else…' She clenched her fists. 'I had no idea how bad things had got.'

'That's because I never told you all what he was like, not even Mirabel, although she had a pretty good idea.'

'Okay, deep breaths.' Sarah stood and squeezed her hand. 'This conversation isn't over, but let's go see Polly and everyone else before they come looking.'

Sarah slipped the card into Lola's bedside table drawer, grabbed the flowers and shoved them into the bin, then took Lola's hand.

As they arrived in the central living area, Lola realised she'd never been more thankful for the bustle of people, for fresh faces to renew the energy in the villa, as she said hello to Jenny and her husband, then swept Polly into a hug and revelled in the happiness radiating off Deni as she and Mark chatted, their arms wrapped around each other.

For a short time, Lola was distracted from the game Jarek was playing. Although 'game' was the wrong choice of word, because wasn't a game supposed to be fun and both players should know the rules? Despite him being on Sardinia, she refused to let him get the better of her, even if it meant shoving that worry and fear deep down to deal with when she got home.

* * *

Something had happened. Rhys would put money on it that it had everything to do with Jarek. With extra people at the villa, there'd been little time to spend with Lola or talk to her properly. But he'd noticed the way her friends swarmed around her, as if protecting her, which made his heart both soar and ache. She had the support of her friends, but she hadn't sought him out. It was too late now anyway, because after the shock of Giada's hospital visit and the two sets of parents making a tentative peace with each other, they'd finally listened to Fabs and Mirabel's wishes. The fancy night-before-the-wedding meal had been cancelled and in its place a quiet afternoon and evening at home had been suggested – with a twist. All of the women were going to Villa Sereno to get their nails wedding-ready, followed by an evening of music and food, while the men were staying at the guest villa for drinks and games, which of course meant he wouldn't have the chance to see Lola this evening either. Mirabel and Fabs were keeping things traditional by not spending the night before the wedding together, yet all Rhys could think about was how much he wanted to spend the night with Lola. That was beginning to seem more and more unlikely, even if the memory of her teasing breath and smooth supple skin pretty much consumed him.

Mirabel gathered her friends together, while her dad, Fabs's papa and Deni and Jenny's husbands were brought into the fold by Freddie and Barnaby offering to make them cocktails. As Rhys watched Sarah and Deni pounce on Zoe, he realised he hadn't once thought about her or Freddie over the past couple of days.

'Of course you have to come with us!' Deni was adamant, despite Zoe's horrified face as she glanced back towards Freddie and the rest of them. Rhys couldn't help feeling smug and a little mean thinking that her having only male friends had backfired when they'd be enjoying themselves without her. Zoe was still looking like a deer caught in headlights as Deni began steering her away.

Lola was on their heels, but she paused to glance back, her

eyes flicking across the crowded living room until she met his gaze.

'You okay?' he mouthed.

Her nod and uncertain smile was the only answer he got. Sarah clamped her arm around her shoulder and manoeuvred her in the direction the others had gone.

Rhys sighed at the sight of her retreating back.

Fabs appeared next to him. 'You'll see her again tomorrow.'

Was it really that obvious how much he wanted to follow Lola out of the door like a lovesick puppy? He exhaled and focused on his friend rather than the woman who set his heart spinning.

'I do think we may have an easier time of it tonight.' Rhys cast his eyes around the room at their mates, Fabs's Italian friends and the male members of Fabs's family. 'The combination of your mum, Mirabel's mum, your *nonna*, Sarah, Zoe. Part of me wishes I could be a fly on the wall.'

'Ha, yes!' Fabs laughed and rested his arm across Rhys's shoulders. 'Although most of me is glad I'm here with you lot!'

27

By eight that evening it looked as if a dressing-up box filled with feathers and glitter had exploded all over the terrace at Villa Sereno. With the music cranked up – a mix of Euro pop hits – Mirabel's friends and family were twirling and dancing about with colourful feather boas draped around necks and ostentatious costume jewellery decorating hair, ears and arms. Fabs's sisters really had brought out their old dressing-up box. Even Giada and Felicity joined in, their feud behind them as they swayed together with matching red lips and purple feathers in their hair, beaming as Deni took their photo.

Embraced in the warmth of two loving families, Lola felt safe among her friends. She was grateful for the distraction, but she knew that was all it was. Jarek hadn't come to Sardinia just for the hell of it, but to break her spirit, yet surrounded by such vibrant women, she felt invincible. Someone draped a turquoise feather boa around her and Lola found herself next to Mirabel, who was sparkling in chunky gold jewellery with a tiara perched on her head. Deni, Sarah and Polly joined them, flinging their arms around each other, shouting 'cheese' as photos were snapped.

While the dressing-up accessories were being cleared away to make room for wine and nibbles, Polly caught hold of Lola and whisked her inside to the library-come-snug where Rhys had slept the night before. It was a cosy, book-lined space that Lola coveted for herself. One day when she had a spare room that could fit more than just a bed and wardrobe in, she'd create a haven like this.

They sat together on the sofa, their legs tucked beneath them. Lola's fingers brushed the smooth velvet, her thoughts turning to Rhys lying in this spot the night before.

'Deni and Sarah have caught me up on a *lot* of stuff this evening.' Polly looked at her knowingly, her pale, freckled cheeks flushed, a glass of wine clasped in her hand. 'Sexy Welsh teachers and psycho ex-boyfriends. You couldn't make it up if you tried, not to mention a full-out war between the in-laws-to-be and a not-so-romantic night away in an Airbnb.'

Lola shrugged. 'Yeah, it's been a lot.'

'And you don't have to talk about any of it. I get why you kept stuff about Jarek to yourself, even if I also know how unhealthy that likely was.' She flashed her a no-nonsense motherly look, one Lola knew she'd perfected on her children. 'I'm not sure we helped with things though, pushing you to hook up with various blokes, teasing you about that incident with Dax. If we'd known – if *I'd* known – we would have gone easy on you. I understand now why you weren't ready for another relationship, even if we only meant it as a bit of fun.' She cleared her throat. 'Obviously I've only just met him, but I am surprised about you and Rhys from the bits and pieces Deni and Sarah have said. Mirabel seemed surprised as well—'

'It's all been a lie, Polly.' Lola loosed a long breath and ran her fingers down the back of the velvet sofa, wondering if it had taken Rhys as long to fall asleep last night as it had for her. 'At least it started that way, now it feels messy and confusing.'

'What do you mean?'

For the second time that day, Lola found herself spilling secrets, this time about the love pact she'd made with Rhys.

Polly took her hand and studied her. 'So you're telling me you and Rhys were pretending to be together to get Deni and everyone off your back about setting you up with some hot Italian guy, but you've actually fallen for him for real?'

'Fallen is too strong a word.' Lola pursed her lips and met Polly's knowing gaze. 'But, yes, something like that.'

Polly grinned. 'I think I need to get to know this Rhys properly.'

They talked a little more and by the time they returned to the terrace, the table had been laid with extra bottles of wine and an array of fresh seafood. Any remaining animosity between the matriarchs had been washed away with wine and laughter, while Mirabel glowed, finally looking blissfully happy and at ease on the night before her wedding. The whole evening was joyful and lively, occasionally verging on raucous, with Deni and Sarah leading the conversation with great hilarity as wine was poured and grilled octopus and juicy prawns were consumed.

With her jaw aching from laughing so much, Lola nipped inside to freshen up and down a glass of water. The last thing she wanted to be was hungover for her best friend's wedding, while Mirabel had stayed off the wine completely. Her married life with Fabs was in touching distance. Lola was happy for her, she really was, but her happiness was tempered with sadness.

As Lola went the long way round to get back to the terrace, she considered if it was the time of year that was making her sad.

In the moonlit garden, there was a freshness in the air that signalled the end of summer.

Bathed in shadows, she stood on the edge of the terrace and watched the women laughing together. It was only late September, but the terrace was lit up like a Christmas tree. Lights adorned the vine-covered pergola, and storm lanterns cast amber, purple and cerise light over the paving. The team of manicurists that had been earlier had given everyone gel nails in a colour to complement their wedding outfits. While Mirabel had opted for a classy French manicure, Lola's own nails were rose gold. Mirabel's only request for the evening had been for a colourful dress code, so everyone was adorned in dresses the colour of summer: bold prints and bright patterns. Lola's own maxi-dress was a vibrant plum and white colour block one. Only Deni had opted for trousers, but she'd swapped her blouse for a hot-pink animal-print top. It suited her, as did the joy she exuded, her cheeks flushing as she laughed with Sarah and Polly. Lola was certain her husband was in for a treat when they eventually returned to the villa.

Lola tore her eyes away and turned towards the sea; the endless black made her shiver. The moonlight was bright enough to make out the jetty, the slosh of water against the wood foaming silver. She felt like escaping there again, but for a different reason this time; although what would be the point without Rhys to talk to? She couldn't stop thinking about him, but there'd been little opportunity to spend time with him at the villa earlier. She could have made an effort to find him, yet he hadn't sought her out either. Did he regret what had happened last night? Did he believe them doing more than kissing had been a mistake or, like her, was he hoping that yet more could happen?

It had been good to confide in Polly, the sensible friend who truly listened – more than Deni and Sarah ever did. Lola loved them all, but it had always been easier to talk to Polly, and considering she didn't want to talk to Mirabel about anything that had happened since they'd been on Sardinia, Polly being here was a huge relief. And yet she felt lost without Rhys's steadying presence.

Since Jarek, all she'd desired was to be on her own, to not rely on anyone but herself, yet Rhys made her feel wanted and safe, desired and loved. She wouldn't let Jarek get his claws into Rhys; she wouldn't allow him to ruin any part of her life, not any more.

Lola retreated further into the garden, past a border carpeted with fragrant yellow flowers and dotted with olive trees up-lit by solar lights. She skirted the neat lawn and headed towards the shadowed seating area next to the gate that led to the sea; it was as if there was an invisible pull towards the jetty. But she halted, not wanting to leave the safety of the garden and her friends, while knowing that sitting on the dock without Rhys would just make her heart ache all the more.

She was about to return to the colour and love radiating from the terrace when footsteps padded up behind her.

'It's quite a view,' a voice with a touch of a Mancunian accent said softly.

Lola turned and met Zoe's considered gaze. Rhys's ex-girlfriend was the last person she thought would seek her out, particularly when Lola had purposefully avoided Zoe, even while her own friends had tried to include her this evening.

'It certainly is,' Lola replied. She didn't quite know what to say to Zoe.

Zoe cleared her throat. 'I overheard Sarah and Deni talking, caught some bits about your ex.'

Lola silently cursed Sarah's big mouth.

'You doing okay?' Zoe asked.

'Do you really care?'

Zoe shuffled awkwardly and turned her gaze to the dark expanse of rippling sea. 'I care that my friend is getting married tomorrow and nothing mucks that up.'

'I care about that too, which is why, until tonight, I had kept things to myself.'

'Does Rhys know about him?'

'Yes,' Lola said tightly.

Zoe nodded. 'Good. Rhys is dependable to a fault and will have your back. Until the trust goes, then it's a different story.'

'Why are you telling me this?'

'I don't know.' Zoe shrugged. 'I saw you out here alone. Honestly, I wanted to check you were okay.' She kicked her sandaled toes through the short grass. 'I appreciate you all including me tonight. I often feel a bit of an outsider, particularly with women. I'm Fabs's friend, not Mirabel's. I'm the token woman when I've always felt like one of the lads, even if sometimes I don't feel a part of the group like I used to. Actually, more often than not that's how I feel.'

'You went on the stag do.'

Zoe grunted. 'And what a mistake that was.'

Lola raised an eyebrow but didn't say anything. She hadn't considered that the stag do might have been as challenging for Zoe as it had been for Rhys. Obviously for different reasons and she was the one who had treated him like shit, but still...

'Change can be a right ball ache. I had a dead good time at uni, all my friends were men mainly because I did a course where the students were predominately guys. I've never really had girl friends, which wasn't a problem till my male mates got into serious relationships. Barnaby's wife doesn't like me; I'm not sure how Mirabel feels, but I figure she's too nice and polite to kick up a fuss—'

'I think she's pretty secure in herself and her relationship with Fabs to not worry about you.'

Zoe gave a sharp nod and folded her arms. 'I deserve that. Fabs is a great bloke and someone I never tried to hook up with because, believe it or not, I never fancied him.'

'You just fancied Rhys and Freddie instead?'

Zoe pursed her lips and let out a long breath into the star-filled night. 'Actually, yeah, I like down-to-earth guys and both Rhys and Freddie tick that box. And the trouble with being attracted to your mates means it kinda messes up that side of things, and not just with them, but the whole damn group. I see it now with all of them; it's harder for me to be one of the guys like I used to be. Me and Freddie being together might make things a bit easier, but everyone knows my history, everyone has an opinion and considers me to be the bad guy – or should I say girl.'

'Perhaps that has something to do with your track record of cheating on Rhys with Freddie?'

The words slipped out, but Lola didn't regret them; she'd stand up for Rhys not because he'd do the same for her but because she wanted to defend and protect him. She hated the thought of him having been hurt by Zoe as much as she had by Jarek. Neither of them had deserved such destructive relationships.

That Zoe didn't immediately snap back came as a surprise.

'I behaved atrociously at uni, towards Rhys at least. We should just have been friends, the same way I was friends with Freddie back then too.'

Lola frowned. 'You mean friends with benefits? You wanted

to have fun with both of them with no commitment or pushback.'

Zoe shoved her hands into the pockets of her summer-yellow dress. 'But Rhys isn't built like that. When he's with someone he's all in, committed and so loving. I wasn't ready for that when we were older, never mind as a student.'

'Why are you telling me this?'

'Because I get the feeling you've had a shitty time of it in a past relationship and I don't actually want to see Rhys get hurt. Again.' She gave a weak smile, her eyes tinged with sadness. 'I really am in love with Freddie; it's not a stunt to hurt Rhys more than I already have. We have good memories together, it's just the bad ones have overridden everything else. And I don't want him to lose Freddie either. We have to move on and be happy. We were once really good friends; that was what our relationship was based on till I fucked it up. I lost his trust and friendship, which I deserve, but I miss him. I miss being his friend. My reaction is to fight back to protect myself and I've perhaps said some unfair stuff to him this week that I regret.'

That was news to Lola, but then she remembered the look on Rhys's face when Freddie had announced his and Zoe's engagement, so she wondered what else had been said.

'Broadcasting you were engaged in front of everyone probably wasn't the smartest move. Even if he says he's over you, he's still hurting.' Lola glanced towards the jetty and remembered Rhys sitting at the end sad and alone. 'This is probably a conversation you should be having with him.'

Zoe pulled her hands from her pockets, held them up and looked at Lola wryly. 'Then consider this the start of me making amends.'

28

The lads' only night at Villa Capparis was like the stag do, but in a more sophisticated setting than a city-centre bar and without as much drunkenness or a punch-up. After a few jolly hours of chatting, sensible drinking and games of pool and cards, by midnight Fabs's family were in taxis on their way back to Villa Sereno and the friends were all heading to bed, with Fabs crashing on the sofa bed in the pool house.

Not that Rhys could get to sleep with his mind whirring. He presumed Lola had returned with the others when footsteps sounded along the hallway. The door to Zoe and Freddie's room opened and closed. He briefly wondered how Zoe had coped with a whole evening spent with Mirabel and her friends. Not so long ago, it would have been Zoe returning to his room. To their room. Not that he actually cared any longer. He rolled on to his back and stared up at the dark ceiling. The anger he'd felt at the stag do and then again at the restaurant when Freddie had announced their engagement had dissipated because he knew he was better off without Zoe – he had been since the moment she'd walked out, chucking away a three-year relationship along with their friendship, but it had taken him being in Sardinia to realise. It had taken Lola to open his eyes to the truth.

Lola.

He sat upright in bed. He'd left the blinds open and he could see across the dark garden. The shadowy trees were backlit by moonlight. Lola would have a similar view on the other side of the villa; he wondered if she was still awake, her thoughts churning as much as his.

Rhys took his phone from the bedside table and scrolled through his photos. There were a few more of them together since that first-night selfie. Had his smile become more genuine as the days had gone by? Because of Lola's influence? He certainly felt lighter inside and his heart brighter, as if he was worthy of being in a relationship again, that he had something to offer someone and space in his heart.

He clicked into messages and onto Lola's name. As his thumbs hovered over the keypad, he was torn about inviting Lola to his room. Could he be as forward and brave as he'd been last night in the Airbnb? Just because he had enjoyed the hell out of their passionate kiss and fumble, that was all it had been. Perhaps she'd been relieved that it had been cut short. And perhaps he was now overthinking things and worrying about what she thought, when the simple truth was she made him happy in every way.

What he was certain about was not leaving it any longer to make contact, not when he'd been dying to talk to her all day. He wrote a message and sent it before he could chicken out.

> Hey, hope your night was good. Ours was actually quite sophisticated and not at all drunken. :)

He stared at his phone like a desperately lovesick teenager, his heart only returning to its normal rhythm when he could see that she was typing something.

> Hey there, ours was completely mad and you should see the photos of Giada, Felicity and Fabs's nonna in feather boas and sparkly tiaras to understand just how crazy crackers it was, but also not that drunken either. We were all being sensible, not wanting wedding day hangovers.

> Sounds epic.

Rhys paused typing, uncertain whether he should say more or simply wish her goodnight. He took a deep breath and decided on the first option.

> Sorry I didn't get a chance to talk to you earlier today, you seemed caught up with your friends, but distracted too. Hope everything's okay?

He sent the message, but kicked himself for not being more specific. *Talk to you about last night* was what he didn't say but wished he had. Neither of them had talked about what had happened in that tiny Airbnb room, at least not with each other. Who knew what she may have said to her friends, while he hadn't told anyone. Fabs hadn't asked about it, but then Fabs had a million other things on his mind. With his wedding tomorrow, Rhys's love life was not a priority.

Minutes later when there was no sign of Lola replying, Rhys snuggled into the pillows and pulled the cover around him with a sigh. He was about to put his phone back on the bedside table when a message pinged.

> I need to tell you something about Jarek in the morning. Stuff happened.

>> You can tell me about it now if you want?

Was that a roundabout invitation for her to come to his room? He wasn't sure what he'd meant by it, but when he saw Lola typing, he assumed she hadn't seen it as a loaded question – or at least had ignored the underlying suggestion.

It took a while for her message to come through, and when it did, she'd pretty much written an essay. His heart dropped at her words. The image she'd attached of the note her ex had sent with the flowers made his heart still. Was Jarek really watching her every move? Was he out there now creeping around in the darkness?

Before Rhys had a chance to reply, another message popped up, adding to her previous one.

> I should have said something earlier, it's just I told Sarah because she'd brought me the flowers, then Polly and the others arrived and I got swept up in everything.

>> Are you okay?

> Yes and no. I'm relieved Polly's here to keep me company – even if she's fast asleep already, I'm not on my own. And Sarah and Deni know about Jarek. And you do too. I keep thinking what else he's prepared to do, then tell myself off for even giving him a second more of my time, because it's exactly what he wants. I'm done with him. It's the big day tomorrow, we should sleep. Night, Rhys x

>> Night Lola x

Whether she'd have preferred his company, she didn't say.

She was right, they needed sleep and he would see her in the morning. Except it took him ages to drift off because his head was filled with puzzling thoughts about that note and whether Lola had wanted him to suggest they spend the night together. Attempting to read between the lines was futile, and all it did was leave him tired and confused.

* * *

Rhys woke with a start, worry about Jarek gnawing at him. His second thought was that it was the day of the wedding, an exciting prospect but one he realised marked the beginning of the end of their time on Sardinia. In a couple of days, Fabs and Mirabel would be heading off on honeymoon, while not long after, the rest of them would be leaving too, scattering back to different parts of Italy and the UK.

He stretched, yawned and rubbed the sleep from his eyes, grateful that he hadn't really drunk last night. The idea of leaving Sardinia left him with an odd feeling. It had been strange to not start back at school at the beginning of September, to not inherit a new Year 5 class. He'd be returning home for only a short time, just long enough to unpack, wash his clothes and repack for his European adventure. Would putting his life on hold and running away from his problems really be the best use of his time? And what was he actually hoping to find or achieve?

The most troubling thought he'd woken up with was that he'd be unlikely to see Lola again. Even the chance of spending time with her this morning would be fleeting when she'd be heading to the family house with her friends to join Mirabel for pre-wedding prep.

For those of them remaining at Villa Capparis with Fabs, breakfast had been scheduled for ten thirty – late enough to see them through to the wedding dinner once Fabs and Mirabel had tied the knot. Rhys was awake early, so he showered, shaved and got dressed in the petrol-blue suit he'd bought specially for the wedding, which was the most expensive piece of clothing he'd ever owned.

As he got ready, he couldn't stop mulling over the messages Lola had sent last night. He kept coming back to the implausible idea that Jarek was actually spying on her. The villa was gated, secure and backed by the sea, so unless he was out in a boat in the bay with binoculars, then there was no way he could see if she was here or not. And how on earth had he known where to spy on her? And if he'd known she hadn't come back to Villa Capparis the night before last then—

Realisation slammed into him, so obvious that he cursed himself for not thinking of it last night.

Pocketing his phone, he raced from the room. The main communal areas were quiet; the only sign anyone was around was the movement on the terrace where the table was being laid out for breakfast.

Rhys didn't pause as he flew round the open door of Lola's room, breathless as he said, 'I know how Jarek knows where you are. Your phone, he's tracking it!'

29

Rhys appearing out of breath in her bedroom door looking hot as hell in a slim-fitting suit took Lola so much by surprise she nearly poked her eye with her mascara wand.

His words barely computed as her eyes lingered on him, sliding from head to toe just as he was doing with her.

'God, you look stunning.' He was still breathless, but in a sexy, 'I want you right now' kind of way rather than because he'd legged it through the villa.

'You scrub up rather well yourself,' she said just as breathlessly. 'But back up to what you said before?'

He stepped into the room and glanced around.

'Polly's just nipped outside to call her husband.'

Rhys nodded. 'Your phone. Jarek's tracking you using your number, that's why he knows where you've been and why you didn't come back here the other night, because he can see where you are. GPS tracking.'

The warm glow Lola had woken up with that morning evaporated. She dropped the mascara on the dressing table and breathed deeply, cursing herself for not having thought of the obvious. Her concern had been what her friends had been posting on social media; she hadn't even considered he could be doing something like this.

She met Rhys's solid, reassuring gaze. 'How can he do that?'

'He probably has an app that he uses to search your number. You told me you never changed it, just blocked him, right?'

'Shit. Shit! I should have changed it, but I didn't think. Why would someone go to such lengths?'

'A normal sane person wouldn't. He's your ex – you believed you were done with him.'

'But I *knew* what he was like. I had an idea of what he was capable of, that was why I left him. I should have taken the threat of his controlling behaviour more seriously.' Trying to get a grip on the panic clawing its way up her chest, Lola took another deep breath. She smoothed her hands down the front of her floral dress and met Rhys's eyes. 'You really think he's tracking me using my phone rather than spying on me?' She shuddered.

'I think so. But if you keep your phone switched off, he won't be able to see where you go today, it'll only show the last location as here.'

'You think he's going to show up? At the wedding?' The rising panic was going to swallow her whole, and tears welled.

Rhys moved swiftly and wrapped his arms around her. 'I don't know. I hope not, but let's not make it easy for him, yeah?'

* * *

Lola heeded Rhys's advice and powered down her phone. In the speedboat on their way to Villa Sereno to help Mirabel get ready, she confided to Deni, Sarah and Polly about Rhys's realisation. Deni cursed her stupidity that she hadn't thought of that herself, then promised she'd take plenty of photos to make up for Lola not being able to take any on her phone. She also pointed out that it would be the perfect opportunity for Lola to live in the moment rather than seeing the wedding framed by a screen. Lola appreciated her friend putting such a rose-tinted spin on the situation and shoved her anxiety deep down, easy enough to do when she was swept up in the excitement of the day by her friends.

With Mark and Jenny's husband joining the men of the Serra family downstairs, Lola, Sarah, Polly and Jenny joined Felicity, Giada and Fabs's sisters in Mirabel's room. A make-up artist was just putting the finishing touches to Mirabel's face – subtle summer-inspired make-up that accentuated rather than overpowered her natural beauty. Giada and Felicity fussed over everyone, handing out glasses of prosecco and peach juice, admiring dresses and tucking pins back into wayward curls. Lola had left her chin-length hair down and had scrunched it into soft waves. Her plum-blue floral dress hugged her curves and flowed into a long skirt, and she'd paired it with heels and a clutch that matched the colour of her nails.

While the family busied about getting more drinks, the friends helped Mirabel into her wedding dress. With her glossy chestnut hair twisted into a loose updo and an ivory dress with an embroidered bodice leading to a silky skirt that gave an elegant silhouette, Lola choked back happy tears as Giada and Felicity gasped.

'Just a couple of hours to go,' Deni whispered as the friends hugged Mirabel.

It had been Mirabel and Fabs's choice to forgo certain traditions. They wanted all of their friends to be a part of the day and to enjoy it, so they'd chosen not to have a best man or bridesmaids, and for Fabs to see his bride before she walked down the aisle. Once Felicity had secured the pearl and blue topaz filigree pendant Mirabel had chosen in the jewellery shop in Bosa, the women joined the rest of the family downstairs and awaited Fabs's arrival with his friends to hand Mirabel her white and blue bouquet.

Lola had always believed they were the perfect couple, but witnessing the look of love Fabs gave as Mirabel accepted her bouquet cemented that thought. Fabs kissed her gently and the cheers from the Italians were echoed by everyone else as Giada and Felicity stepped forward with a dish filled with wheat, rice, coins, sugared almonds and rose petals. Together they raised it high and smashed it on the ground in front of Fabs and Mirabel.

Mirabel had explained that the tradition was a blessing for the bride and groom, and the contents now scattered across the paving stones were symbols of abundance, love, wealth and wisdom. Lola fought back tears; what it symbolised to her was the families' love for their children and the safety her friend had marrying Fabs. Giada and Felicity embraced, and the men did too. On the cusp of becoming a family, they'd allowed bygones be bygones. Lola dabbed her eyes with a tissue. Yes, waterproof mascara had been a must for today.

* * *

Sardinia was an island of contrasts, from the seductive romance of white sand beaches and clear turquoise sea to the swathes of forest and green-clad hills inland. Having taken a travel sickness tablet, Lola was actually able to enjoy the journey, her battering heart calming the further they drove. The luxurious family estate on a vibrant and wealthy part of the coast contrasted with the peaceful countryside location of the wedding.

Despite having seen countless photos of the wedding venue,

the reality of Il Giardino in Sardinia's Nuoro region took her breath away. With its backdrop of soaring limestone mountains, the sprawling hotel was nestled amongst juniper and olive trees, green and peaceful.

From the moment they set foot in the grounds, everything was seamless; their overnight bags were taken care of, while glasses of prosecco were placed in their hands as they milled around on a terrace shaded by an ancient olive tree. Vivaldi's *The Four Seasons*' joyous and upbeat Spring movement accompanied the guests' chatter as canapés of sweet pepper crostini, mini bruschetta and olives were served.

Il Giardino was a treasure trove of outdoor terraces and gardens, interspersed between whitewashed buildings with terracotta roofs. Wooden doorways painted in shades of ocean-blue and dusky-pink were like portals into a secret world: a rooftop terrace with epic views; an orchard with a path meandering through swaying grasses; and an enclosed patio shaded by trees and blooming with cherry-red flowers.

After the welcome drinks, the guests were led to where the wedding ceremony would take place. Rows of white chairs were set out on a red-bricked terrace dappled by sunlight. Decorative sprays of white, blue and blush-pink flowers adorned the terrace, and roses climbed a white wall on one side, while the green trees were the only other decoration. Nothing more was needed besides Fabs and Mirabel and a backdrop of mountain and sky.

Lola sat alongside her friends behind Mirabel's family, with the groom's family and friends on the other side of the aisle. Lola's eyes were drawn to Rhys, and the stolen glances between them assured her that he was thinking about her as much as she was about him. The air was alive with insects and butterflies, while sunshine and shadows played across the guests through a canopy of leaves. Beyond the bride, groom and the mayor who was officiating the ceremony, the mountain soared towards the sky, its pale, dove-grey rock broken up by the green trees and bushes clinging to the hillside. The wedding must have cost a fortune, but for all their wealth it was somehow rustic, perfectly balanced with a touch of luxury. The blend of Italian and English, the traditional and unique, was everything.

The whole afternoon was a wonderful blur, punctuated by moments that Lola knew she would remember forever: Mirabel saying 'I do'; Fabs kissing Mirabel as his wife for the first time; Giada and Felicity's tear-streaked faces; and the bride and groom running hand in hand along the aisle between the upstanding guests with huge grins on their faces.

After the ceremony, drinks were served in the garden bar, which was shaded by overhanging trees, while the photographs took place in various locations, meaning there was a continuous movement of guests as first the family, then the friends, were called upon to join Fabs and Mirabel.

Half an hour later, Lola found herself on the roof terrace bar, just her and Rhys on either side of their best friends, the softening light warming them all as they stood with their backs to the mountain, their arms around their friends' waists as they smiled at the photographer.

Lola squeezed Mirabel tight as the emotion that had been weaving through her all day threatened to spill over. Not because she was sad, but because it was a joyous occasion, because her best friend was finally married, and because Rhys was in touching distance.

The photographer finished and Mirabel handed Lola her bouquet. 'Do you mind holding it for a moment?'

Clutching the flowers, Lola watched from the other side of the roof terrace as the photographer asked Mirabel to stand next to the wall. The V-shaped back of her dress scooped low, while her chestnut hair was pinned up with loose tendrils framing her face. The photographer positioned Fabs so he was perched on the low white wall that overlooked the juniper and olive trees carpeting the valley. Fabs rested his hand on the small of Mirabel's back and gazed adoringly up at her. Across the valley, the ash-grey mountain peaks were kissed by clouds, which were tinged rose and amber as the sun dipped towards the horizon.

This was what love looked like.

Lola sighed, turned and met Rhys's eyes. She wondered what he was thinking; if, like her, he could only dream of finding a love so perfect, a life partner who slotted in as effortlessly as a missing puzzle piece.

His sad smile suggested that perhaps he was thinking the same thing.

Lola couldn't bear to witness his sorrow; she wanted more than anything to make his smile reach his eyes. She was about to go over to him when Deni's arm clamped across her shoulder.

'Felicity's on the lookout for you; apparently she has a thank you gift to give you before dinner.'

Deni steered her down the steps and back towards the rest of the guests. Lola's chance to go over to Rhys was lost.

30

Over the last few years, Lola had been to countless weddings as both a guest and occasionally a bridesmaid, but she'd never been to one in a place quite like Il Giardino. The wedding reception was held on the largest terrace. The tables were dotted between olive trees and raised borders spilling over with herbs that released a fresh earthy scent into the warmth of the early evening. Each table was decorated with a centrepiece of dried grasses and seeds, the warm cream tones beautifully showcasing the darker greens of the surrounding trees and the mauve hues of the mountain backdrop.

Lola was on a table with Deni, Mark and a couple of Fabs's Italian friends not far from where the bride and groom were sitting with their immediate family, while Rhys was sitting a little further away with Barnaby, Gareth, Sarah and Polly.

Valentino was seated to her left. Of course, the seating arrangements had been organised months before, but it did make her wonder if Mirabel had considered Valentino as a possible suitor. He was nice enough but their conversation was stilted, unsurprising considering the last time they'd spoken she'd turned him down.

Even with over a hundred guests, it felt intimate, with the tables spaced between the trees. The waiters began to bring out the courses: ravioli with wild fennel followed by spit-roasted pork served with an array of dishes. Lola's mouth watered at the sight of pan-fried peppers and onions, crispy potatoes and ricotta-stuffed aubergine, along with the delicious aroma, a smokiness mixed with citrus and herbs.

As they began to eat, her attention kept drifting towards Rhys, who seemed to be listening intently to Barnaby. He was good at paying attention to people, but he was also open to talking about his feelings and worries. Mirabel often referred to Fabs as her best friend. Lola had never thought of any partners in that way. Perhaps that was where she was going wrong. How could she put her heart and soul into a romantic relationship if they weren't the closest person in her life – friends as well as lovers? She'd never talked to Jarek as openly as she had with Rhys this week.

Rhys looked her way and she blushed. She raised her glass of wine and he did the same in a silent exchange. That curdling thought about Jarek and the unhealthy relationships she'd had in the past eased a little. Rhys was good for her: his friendship, his thoughtfulness, his easy-going demeanour and humour. He made her laugh and—

'What do you think, Lola?'

At the sound of her name, she switched her attention to Deni, who was doing a valiant job of keeping the conversation flowing around their table. Even self-assured Valentino, who was being standoffish, was making a decent effort to chat politely. Lola inwardly sighed but silently promised to stay present and help Deni out on the conversation front.

Once the honey and myrtle gelato had been consumed and Fabs and Mirabel had done the rounds of the tables to thank everyone, they announced that the bar on the adjacent terrace was open and invited everyone to join them. Live music from a string trio filled the dusk-tinged evening, a jazzy beat with electronic strings. The candles on the tables flickered and the woven lanterns hanging in the trees glowed as people began to drift away. Through the slender branches, Lola could make out Fabs and Mirabel dancing. Lola had never seen her look happier, dazzling in her ivory dress, her skin sun-kissed and shimmering, her hair and make-up natural, the focus on dark lashes and strawberry lips. Smiling, Lola touched the small round filigree necklace that Felicity had given her as a thank you for helping Mirabel over the last few months.

'Would you like to dance?' Valentino's smooth, deep voice pulled her attention away from her friend. With a sinking feeling, she realised they were the only two left. Glancing back, she spotted Deni and Mark standing on the edge of the terrace with their arms wrapped around each other; Polly and Sarah had disappeared completely, Gareth was chatting up his Italian fling, while Rhys was with Barnaby and Freddie at the bar.

'Not at the moment,' she said politely.

'But later?'

He was certainly persistent.

'Maybe.' She would dance at some point tonight, but with her friends and hopefully Rhys *if* he asked. She cursed herself for daydreaming and winding up stuck with Valentino. *That's unfair*, she thought as she turned back and met his gaze again, an odd mix of amusement and seduction on his face. Did he still believe he had a chance with her? Of course he did because he was so confident in his looks that he wasn't used to being turned down.

'Did you get my flowers, Lola?'

A voice behind her sent her breath whooshing from her body at its familiarity; a voice that once sent chills through her and still did, just for a very different reason. Trying to keep it together, she turned away from Valentino, her eyes snapping to Jarek as he slid onto the empty chair next to her. She knew his face so well, yet the person behind those cool dark eyes was a stranger, one who unsettled her to her very core.

He looked right past her to Valentino.

'Excuse me for interrupting,' Jarek said smoothly, a picture of sophisticated politeness. 'It's just I haven't had the chance to talk to Lola properly for quite some time.' His eyes flicked back to hers. 'The other day didn't count, not when you were in such a rush to make your dinner reservation.'

With his sharply cut suit and open-necked shirt, he fitted in beautifully and had chosen his moment with a sniper's precision when she was talking to Valentino, who wouldn't know who he was. There was no one in the immediate vicinity who would recognise him either, Lola realised with growing fear.

She reined in her breathing. Silently and sternly, she told herself that Valentino was next to her, she was surrounded by people, even if her friends weren't here right this moment.

She sensed Valentino making a move to go and through sheer terror of being left on her own, she clamped her hand on to his rock-hard thigh. That stopped him.

Jarek's eyes slid to her hand, then snapped back to her face without a flicker of emotion. 'I thought we could take a walk and talk properly,' he said smoothly.

'I'm perfectly fine here with Valentino. We were about to have a dance.'

'Mmn.' Jarek leaned back in his chair and studied her. 'You do seem to be getting through men like they're going out of fashion.' The edge to his voice had become dangerously low. The muscles in his jaw tightened, betraying his annoyance or an anger he had no right to direct her way.

Valentino started to say something, but Lola quickly cut in, shifting closer to his warm solidness while not taking her eyes off Jarek. 'We had been enjoying each other's company before you interrupted.'

'What happened to the other one?' Jarek cocked his head. 'Rhys, wasn't it?'

Lola's breath hitched at Rhys's name on Jarek's lips. She desperately wanted his focus away from Rhys. She shrugged. 'He's just a friend.'

Her heart was thudding so hard, she felt it fluttering in her throat; the pounding in her ears drowned out the joyful conversations happening on the table behind her.

Jarek leaned close. 'Are you being truthful with me, Lola?'

With her heart ricocheting against her chest, she slid her arm around Valentino and didn't flinch under Jarek's glare. 'It's hardly any of your business any longer.'

* * *

The man to Lola's right had his back to him, but there was something about her demeanour that made Rhys shift his attention from his conversation with Barnaby towards her. From just the way she was sitting, stiff and upright, leaning away as if she was getting ready to run, he sensed something wasn't right. Actually, she was leaning as close to Valentino as she could get.

Rhys's heart dropped into his stomach. She looked scared shitless. There was only one person who would have that effect.

With so many people and tables between them, he felt utterly helpless and frozen to the spot; he didn't have a clue what to do while avoiding causing a scene, yet he couldn't ignore the fact that her ex had followed her here. Even though he didn't know what he was going to do or say, Rhys was about to stride over when Lola grasped Valentino's face and kissed him. Passionately. And from the way his hands immediately cupped her hips and tugged her close, he reciprocated equally as passionately.

The air was knocked from Rhys, like he'd been sucker-punched in the gut.

'Rhys?' Barnaby said. 'Are you okay?'

A roaring in his ears engulfed him. His heart thumped and adrenaline pulsed. Every part of him was tense and ready for a fight, because witnessing Lola kiss Valentino angered him almost as much as Jarek having the audacity to infiltrate the wedding did.

'Rhys?' Barnaby repeated, following Rhys's line of sight. 'What's going on?'

Rhys's whole focus was on Lola, and the second she pulled away from Valentino, Jarek got right in her face and said something, before standing and pacing away.

Rhys ignored the concern on Barnaby's face and handed him his glass of beer. 'Hold this, please. I'll be back.'

Rhys's blood was on fire as he stalked in the direction Jarek had disappeared. He knew he'd turn up here because he wanted to cause Lola the most amount of upset, but to be this brazen about it was unsettling. He understood why Lola had kissed Valentino, someone who matched Jarek in looks and build, handsome and confident with it – the sort of man Jarek would actually believe she was with.

With his fists clenched and eyes blurring, he strode even faster beneath the vine-covered arch that led onto the grassy path through the meadow. In the dusk, with only occasional solar lights to mark the way, there was no sign of Jarek and the only sound beyond the roaring in his ears was the tinkle of shepherds' bells which hung from the branches of the surrounding olive trees.

Freddie grabbed him.

On Freddie's heels, Barnaby pulled him to a stop. 'What the hell's going on, Rhys?' he said. 'And what on earth was Lola playing at with Valentino?'

'Yeah.' Freddie nodded. 'I thought you and her were a thing?'

Rhys couldn't think straight, not with a bullet train of upset ripping through him. 'Her psycho ex is here, so get your fucking hands off me so I can get rid of him.'

Freddie raised his eyebrows but released his hold. 'Let's go then.' He motioned the way ahead.

Rhys faltered, but at Freddie's intense look and serious nod, he set off, both him and Barnaby matching his pace through the meadow.

* * *

'I thought you weren't interested?' Valentino said to Lola the moment Jarek had stalked off.

Lola pulled away from his hold. 'I'm not,' she replied, swivelling in her chair to search the terrace. She spied Rhys still by the bar tight-jawed and rage-filled. He shoved his drink into Barnaby's hand, then weaved between the tables in the direction Jarek had gone, not once looking her way. Without a doubt he'd seen her performance with Valentino. That was all it had been, a performance to put two fingers up to her ex in an attempt to unsettle him, while trying to get his focus away from Rhys. And yet...

'You mess around with me, that is it?'

She was now treading a fine line between making a scene with Valentino or pacifying him with an explanation.

The confusion on his face when she turned back to him made her soften her retort. 'I'm sorry. I did just use you.' She waved her hand in the direction Jarek had gone. 'That was my ex-boyfriend, who's stalking me.' There, she'd said it out loud, the truth of what Jarek was actually doing and the lengths he was prepared to go. 'I'm really glad you were here with me. He's not someone I want to be left on my own with.'

Valentino opened his mouth as if to snap back, then nodded. 'I'm glad I was here.'

Deni flew into the seat that Jarek had vacated. 'Barnaby said something's up.' Her eyes narrowed as she glanced at Valentino, then back to Lola. 'What's going on?'

'Jarek's here.'

'Oh my God.' Deni's face fell. 'Are you okay?'

'He is unhinged,' Lola hissed. 'And he can't – he absolutely can't ruin this wedding.'

'We won't let him,' Deni said fiercely.

Lola loosed a long breath. 'I think Rhys went after him.' *Looking like he was going to punch his lights out*, she thought. Oh God, he wouldn't punch Jarek, would he? 'Shit. I was trying to get Jarek's attention away from Rhys. I have to find him.'

Deni placed a firm hand on her shoulder. 'You need to stay here. A reaction from you is presumably what he wants, so don't give him the satisfaction. Barnaby went after Rhys. Freddie too. He's not facing Jarek alone.'

31

The way Rhys's friends rallied around him meant so much. By the time they caught up with Jarek on the far side of Il Giardino's grounds, Lola's ex was more than ready for a fight. With Jarek in his face spitting vitriol and talking shit about Lola, baiting him with 'she's going to tear you up and spit you out', Rhys realised he was the one in control. Jarek was alone, while his friends were supporting him. However much he wanted to lash out, he wouldn't, because Jarek was in the wrong, no one else; Jarek was the one cornered and fighting; Jarek was the one who Lola loathed.

Rhys didn't snap, not like he had at the stag do with Freddie. This was different because he didn't want to make things worse for Lola, because he cared deeply about her, even if she didn't think of him in the same way. There was nothing more he'd like than to punch Jarek's viciously handsome face, but he restrained himself. His friends only stepped in when Jarek continued to provoke him, almost as if he wanted to get hit, manipulating the situation so he would be the one wronged. Rhys wouldn't give him the satisfaction. To protect her, he'd walk away. And this time with countless witnesses, Jarek had messed up.

Freddie and Barnaby elbowed their way in-between them and Rhys allowed them to take charge.

'You've gate-crashed this wedding; you're leaving. *Now*,' Freddie growled as he clamped his hand on Jarek's shoulder. Barnaby closed in on Jarek's other side.

Jarek was playing it cool. He shrugged Freddie off and held his hands up, seemingly unruffled as he looked between them all, his focus zoning in on Rhys, which made his skin crawl. He refused to flinch from his hateful gaze. It was clear to see how easily he could turn on the charm and how effortlessly he'd been able to reel Lola in.

'I was leaving anyway,' he said breezily as if he hadn't turned up purely to upset. With his hands in his trouser pockets, he strolled towards the exit, Freddie following a few steps behind. Before closing the gate, Jarek turned and looked at Rhys. 'Tell Lola I'll see her soon.'

Rhys nearly lost it at that, but Barnaby grabbed him before he could charge forward.

'He's not worth it.' Barnaby's firm words and pleading look was enough to make Rhys pause. 'Walk away and find Lola. We'll make sure he doesn't come back.'

Rhys wanted to do anything but find Lola. That was a conversation he didn't want to have, because the emotions that had been stirred when he saw her kissing Valentino had left him feeling downright confused. But Barnaby insisted, so he left.

The spiralling negativity tightened its grip as he retraced his steps through the meadow. Darkness had descended and lights glittered through the trees up ahead. The garden terrace was now awash with colour. The craggy mountains were silhouetted against the midnight-blue sky, while the horizon was tinged amber and gold. A breeze rustled the grasses and sent the shepherds' bells jangling. The music, laughter and light was inviting and he knew Lola was in amongst it somewhere, her friends rallying around her. Valentino may well be comforting her too.

Rhys clenched his fists and the knot in his chest tightened. How had he ever believed he'd be good enough for someone like Lola? The look Jarek had given him, one of pity and disbelief at the possibility that Lola had replaced him – a handsome, rich investment banker – with a plain, shy teacher was laughable.

He wanted to stay concealed in the darkness on the periphery, like he so often was. Not that he could continue leading his life like that. He was putting his career, his ambitions and his life in Bristol on hold to go travelling, but what he was really doing was escaping so he didn't have to deal with difficult emotions when that was exactly what he needed to do.

Lola was just visible beyond the trees, radiant despite her lack of a smile. She stood out amongst her friends, her beauty accentuated by the soft candlelight. Barnaby had urged him to find her, but how on earth could he walk up to her now?

A breeze stirred the leaves; out in the countryside, autumn was in the air, particularly now the sun had nearly disappeared. Rhys breathed a deep lungful of fresh air tinged with earthiness and herbs. Being outdoors was what he loved, it was where he felt at peace, a similar feeling to when he was making things with his hands. He had to stop hiding or shoving down his desires because they felt too hard to bring to fruition. He 100 per cent knew he would feel even worse if he ignored Lola completely.

Rhys left the meadow and followed the dusty path that wound through the trees. The flickering light and the warmth of the colours coming from the garden terrace chased away the shadows. Music drifted and laughter pierced the air.

Lola was surrounded by her friends, Deni, Polly and Sarah circling her as protectively as a pack of wolves. She caught sight of him first, immediately breaking away from the group and stepping towards him, her hands outstretched.

'Are you okay?' She glanced behind him. 'Is he gone?'

Rhys nodded, his mouth suddenly dry. The worry in her eyes broke his heart, but more than anything he wished he'd been the one to protect her when Jarek showed up. At least Valentino was nowhere to be seen. He clenched his fists again.

'He's gone. Barnaby's going to speak to the staff, ensure he doesn't come back.'

'Thank you.' Lola stepped a little closer. Rhys noticed her friends kept their distance, pretending to talk amongst themselves, but they were watching like hawks, unsubtly trying to listen in.

'Are you okay though?'

'I'm okay now...' She trailed off. 'I don't know why I was surprised that he showed up here.'

He shook his head. 'He is one determined son-of-a-bitch.' At her wide-eyed look, he backtracked, his voice softening. 'He's really left, Lola. And you're not alone.' He gestured towards her friends, who were still doing a rubbish job of pretending they weren't watching.

The short distance between them felt vast, as if there was an invisible divide keeping them apart. Half of him wanted to breach it so he could hug her, while the other half wanted to run away.

'I, uh... About what happened.' She gestured towards the table she'd been sitting at.

'I know why you did it.' Rhys shoved his hands in his pockets. 'To protect yourself, to show him you've moved on with someone who's his equal.'

Lola drew back. 'That's not what I was thinking at all.' Her expression morphed from worry to tight-lipped stoniness. 'I did it to pr—'

'Honestly, Lola, it's okay,' he cut in softly as the sorrow in his chest grew. 'You don't need to explain. It was perfectly clear. I would have done the same in your position.'

He didn't know how to deal with the rejection, and he definitely couldn't stand to see Lola's face crumple. So with his heart racing, he walked away and tried to blot out the sight of her damp eyes. He was escaping again, although unlike at the first night party, this time there was no chance of Lola joining him.

The roof terrace where many photos had been taken earlier was quiet, with only a few guests cosying up on the white cushioned seats; no one he knew well enough to start up a conversation with. The wistful look of longing on Lola's face when she'd been watching Mirabel with Fabs earlier had made his heart stall. Her best friend would be starting her married life with her soulmate. To have that... Rhys loosed a long breath and rested his elbows on the stone wall.

Tiny bulbs crisscrossed the bar terrace below. The earlier electric string trio had been replaced with a DJ playing an eclectic mix of music. He couldn't resist tapping his foot. Fabs and Mirabel were dancing together, while Fabs's sisters and their husbands circled them. Both sets of parents looked on, their smiling, flushed faces filled with love, while not a hint of animosity lingered between them. Watching the swirling dancers and listening to the happy chatter and laughter merging with the music allowed his heart to calm and the adrenaline to subside.

Rhys remained leaning against the rough wall long enough for his elbows to begin to ache. He straightened, stretched and rested his hands back on the wall. The surrounding darkness was absolute and suited his mood; even the jagged outline of the mountain had merged with the inky sky.

Heels clipped across the rooftop terrace. Zoe appeared by his side. He mumbled some sort of greeting, but she remained silent as they gazed down at the guests either dancing or milling about between the potted olive trees and flickering lanterns. He caught a flash of Lola's plum-blue dress before she was swallowed up by the trees, Sarah, Deni and Polly with her.

'Why the hell are you up here and not down there with Lola?' Zoe finally broke the silence.

'If you've come to gloat, I'm not in the mood—'

'Freddie caught me up.' Zoe clasped her hands together on the wall. 'I'm not gloating. I'm checking you're okay. The guys said you seemed upset.'

'No shit.'

'Which is understandable after what happened.' She ran her thumb over her engagement ring. 'A bit of a shock her ex showing up like that. Perhaps you two should have said something before, instead of pretending everything was okay.' She paused and Rhys sensed her eyes on him. 'You've been hiding quite a lot of things since we've been here.'

Rhys breathed deeply. The colourful dresses and the flickering candlelight merged together in a blur as he tried to hold it together. He'd come up here for some peace and to escape people – Lola and his friends included, certainly his ex-girlfriend. He sighed; he might as well get it all out in the open.

'You were right about that night in Bosa; it was all for show.' He didn't look at her, just continued to watch the dancing below. 'We were just pretending.'

'Yeah, I figured as much.' Zoe paused. 'But it's not for show now, is it? Not the way she looks at you or how you feel about her, given how bloody miserable you are right now. No one hurts the way she's hurting tonight without being head over heels in—'

'Don't, Zoe. Just don't.' Rhys shook his head. 'She doesn't want someone like me. She wants someone like Valentino, someone who is impressive in every fucking way.'

'Oh, get over yourself, Rhys!' Zoe spluttered. 'You're the nicest damn man I've ever known and sexy with it – just don't tell Freddie I said that. I loved being with you, it was just the wrong time. I wasn't ready for a serious relationship back then, both times we were together—'

'And you are now?'

'Me and Freddie are dead good together. I treated you like shit messing about behind your back when we were at uni, but we've all grown up since then. And changed.' She pouted as if contemplating saying something more. 'You see yourself in a completely different way to how everyone else sees you. And what Lola did with Valentino tonight was to stick two fingers up to her crazy ex in an attempt to get him off *your* back. Sarah said as much.'

Rhys lifted his hands from the wall, turned to her and frowned.

Zoe shrugged. 'Sarah and I have been tight since yesterday evening's girls' night. She's as much of a gossip as I am.' Zoe studied him with a directness that made her formidable working in an industry dominated by men. 'You're a fool if you don't fight for her or, worse, let *your* insecurities get the better of you.'

'You do understand where my insecurities come from?'

Zoe held up her hands. 'Why the hell do you think I'm talking to you now? I fucked up when we were together. I dealt with my own insecurities and uncertainty in a cowardly way, by upping and leaving instead of staying and talking things through. We would never have worked out, but I should have dealt with the situation differently. We did have fun, Rhys. I'm happy now and I want that for you too. We were once really good mates. I cared about you and still do. Neither me nor Freddie want to lose you. I know we're never going to be able to get our friendship back to the way things were, but it'd be ace if we could at least be in a room together without wanting to flay each other.'

'Or chat openly about stuff the way we used to.'

'Exactly. The way we're doing right now.' She waggled a finger between them. 'And at least I can put my hand on my heart and say I'm nowhere near as crazy bad as Lola's ex.'

Rhys huffed a laugh. 'You could put it on a T-shirt: "I'm no psycho ex".'

'Something to be proud of.'

'Indeed.'

'Go talk to her, Rhys.' Zoe looked at him intently and touched his arm, a platonic gesture that made him feel nothing, neither longing nor regret. 'Don't let her ex ruin what you have with Lola, because I'm pretty sure that was his intention. I ran away from big scary feelings and adult conversation once. Don't make the same mistake I did and mess things up with Lola, even if it only ends up being a friendship you lose out on.' Her eyes were soft and sad. She pushed away from the wall and patted his shoulder. 'Promise me you won't be so stubborn that you miss your chance with her, Rhys.'

32

Rhys walking away from her looking so sad was the worst moment of Lola's life. Kissing Valentino had been purely to unnerve Jarek and protect Rhys *from* him and yet it had backfired spectacularly.

Her friends swarmed around her like she was a queen bee needing to be protected, yet despite being enveloped by their love and concern, she felt empty. Jarek had won. He'd managed once again to make her feel scared, insignificant and unworthy, but worst of all he'd managed to push a wedge between her and Rhys. It didn't matter if Rhys and his friends had thrown him out and stood up for her, or that her friends were supporting her, not when he'd messed up the best thing that had happened to her in a very long time.

Someone placed a drink in her hand, and when it was clear that she didn't want to talk about Jarek, Valentino or Rhys, the conversation was swiftly moved on by Deni about how they must get a picture of them all in the photo booth, with Mirabel too. Lola listened, chipped in a word or two and sipped her rum and pink grapefruit cocktail. She caught the concerned glances from her friends so went through the motions of trying to enjoy the evening, yet it felt as if she was looking down on herself rather than fully experiencing everything.

It was only after she'd drained her drink and Deni and Sarah went to the bar for another round of cocktails that Polly led her to the nearest table and made her sit down.

'I know you're not okay, so there's no point pretending that you are,' she said matter-of-factly. 'But he's gone, so you can at least relax tonight.'

'He may be gone, but he's not out of my life. He's a never-ending nightmare.'

'And you'll put a stop to it as soon as you get home.' She smiled gently. 'There are enough flipping lawyers here to give you advice and fight your corner. Jarek won't get away with this behaviour. His one mistake tonight – of many, I should add – was making himself so public. Rhys, Valentino and Fabs's friends are all witnesses. It'll be okay.'

Lola nodded glumly and focused on the olive tree next to them, its branches threaded with fairy lights. She needed Polly, her sensible, thoughtful friend, to see the situation from a different viewpoint. 'I actually couldn't care less about Jarek right now.' Lola twisted back to face Polly, her voice cracking as she said, 'It's Rhys I've messed things up with.'

'*You* didn't mess up anything. Jarek did that. The way you're feeling right now is because he forced you into a situation you had no control over. And Rhys reacted that way because he likes you, Lola,' Polly said softly. 'I don't know Rhys at all, but he had no hesitation in going after Jarek. His reaction was to protect you and that speaks volumes. And yes, his anger got the better of him, but that seems to have come from a place of self-doubt, if he thinks either Valentino or Jarek are more worthy of your love. I'm sure Valentino's a nice guy and has abs that look like they've been chiselled from marble, but Jarek.' Polly whistled low. 'He's a nasty piece of work who doesn't deserve one more second of your time. He's messed with your head so much and for too long. Don't let him destroy a relationship with a hell of a decent guy.'

Deni and Sarah returned, interrupting their conversation. Through the trees, Lola could make out the other terrace where the DJ had everyone up and dancing, ruby, cerise and powder-blue dresses catching the light as people moved. Four cocktail glasses topped with lime and a sprig of thyme were placed on the table. Polly squeezed Lola's hand as they turned their attention to their friends.

'To Fabs and Mirabel, and of course friendship,' Deni said as they knocked their glasses together.

Lola sipped the lemony gin cocktail as she was embraced by her friends' merriment. She tried to relax, yet her thoughts still snagged on Rhys. She wondered where he was, and if he was okay.

'Where on earth have you lot been!' Mirabel threw herself among them, planting her arms across Deni's and Polly's shoulders and cutting Lola's thoughts short. 'There's a dance floor that-a-way with all of your names on it.' With her arm still round Deni, she grabbed Lola's hand and tugged her in the direction of the other terrace.

Lola pushed her worries aside and chose laughter, dancing and her friends. She lost herself to the music, something that always brought her comfort and ignited joy. She was surrounded by her friends, and they laughed and twirled, their heels scuffing the red bricks, while the light from the bulbs crisscrossing overhead made necklaces glitter and earrings sparkle. Mirabel threw her arms around Lola, and she allowed herself to be swept up in the love and happiness that emanated from her newly-wed best friend.

* * *

The evening went by far too quickly in a whirl of joy that had only been marred by the incident with Jarek and which, by some miracle, Mirabel was none the wiser about.

Fabs obviously knew what had happened, if his extra-big hug was anything to go by. 'Rhys has got your back, Lola,' he said quietly. 'Barnaby and the rest of the guys too.'

Tears had already been threatening and she nearly lost it at the look Fabs gave her when he pulled away: one of support, love and understanding. He was an extended part of her family now he'd married the friend she considered to be a sister.

She only managed a nod before he was swept into a hug by someone else. Then Mirabel was in front of her, her hazel eyes damp and sparkling, her cheeks flushed as she pulled her close.

'Thank you for everything,' Mirabel whispered as she hugged her tight. The build-up to the wedding had been long and intense and it was coming to an end, a spectacularly wonderful day that was tinged with sadness. They'd see each other tomorrow for brunch before Mirabel headed off with Fabs on their month-long honeymoon, but that was it. Mirabel would return to Sardinia, not London, while Lola would be heading home to face a completely different challenge alone. No, she wasn't alone, as Fabs had just told her. So when Mirabel pulled away, Lola smiled despite her internal battle and they laughed together, their cheeks streaked with tears.

Once Fabs and Mirabel had been waved off to their bridal suite, people began to drift away. While Sarah, Gareth, Freddie and Zoe were keen to prop up the bar for a little longer, Lola followed Polly, Deni and Mark's lead and called it a night. With Rhys and Barnaby joining them, their calls of 'goodnight' and 'see you all in the morning' echoed into the star-speckled night.

Deni, Mark and Polly chatted non-stop as they strolled through Il Giardino's honey-lit grounds. Lola was acutely aware of Rhys and Barnaby walking behind them in silence. She didn't know how to ease the tension with Rhys. She wasn't even sure if she should, not when they'd be going home in a couple of days and he'd be heading off on his travels. What would be the point?

They reached the entrance to the main hotel building and while her friends headed towards the lift, Rhys and Barnaby turned right. Lola slowed and glanced back. Rhys had stopped. Barnaby squeezed his shoulder and continued walking.

They met each other's eyes. Rhys opened his mouth, then closed it. Lola waited, hoping he would say something, although perhaps it was for the best to end whatever tentative thing they had before emotions became even more tangled and confused.

The sound of the lift pinging open made the decision for her.

'Night, Rhys,' she said quietly.

Without waiting for a reply, she paced the short distance to the lift and joined her friends just as the doors closed, shutting out the sight of Rhys still standing in the hotel's lobby.

No one said a word on the way up, but she noticed her friends' concerned glances.

The lift doors opened onto the first floor and Lola led the way along the hallway. She felt a rush of overwhelming sadness as she paused outside her room. Time was slipping away, their night at Il Giardino the final flourish to a spectacular stay on Sardinia. With just a couple of days left before the flight home, tonight was the beginning of the end.

'Are you sure you're all right?' Polly whispered as she gave her a squeeze.

Deni was already outside her room, her call of 'goodnight' echoing down the hall as she gave a cheeky wink and pushed her husband inside.

Lola huffed. 'I'm fine, honestly. I just need to sleep. Tomorrow's a whole new day, eh?'

Polly nodded, although she didn't look convinced. 'I'll see you at brunch then.'

The second Lola closed the door to her room it was if all the emotions she'd been bottling up and fighting against for months swamped her. The sense of loss was acute as hot tears fell. This was the second wedding of the year that she'd cried at, although at the first one when she'd been sitting half submerged in a muddy lake she'd been laughing as hard as she'd been crying. There was nothing funny about how she was feeling right now.

She swiped the back of her hand over her eyes and stumbled across the room. The spacious sitting area was shrouded in darkness, and through an archway the four-poster bed enveloped by cream curtains looked too large and imposing for one person.

Lola threw open the door to the private terrace and took a breath of sweet mountain air. The wide-open sky was velvety black and dusted with stars. Goosebumps prickled her arms, and the feelings of freedom and possibility made Lola's heart ache with sadness. London was vibrant and bustling and had its own sort of beauty, yet the idea of returning made her insides clench, not because she didn't love her job, but because of how claustrophobic it would be trapped in a city without Mirabel and where Jarek would be. A heaviness settled that wouldn't be blown away by the herb-scented breeze. Just the thought of having to deal with all of that terrified her.

But not tonight.

Shivering in her short-sleeved dress, Lola returned inside and shut the door on the breeze. She wandered into the bedroom and switched on the lamp.

And then her heart bottomed out. A cream envelope was

propped against the pillow on the side of the bed she slept on, her name written in Jarek's punchy handwriting.

She wanted to run; she wanted to hide, to scream, to sob, to drag the suffocating knot of fear and worry from deep inside and stomp all over it. She wanted to be far from his influence, to be utterly rid of him, yet she was still riding the emotional wave of his making. Running away wasn't the answer, neither was burying her feelings or wishing she could forget all about him, which as he'd proved many times was futile. Facing him head on with the intention of removing him from her life rather than wishing things were different was the path she needed to take.

So, despite wanting to flee, Lola reached out and plucked the envelope off the bed.

33

Lola trembled as she pulled out the handwritten note and read it.

Dear Lola,

What a pleasure it was to stumble across you the other day in Porto Cervo, although your enthusiasm was somewhat lacking, I'll forgive you because I'm nice like that.

But I just wanted to remind you that I'll decide when we're done, not you. Did you learn nothing when we were together?

I do hope you'll be thinking of me tonight, just as I've been thinking about you every night since we met.

Yours forever,

J x

Gone was any subtlety, as if he no longer cared about the consequences. He was baiting her, while proving that he was the one in control. Yet going to these lengths would be his downfall, because the amount of evidence he was providing would help her get him out of her life. Polly had been absolutely right about that. His note simmered with anger though, as if he was surprised that she'd walked away from him and hadn't looked back, something he obviously wasn't used to.

The more she'd got to know him, the more the 'real' him had become apparent. It was hard to understand how someone could thrive off control, manipulation and hurting the person they wanted to be with. Whenever a touch of humanity slipped through, something dark and twisted inside him tightened its grip. He'd shared so little about his family and she knew nothing of his childhood that the possibility of trauma somewhere in his past was highly likely. People weren't inherently evil, were they? Something must have happened to make him want to treat the person he chose to be with so appallingly. He'd never be satisfied, he'd never find real love, he'd never be able to let go of whatever hurt he was holding on to.

Whether Jarek had somehow managed to get into her room to place the letter on the bed or he'd sweet-talked one of the hotel's staff into leaving it there, he'd infiltrated her private space and contaminated it. She didn't want to stay here a second longer and certainly not sleep here alone. What she needed was the company of a friend.

Taking her phone from her overnight bag, she paused before switching it on. What harm would it do when Jarek already knew where she was? She thumbed a quick message.

> Which room are you in?

Lola stared at her phone. Rhys had seen the message, but he was taking a long time to reply. Although, of course, he might not reply at all. And her message was abrupt with little explanation of why she wanted to know where he was.

Lola sighed and typed another message.

> I'm sorry, I'm scared and worried. Jarek left a note in my room and I can't stay here on my own another minute.

Within seconds, he sent a reply.

> The olive suite, ground floor.

Turning off her phone again and stuffing the room card in her clutch, she flew from the room. As she navigated her way downstairs, she realised her desire to see Rhys and make things right had been bubbling beneath the surface all night, yet they'd both retreated to the comfort and familiarity of their friends.

Reaching the Olive Suite, her heart pounded and she faltered before knocking.

Within seconds, the door swung open. As Lola looked at Rhys, a feeling rushed through her that took her breath away. He was still in his suit, although he'd discarded his jacket and tie, and the top couple of buttons of his shirt were undone. In the dim light of the doorway, she could make out his flushed cheeks and pursed lips. He stepped back and she slipped inside.

'He left a letter?' Rhys glanced at the clutch she was holding.

'I left it in the room.' She shook her head as the anxiety in her chest began to crack wide open again. 'I just needed to get out of there, see a friendly face—'

'You mean you wouldn't have come here unless he'd frightened you.' Rhys folded his arms.

'That's what you've taken from me being here?' Lola mirrored his stance. 'Not that out of everyone, all of my friends, *you're* the person I wanted to see.' She fought back a wave of sadness. 'I don't know if I'd have come here tonight if Jarek hadn't left that note, because I was upset and angry, at you, at myself. But mostly him.' Lola tried hard to separate the hurt from the way she felt in her heart, to find a way to put into words how she was feeling. 'What this last couple of weeks has taught me is that I can open up to someone again; I can share my fears as much as my dreams. I can learn to trust again. You're the reason for that, Rhys. That's why I came here. To you.'

The expression on his face changed from confusion to openness as he ran his hand down his stubbled jaw. 'I'm sorry, I spoke without thinking. I wanted to talk to you in the lobby before. I wanted to say sorry for taking my anger out on you. I just didn't know what to say.' He loosed a heavy sigh. 'I thought the reason you kissed Valentino was because—'

'I know what you thought,' Lola said firmly. She stepped towards him. 'Valentino is not your equal; Jarek neither, far from it. *You* are worth a thousand times more than him. What I did with Valentino was purely to get Jarek's attention away from you. Not that you can't stand up for yourself, but I didn't want to let anything happen to someone I care about. I wanted to tell you earlier that I don't think about Valentino in that way at all. You're everything. But you were too angry to hear me out. You wouldn't have listened.'

'I'm listening now.' His voice was rough and choked with emotion. His whole body was still, his focus on her completely, both of them standing rigidly on the threshold of his suite.

'Then ask me to stay, Rhys. Or tell me to leave. It's your choice.'

The note may have been the deciding factor for her seeking out Rhys, but it had been on her mind all evening how to make things right between them. She didn't expect anything from him beyond his company, to talk and share and heal, the way they had done so easily over the last few days.

Rhys stepped closer, his eyes devouring her but in a way that suggested he was battling with something. His breath caressed her face, while her heart thudded. He reached for her hand, his fingers sliding between hers, warm and comforting yet coupled with promise and delight. When he smiled, his face lit up completely, just as it had done that first night on the jetty.

'Lola Wild, would you like to stay the night?'

34

Rhys could have told Lola to leave; that would have been easier than risking getting hurt more than he already had, but he was fed up of giving into his worries and fears. He couldn't let her walk away. It would have felt as if she'd be walking out of his life, as she'd be doing in just two days' time when they got on separate flights to return to the UK. But that didn't mean they couldn't at least explore what was between them in the short time they had left. His earlier conversation with Zoe had played over and over throughout the evening. With her no-bullshit attitude, she'd told him some hard truths, so perhaps she was a true friend. And she was right: he'd be a fool to not fight for whatever tentative thing he and Lola had.

'Lola Wild, would you like to stay the night?'

Her eyes were wide and for a moment it looked like she might run out of the door.

He gulped. 'We can just chat or sit outside, have a drink, nothing more—'

'Stop talking, Rhys.'

They were already so close, he could feel the warmth radiating off her. A fresh floral scent with seductive notes of jasmine and honey made him want to wrap his arms around her and bury his face in her hair. She kicked off her heels, stood on tiptoes and closed the distance between them to kiss him, slowly, gently, teasingly...

He pulled away laughing. 'Talking too much is not something anyone's ever complained about with me.'

'And yet you're still talking.'

The smile she gave him reached her eyes and it wasn't just relief that went through him at the sight, but a desire to be the person who made her smile like that every single day.

He took her advice, though, and shut the hell up. He returned the kiss with fervour, the memory of their first kiss at the restaurant an echo of this one; a kiss that made his heart and body ignite with desire and longing and love.

Taking her hand, Rhys led her through his suite, which was set around a courtyard garden with an ancient-looking olive tree threaded with lights. In the subtle lamplight, it was difficult to see where the room ended and the outside began. A small plunge pool was lit a deep turquoise, while the tiny lights entwined in the tree mirrored the stars in the clear night sky.

They sat together on the oversized beanbag lounger beneath the olive tree. Rhys pulled a throw over them as Lola snuggled against him. On the cusp of autumn, the cloudless night in a mountainous region was refreshingly cool. It reminded him of all the things he loved about autumn and winter, a time of year that made him feel alive and free, particularly when he was doing physical work or spending the day outdoors – he needed more of those things in his life – something he intended to work towards over the coming year.

'I don't really like cities and yet I'm visiting Paris first.' Even keeping his voice hushed it sounded loud as he broke the silence. 'This is my kind of place.'

Where they were nestled together half lying in the lounger, all Rhys could see was the sky, so dark and clear that if he'd known anything about the stars, he'd be able to make out the constellations. Dark cotton-wool blooms of juniper framed the view, looming beyond the white walls that enclosed the courtyard. The night was far from silent, with the cicadas keeping them company, the sigh of the breeze in the branches above, a distant tinkle of a shepherd's bell, a cough, a peal of laughter. Even though Rhys knew their friends were close by, it felt as if it was only the two of them, and Lola was safe in his arms where she should have been all night. He pulled her closer. Her skin was warm through her dress. He breathed in her honey-sweet perfume that mixed with the aromatic thyme that sprouted in the cracks between the paving stones.

'I like city living and love London, but I understand the appeal of somewhere like this.' Lola glided her hand across his stomach and came to a rest against his chest, where his shirt buttons opened. 'For me, though, it would need to have a sea view to be perfect. However much I love summer, there was something rather special about living by the coast in Devon and getting the beaches almost to myself in the colder months. I think that's what I miss living where I do now – the freedom and space of where I grew up.'

'That's always been my dream.' Rhys rested his chin on the top of her head. 'It was never my intention to stay living in Bristol after I graduated, but I got my first teaching job, loved the school I worked at and before I knew it I'd bought a house. A place I thought would be temporary became my permanent home.'

Stuck was what he'd almost said, but that sounded far too

negative. He did have the freedom to change things and do what he wanted. He had savings and skills, he just needed enough desire and courage. With Lola gently circling her fingers over his chest, he was having a hard job thinking straight, but now he had to be brave.

'I really am sorry for letting my insecurities get the better of me earlier,' Rhys said quietly, trying not to focus on the heat of her drifting fingers. 'It's easier to play the victim than face the truth when feelings are involved.'

Lola lifted her head from the crook of his shoulder. 'Because letting someone new into your life is scarier than pushing them away?'

'Yes.'

'Because that's how I feel,' Lola said slowly. 'But mine's a trust issue rather than a belief in myself.'

'I should have trusted your reason for doing what you did.'

'And I shouldn't have let you walk away when I knew you were hurting.'

'I just wish I'd been there with you, like in Porto Cervo.' Rhys skimmed his fingers over the curve of her hip.

Lola nodded. 'I know, but you're the one who's with me now.'

She sealed that thought with a kiss. Her hand slid up his chest until she was cupping his stubbled cheek and they were kissing deeply, as if they couldn't get enough of each other now the misunderstanding had been cleared up.

He had no idea how long they kissed for. It could have been ten minutes or an hour, but all he knew was he didn't want to stop. It was lingering and explorative, sensual and certain, and the way he felt in his heart for once matched what he was thinking: that this was everything; Lola was everything to him.

His hands caressed the bare skin revealed by the low-cut back of her dress, while hers dipped beneath his unbuttoned shirt and across the top of his chest, coming to a rest over his heart. There was an unspoken understanding that this night was about comfort and companionship even if desire wove between them. His imagination went way beyond what they were doing, but his hands stopped short of his mind's intentions.

It was only when goosebumps stole across Lola's bare arms and he could feel her shivering that they pulled away from each other. He had no idea of the time, but with the night sky clear and dark, chill air stole beneath the cosy throw.

'We should really get some sleep.'

At Lola's nod of agreement, Rhys pulled her to her feet. Stifling a yawn, she looked as sleepy as he felt, but delicious with it, with her mussed-up hair and cheeks flushed from the cold.

He closed the glass doors on the terrace but didn't bother switching on the bedside light. Lola peeled off her dress and let it pool on the floor, then she slid beneath the bedcover in just her bra and thong. He gulped back a wave of desire and unbuttoned his shirt, leaving it on the back of the chair with his trousers neatly folded. He was a creature of habit while Lola was a free spirit; they were opposites in so many ways and yet somehow they were perfect for each other.

He joined her in bed but left a gap between them. Lola's breathing was already rhythmic and hushed, and it was only when she reached behind her for his arm and laid it across her bare stomach that he allowed himself to relax. Letting out a long, contented sigh, he snuggled close and breathed in her honey-scented hair. Holding Lola in his arms and falling asleep together was perfect. For tonight it was enough.

* * *

Lola wanted Rhys in all senses of the word, but in his arms, snuggled together in the dark, was perfect. She didn't want to complicate things with sex, especially after today's events, and she sensed Rhys felt the same. Their desire had been blatantly obvious when they'd been kissing, their hands roving just enough to sense, well, everything.

Lola smiled and slid her arm tighter over Rhys's where it lay against her stomach. He planted a kiss on the back of her head and stayed there, his breath hot, his arms encircling. The feeling of safety, of comfort, of peace, of being home was everything. She'd never felt anything like it, even if she knew this moment would be fleeting. This feeling would disperse as they scattered to the wind when their time on Sardinia came to an end.

35

Waking up next to Lola should have made Rhys the happiest man in the world, but despite their connection and spending the night together – even if they'd only shared each other's company – uncertainty still tugged at him. Regardless of the yearning he'd felt last night – and the desire that was so obvious this morning it was downright torturous – Lola was hurting and had come to him in fear; his desire was not something he felt comfortable acting on, however much he wanted to.

Instead of initiating sex, he snuck out of bed, pulled on a clean T-shirt and shorts and made a Nespresso coffee. Opening the sliding doors to the courtyard, he clasped his cup and breathed in the scent of herbs, damp soil and the coffee steaming into the fresh morning air.

Rhys gazed up at the vibrant green of the juniper trees against the wash of blue sky, the leaves translucent where the sun hit. He sat down on the edge of the pool and dunked his feet into the water, which was warm enough to combat the chill of the morning. He sipped his coffee while watching the birds flit between the trees and listened to the rustle of leaves as the branches were stirred by the breeze.

Rhys wasn't sure how long he sat there watching the ants soldiering across the paving and the butterflies dancing over the thyme, when he heard the coffee machine whirring. He turned just as Lola stepped outside and his heart juddered at the sight of her in the shirt he'd been wearing last night. With her bare legs, ruffled hair and smudged make-up, she'd never looked more beautiful.

She sat down next to him with her coffee and plunged her feet into the pool with a sigh. 'That is gloriously warm. You been out here long?'

Rhys drained the remainder of his coffee. 'A little while.'

'It's peaceful.'

'More so than last night,' he said quietly. 'Everyone's still asleep.'

'You didn't want to lie in?'

Not when all I could think about was wanting you, Rhys didn't say. 'Bit of an early bird.' He shrugged.

'You keep school hours, that's why.'

'You must have to get up early for your job?'

'Of course, but not all the time. My hours are quite erratic with lots of late nights thrown in and travel. Keeps me on my toes. And I've always been a bit of a night owl, although now I'm in my thirties I definitely can't do the late nights and early starts like I used to. At least not without feeling like shit. The grumpiness is unreal – you would not want to witness it.'

Oh but I would, Rhys thought.

'So, Mr Early Riser, is your sabbatical your way of taking a chance on doing something different with your life or do you really intend to go back to teaching?'

That was a big question for first thing in the morning; he gazed up at the pearly blue sky while he considered it.

'It's not a stipulation of taking the time off, but my intention is to return, although the year away is an opportunity for me to focus on doing something different and what I might want to do differently, you know, in the future.'

'You're being very non-committal.' Lola slipped her arm in his and kicked her feet beneath the surface of the pool, sending warm water lapping further up his legs. 'Saying out loud that you want to change your life scares you silly, doesn't it?'

'It's that obvious?' Her arm was tight, grounding him. His elbow brushing the side of her breast sent heat coursing through him. Being open and honest was less scary than bottling everything up only to wind up unhappy and filled with fear and anxiety. He didn't want to remain in an endless downward spiral. 'You're absolutely right. I don't know what I'm afraid of – failing, maybe? Worried I'll feel worse about myself than I already do?' He glanced at her. 'Than I did. I feel pretty good right now.'

Lola put her cup down and turned to face him, her eyes bright despite the smudges of mascara beneath them.

'To manifest change, you have to vocalise it and believe in it to make it happen.'

'But that's what I still need to figure out. I love teaching. The kids are the best; the workload, the stress, the challenges not so much, but I don't hate it by any means, I've just got into a rut and filled with negativity in here.' He pressed his fist to the centre of his chest. 'Travelling around Europe selfishly doing something for myself for a few weeks I hope will be the start of me healing.'

'It's not selfish if it's to protect your mental health.' Lola placed her hand on his thigh. 'I'd say that's essential.'

A phone pinged from inside the room.

'That must be yours,' Rhys said, lifting up his own phone.

Lola covered her mouth as she yawned. 'Who's messaging me this early in the morning?' She went still, then scrambled to her feet.

Rhys watched as she disappeared inside and scooped up her phone. Her shoulders tensed. He knew who it was without having to ask.

Leaving his cup next to the pool, he joined her inside. He put his hand on her shoulder and flinched as she jumped.

'Lola?' he said softly.

She turned to him, her face sheet-white, and held out her phone. 'Read this.'

> I've had enough, you ungrateful bitch. After everything I gave you and everything I've done for you. I was the best thing that ever happened to you and you've thrown it all away. You'll just have to live with the regret. We're done.

Rhys looked up from the message and met Lola's wide eyes. Tears streaked down her pale cheeks.

'Bloody hell, Lola.' Putting the phone down, he wrapped his arms around her and held her tight. 'You still need to get an injunction, but this might just mean he's given up pursuing you.'

* * *

Lola didn't exactly creep through the hotel, but she was conscious that she was in the dress she'd been wearing the night before and looked like she'd just got out of bed, but that didn't really matter when she had other things on her mind. In daylight, the threat of Jarek and his disturbing letter wasn't quite so frightening, even after that morning's message. The possibility that he'd decided to cut his losses and move on for good was more than she could have hoped for.

Brunch had been arranged for eleven, a decent time after a wedding, although she'd been up for quite a while already talking to Rhys. The kiss they'd shared before she'd left his room had been chaste, as if neither of them wanted to allow the rumbling feelings of desire to take over. The night before had definitely not been the right time, while this morning hadn't felt quite right either, even if there was a tug of war happening between her heart and head.

Brunch was in the herb garden, with groups of family and friends clustered around tables dotted between raised borders packed with salad leaves, mint and marjoram. Mirabel glowed with happiness and Fabs's own contentment shone through; perhaps they were the only two people that morning who were truly happy. For everyone else, the wedding was over and real life beckoned.

Lola found herself sitting with Deni, Mark, Sarah and Polly enjoying a breakfast of fresh bread, local honey and deliciously salty charcuterie in surroundings awash with sunshine. Rhys was on another table with Barnaby, Gareth, Freddie and Zoe. They caught each other's eyes and Lola smiled, holding his gaze and drinking him in; dark hair and smiling eyes, pale skin that had caught the sun and perhaps flushed a little as he looked at her, and sensual lips that she'd spent a *long* time kissing last night.

'You made up with Rhys then,' Sarah said with raised eyebrows. 'I saw you coming back to your room this morning. Hell of a night, eh?'

Lola switched her focus to her friends: Sarah with a mischievous grin, Polly smiling encouragingly, while Deni and Mark watched on with amused interest, their hands clasped together.

Full disclosure – that was what she'd promised herself from now on, to not withhold stuff from her friends or feel as if she had to hide any part of herself, both the good and the bad, either the things that worried her or brought her joy.

Lola rested her hands on the table, leaned in and kept her voice low. 'I haven't slept with him. I mean, we have slept together in the same bed, but we've not had sex.'

She could have laughed at the incredulous look her friends were giving her. Mark took a large gulp of coffee.

'How is that even possible?' Sarah sat back wide-eyed. 'And there was me thinking I was the only one out here not getting any action.'

'I'm not,' Polly said.

'I wasn't either.' Deni shrugged. 'Till Mark arrived.'

Lola laughed as Mark's cheeks flushed poppy-red. 'And that's my cue to leave.' He kissed Deni and scraped his chair back. 'I'll finish packing and check us out.'

Deni waited until Mark had escaped across the herb garden terrace and was out of earshot before whispering, 'I'm actually getting quite a lot of action.' She flapped a hand in front of her own flushed cheeks. 'You were right, Lola, about this island being made for romance.'

Polly whooped and Sarah high-fived her. Lola smiled, but her heart was twisted with longing for the happiness that was now radiating from her friend. From all three of her friends, actually. And she knew without a doubt how happy Mirabel was.

Her friends' attention turned back to her.

'So you haven't done *anything* with him?' Sarah asked.

'Our first kiss was at the restaurant when Freddie and Zoe announced their engagement and it wasn't even meant to be a proper one, just my way of taking Rhys's attention away from his friends having stomped all over his heart. And if you all believed Rhys and I were together, then everyone would leave us alone.'

'Wait?' Deni frowned. 'So it was all pretend?'

'The first night at Villa Sereno when I went out for some air I got talking to Rhys. We were both escaping.' Lola cleared her throat. 'We were both escaping from our friends. I'm so sorry.' She looked between Deni and Sarah. 'Jarek treated me appallingly. He shattered my confidence, my self-belief and he destroyed so much of me. You were all pushing for me to hook up with someone and move on, except that was the last thing I wanted.'

'Oh my goodness, Lola.' Deni reached across the table and held her hands. 'You should have said something.'

'I know, but it would have unravelled everything and I couldn't face that, talking about Jarek with you. I foolishly thought by bottling everything up and pretending I was okay, I'd be able to move on and forget about him.'

'But he didn't let you.'

'No, he didn't.' Lola gazed across the herb garden. Her friends were quiet, watching her, waiting. 'But I found I could talk to Rhys. Because that was all we were doing. That first night we made a love pact.' Lola laughed. 'It sounds ridiculous now, but at the time it seemed like a good idea and a way to help each other out.'

Sarah folded her napkin. 'So you pretended to be together?'

Lola nodded.

'And you didn't do anything that first night apart from talk?' Deni asked, her eyebrows furrowed.

'Nope.'

'Oh shit, the night in Bosa when I rearranged the room so you two could share!' Deni put her face in her hands.

'Yeah, thanks for that.' Lola laughed. 'We had an understanding and everything was pretend until it wasn't.'

'Oh my good God!' Sarah grinned manically. 'This is the best love story – please tell me it has a fairy tale ending.'

Polly nudged Sarah in the ribs and raised an eyebrow. Of all Lola's friends, she understood that nothing was straightforward, and a fairy tale ending after what Jarek had pulled would have been a miracle.

'Something changed that night with Rhys. Nothing had really happened, but I think he began to see me in a different way and then when I kissed him that night at the restaurant...'

'You realised he meant something to you,' Polly said quietly.

'Yeah, and after that I don't think either of us understood what was pretend and what was real. And we talked. Like, really talked. I told him stuff that I hadn't told anyone, not you lot, not even Mirabel. And when Mirabel ran off that day, it was Rhys I asked to drive me there to find her, and when Mirabel persuaded Fabs to find us somewhere to stay, it was so completely different sharing a bed with him to the first time. And stuff did end up happening; we desperately wanted each other and I'm pretty sure of the direction that night was going until Fabs got the call about—'

'His mamma. Fuck.' Deni huffed. 'That was what stopped you two from getting it on?'

Sarah grimaced. 'Oh my God, I'm sexually frustrated on your behalf.'

Polly's hand brushed the top of Lola's as she leaned closer. 'And last night?'

'We kissed and talked and cuddled. But last night I went to him because I was scared, after... well, you know.' She waved her hand in the air, not willing to say *his* name or go into the full details about the letter he'd left or his final message. 'It was not the right time. I don't know, there's so much expectation and we've shared so much over the last few days. I treasure his friendship and I really don't want to mess that up.'

'But on the flip side we're going home tomorrow.' Deni gave her a firm look that she imagined she used quite often with her clients when she didn't want them to argue back. She folded her arms. 'If you really think about it, what do you have to lose?'

Nothing, Lola thought, particularly if she didn't want to leave Sardinia with any regrets.

36

After brunch, Fabs and Mirabel said their goodbyes. Lola thought she'd never stop crying after waving her best friend off. They would talk properly and she'd catch Mirabel up on everything that she'd already shared with Deni, Sarah and Polly once Mirabel got back from her honeymoon, but it wouldn't be the same video-calling instead of gossiping over a glass of wine at a bar after work.

It was late afternoon by the time they returned to Villa Capparis. Everyone was subdued and there was a definite air of melancholy, with their time on Sardinia about to come to an end. The flights the next day were staggered, with Lola, Deni, Mark, Polly, Sarah, Jenny and her husband flying to Heathrow and Barnaby, Rhys, Gareth, Freddie and Zoe to Bristol. Tonight was their last together. Not only did Lola feel partied out, but she was emotionally exhausted from the events of the last few days.

'I've never known such a miserable fucking bunch!'

Of course it would be Gareth who would try to instigate some much-needed enthusiasm when everyone was feeling decidedly hungover and sombre.

'It's our last evening here.' He swept his arm around as they trooped into the main living area. 'Let's have some fun!'

Chef Carlo appeared in the doorway, greeting them with a breezy smile and a nod.

'Fabrizio say you may be sad.' He gestured towards the garden. 'So if you come with me.'

He pushed open the doors to the terrace and they were greeted by the sight of the table set for dinner with cream plates and brushed gold cutlery laid out on a muted floral tablecloth with vases of blue and dusky-pink hydrangeas interspersed between bottles of oil and vinegar. The enticing smell of grilling meat drifted from somewhere in the garden.

Gareth dropped his overnight bag in the living room and strolled outside. 'Now we're talking!'

'Boy am I going to miss you.' Deni shook Chef Carlo's hand and planted a kiss on each of his cheeks. 'Thank you for looking after us so well. *Grazie*.'

'You are welcome. Now enjoy.'

After taking their bags to their rooms and freshening up, their earlier frowns were banished as they settled around the table. They were no longer in those tight-knit friendship groups that they'd started out with nine days ago.

Chef Carlo and his team outdid themselves with a final meal of barbecued pancetta and pork chops with roasted aubergine, slices of courgette and home-cooked chips. The friends laughed, chatted, drank and ate together until the sun disappeared and the candles and lanterns were lit. With the earlier melancholy banished by good food and good company, contentment wound through the laughter and conversation.

When the sky had darkened to pitch-black, the stars shone and the moon cast twinkling silver on the sea beyond the trees, a hush went round the table as Freddie stood up. A knot of tension tightened in Lola's chest as he raised his glass. She caught Rhys's eye and he shrugged.

'Yeah, yeah, I know what you're all thinking, am I going to misread the mood and make another badly timed announcement.' He glanced at Zoe, whose cheeks had flushed a deeper pink than the hydrangea flowers. 'But no, it's just a toast to Fabs and Mirabel, who are obviously not here, but they brought us all together for what has turned out to be a wonderfully memorable week or two. So I wanted us to toast them – to Fabs and Mirabel and to friends old and new.'

Everyone raised a glass. 'To Fabs and Mirabel and friends old and new,' echoed around the table as glasses clinked.

Barnaby stood, holding his own glass aloft as he clamped a hand on Freddie's shoulder. 'Hey, I'm sure I speak for everyone here when I say we are incredibly happy about your engagement news. You do understand that, right?'

'Here, here.' Rhys stood and glanced between Freddie and Zoe.

A lump formed in Lola's throat at Rhys's generosity. His ability to forgive even if he wouldn't forget was touching. Going by Zoe's teary-eyed expression, she was equally moved.

'To Freddie and Zoe!' Barnaby said with laughter. 'And Chef Carlo and everyone here who's looked after us so well.'

'It's going to be hell going back to my flat with no cook, no fresh sweet-smelling towels,' Gareth grumbled. 'Might have to get myself a cleaner.'

'Doesn't your mum still do your washing?' Freddie jibed next to him.

Lola joined in with the laughter and teasing as Barnaby, Freddie and Rhys sat down and conversations started up again. All those worries she'd arrived in Sardinia with and her anxiety over meeting new people had disappeared, even with the challenges thrown at her. Clutching her wine, she leaned back in her chair and surveyed her friends. Laughter and chatter bounced around the table, enveloping her in contentment; she didn't want to break the moment and she certainly didn't want to head home and face reality. She glanced along the table and her heart skipped as she met Rhys's gaze. The smile he gave her made her ache with longing for this evening to continue forever, although with just her and Rhys so they could see where the night would take them.

Still holding his gaze, she raised her glass in her own silent toast: *To Lola and Rhys.*

* * *

Lola looked stunning tonight. The soft candlelight accentuated her tan, catching her high cheekbones, and her eyes sparkled as she laughed, a joyous sound that sent warm tingles through Rhys. For a last evening it was perfect. The only way it could have been any better was if Fabs and Mirabel were with them, or if it wasn't their last night at all. Time with Lola was slipping away and he didn't want to let go of this happiness. He wasn't the only one feeling it, he was sure, but he was fearful that he'd be the one who lost the most when they left Sardinia. The minutes were ticking by; the night would be drawing to a close all too soon.

Forgiving Freddie and Zoe was the right thing to do, which was why he'd seconded Barnaby's toast. There was no point in holding a grudge, when actually, in a roundabout way, they'd done him a favour. That hurt and disappointment caused by Zoe had been erased by Lola, but the actions of his friends this week had forced his feelings out into the open and he'd had to deal with them. During their time on Sardinia, he'd had sharp words with Zoe but also tender ones. Their last conversation overlooking the wedding dance floor had eased the ache in his heart, while a softer, caring side to Zoe had emerged that she usually hid well. She was happy with Freddie and she wanted him to be happy too. Whether that was with Lola or not, only time would tell.

37

Polly was the sort of drunk friend who was a pleasure to be around – her usual quiet demeanour switched to a bit naughty and she'd say things she'd never say when she was sober. Mirabel had always been a weepy drunk, Sarah managed to be even louder and more forthright than normal, while Deni would let go of all her inhibitions. Lola, of course, was the drunk friend who usually caused a scene.

Lola was about to head back outside with her favourite limoncello cocktail when Polly made a beeline for her. It was obvious from the sleepy smile and the shake of her hips as she twirled towards her that her lovely friend was wonderfully tipsy.

'You're not heading to bed already, are you?' Lola asked as she reached her.

'Already?' Polly raised an eyebrow. 'It's midnight and waaaaay past my bedtime.' She put her arm around Lola's waist. 'But the night is still young for you, so go back out there. Oh, and if you stay in our room tonight just to keep me company, I will make your life hell for the foreseeable future. There's a gorgeous man out there who is dying to get his hands on you. Please, for the love of God, leave me in peace and have some last-night fun!' She cocked her head and gave her a sly look. 'Anyway, I can't stand your snoring.'

'I do not snore!'

'If you say so.' Polly chuckled. 'I am perfectly happy having a room to myself away from my husband – who does snore – and my kids who wake me up at some ungodly hour *every* morning. So please, go, and you and Rhys get rid of all this sexual tension, then you can give me, Deni and Sarah *all* the gossip on the flight home. Deal?'

Laughter bubbled up inside Lola at her friend's serious expression. It would have been formidable on Deni, but her loveable friend just couldn't quite pull it off, not after a few glasses of wine. As Polly kissed her cheek and set off towards their bedroom with a wave, Lola wholeheartedly agreed that something needed to happen between her and Rhys, yet there was an unstated pressure, because tonight would be their last chance.

Opportunities had arisen but had been thwarted one way or other. But tonight, Polly was right. What was stopping her? Having feelings for someone left her vulnerable to getting her heart broken, but what she was most fearful of was allowing someone close and risking losing herself again. She reminded herself that Rhys wasn't Jarek. The truth was she knew that taking things further with Rhys would make it all the harder to say goodbye tomorrow, but did that really mean they shouldn't?

Lola returned outside to find Deni and Mark, plus Jenny and her husband, saying goodnight, which seemed to give Freddie and Zoe their cue to head to their room as well.

A couple of minutes later, Sarah gave an overdramatic yawn and stood up.

'Oof, I don't know about you guys, but I need my beauty sleep.'

'I'll walk you to your room.' Gareth grinned manically at Sarah as he too scraped back his chair and downed the remainder of his beer.

Barnaby stretched. 'Think I might join you. Not join you, you know what I mean, just it's time for bed too.'

It was almost as if there'd been an understanding between everyone – a pinball effect the moment the first person had called it a night.

Lola rolled her eyes at Sarah as she winked and, clasping Gareth's arm, they strolled across the terrace, a red-faced Barnaby on their heels.

'Well, that was unsubtle.' Rhys chuckled.

Heat flooded Lola's chest. 'Wasn't it just.'

There were two empty chairs between them, a chasm that needed breaching. It was incredibly quiet, as if even whispering would be too loud against the night-time scritch of insects. The villa was filled with people all anticipating how Lola and Rhys's night would go; their friends willing them to get together to make magical memories on their last night in Sardinia. That was the hope, wasn't it?

To hell with it.

Lola scooped up her limoncello cocktail and closed the distance between them. Placing her drink on the table, she slid onto his lap and wrapped her arms around him. It might be a mistake to spend the night together when there wouldn't be any chance of repeating it, but her body was craving him, her heart was full of him and her head was screaming yes.

She was still weighing up what they should or shouldn't do when Rhys kissed her.

And then, much like it had been the first time they'd kissed at the restaurant in Porto Cervo, everything else peeled away and there was just her and Rhys. This time there were no witnesses. There was no need to stop and no awkwardness to navigate afterwards. As their hands slid around each other and their kiss deepened, it was everything she wanted.

They kissed for a long time, sensual, passionate and expectant, and only paused when one of the candles on the table guttered out. Goosebumps prickled Lola's skin from the nighttime breeze and the thrill of Rhys's touch.

'Maybe we should move so Chef Carlo can clear away and get some sleep.' Rhys's whisper was edged with laughter.

Lola caught his face in her hands. 'Do you know that's one of the things I love about you most. How thoughtful you are.'

'My intentions aren't quite that innocent, though.'

Well damn, if the look he was giving her and the promise in his tone didn't undress her there and then.

'I should hope not.' Lola's tongue flicked and teased across his lips as her fingers started unbuttoning his shirt.

'I really do think we should continue this somewhere a little more private.' This time his whispered words were deep and guttural and when he took her hand and led her with purpose through the villa towards his room, any thoughts about how kind and considerate he was turned to just how much she wanted him. She adored this confident side to him that knew what he wanted too.

The restraint from the night before evaporated the moment he closed his door; Lola's fear had been replaced by unbridled desire, while Rhys's reticence had disappeared completely. His shirt was off within seconds and Lola nearly tripped over her own skirt as it caught around her feet. Rhys steadied her, his hands on her waist warm, firm and wanted.

Lola led him to the bed and relished the way his eyes roved.

His breath hitched as she unhooked her bra and discarded it on the floor.

Rhys fumbled with the buttons on his jeans and gave up entirely when Lola took over, while he focused on her, his hands exploring her body.

Lola pulled his phone from his pocket and placed it on the bedside table, then she yanked down his jeans.

'I hope your phone's off, Rhys. No interruptions this time.' She let his jeans drop next to her bra and pulled him down on the bed with her. 'If someone knocks on the door, ignore them. Hell, if the fire alarm goes off, we ignore it.'

'Or head to the beach and continue there.'

'I like your thinking.' Lola grinned. 'Oh, and if Freddie and Zoe hear, I'm okay with that too.'

'Are you still talking?' He grazed his lips across the side of her neck and when he trailed them between her breasts, every single thought exited her head.

38

Lola woke before Rhys did, the happiness from the night before still there, yet it was bittersweet, as she was dreading having to say goodbye later. One final night with Rhys had been the perfect way to end their time in Sardinia, but it didn't soften the blow that what they'd started was finishing as quickly as it had begun.

What struck her was that she was in a much better place emotionally, mentally and most definitely physically than when she'd arrived. That was quite something, and an awful lot of that was thanks to the man asleep next to her.

His room was almost a mirror image of hers, with soothing white walls and an ocean-blue bedspread, the sheets rumpled from last night's memorable activities. God, she adored everything about him.

'Morning, beautiful.' His lilting Welsh voice took her by surprise, and the way he said it so sleepily with a smile of drunken happiness filled her heart.

Sunshine slanted through the gap in the blinds and dust motes twirled. She could hear distant voices, so someone was up, but it was peaceful. If she squeezed her eyes shut, perhaps she could pretend they could stay curled up together indefinitely, sated after one blissful night, never having to go home and face reality.

'Morning, handsome,' she said with a smile. She couldn't hide or forget or pretend. She needed to accept what this was: the perfect ending to ten days that had been wonderful and challenging in equal measure, but had also taught her a hell of a lot too. She shouldn't shy away from heading home and what she needed to face, which she'd be doing with an army of friends by her side.

'I bet there'll be a wager round the breakfast table whether we'll walk in together hand in hand or sneak in separately.' His eyes were bright and warm as he gazed at her. 'I know what I want to do.'

Lola eased her fingers between his. 'Oh, I know what I want as well, but more than anything I don't want to leave this bed.'

'Mmn, that makes two of us.'

His kiss was slow and delicate, yet heat fused through her body. She wanted to snapshot this moment of absolute contentment. Because even if they stayed on Sardinia for a week or two more, for months even, the reality would be different. The dynamic would change, the same way it would be different if they continued their relationship back in the UK – not that it would be a possibility when Rhys would be heading off again soon. Their lives weren't really compatible, yet that didn't mean they couldn't stay friends.

Being open and honest was her new mantra.

'Part of me doesn't want to leave,' Lola said quietly as she pulled away from his kiss. Curled together hot and naked was perfect for baring her soul. 'But I know I need to so I can deal with the person who's made my life hell and put it all behind me.

This is fantasy right now and utterly wonderful. I just wish it was real life.'

The way he was looking at her made her wonder if he was going to blurt out something like 'but this could be real', or persuade her that they could turn the fantasy into reality. But how? It wasn't as if it hadn't crossed her mind when she'd drifted off last night.

'Real life can suck,' Rhys eventually said. 'But it doesn't mean there aren't good things in it. And you're going to go back and get your life sorted and feel so much better for it. You'll get your freedom and confidence back, I know you will. That's what's important right now.'

But what about you? What about us? Lola wanted to say, but didn't because she knew he was right; there were things she had to do, however hard, upsetting and likely frustrating they'd be. And she wouldn't be doing it alone, while Rhys...

'You're going to reshape your life over the coming months too and come out a hell of a lot stronger for it.'

'That's the hope.' Beneath the sheet, his fingers glided over the curve of her hip. 'The thing I love most about being a teacher is the way the kids are so full of enthusiasm. I always wonder why we lose that fun-loving side of ourselves when we grow up – that ability to be spontaneous and fearless. To give anything a go without worrying about doing the wrong thing or making a fool of ourselves. At least I lost that side of myself. I love how you didn't – at least you didn't until...'

'Yeah, until you know who.' She was glad he didn't say his name, not while they were entangled together beneath the sheets. Too much time had been spent worrying over her ex to be thinking about him in a moment of loved-up vulnerability. 'I've told you before, it feels as if I'm wearing a mask in public, playing the part people expect of me. It's hard to know who the real me is any longer, although I've been more open with my feelings with you and my friends this past week than I ever have.'

'Enough to get rid of the mask entirely?'

'Oh, I'm not sure I'm quite back to my old self; I might never be. He changed me for the worst, perhaps for good too. I'm not so trusting and blinded by the things he was good at projecting; the things that don't actually matter.' She didn't need to say looks or money or charm for him to understand.

Rhys pulled away from their embrace and lay back on the pillow with his hands tucked behind his head, staring up at the ceiling. Lola shifted onto her side and slipped one hand beneath her pillow. She made lazy circles with her fingers through the smattering of his chest hair and watched him. The tightening of his jaw and slight creasing of his forehead showed his thought process. He opened his mouth to say something, then closed it, and it was obvious he was building up to saying something he wasn't sure about.

Finally, he turned to her and slid his hand over hers so both of their hands rested on the centre of his chest. 'Perhaps you need to do something drastic.'

'Do you have something in mind?'

He held her gaze, firm and unwavering. 'Go travelling. I mean proper travelling, not a holiday to Sardinia. It could be two weeks or two months, whatever you can manage, to bum around Europe.' He took a drag of air. 'With me.' His eyes traced every inch of her face, and the way he did made her feel seen and understood, as if he was reaching into her, trying to untangle her messy thoughts about what she wanted. 'Come with me, Lola.'

'I can't.' The words were out too quickly. A defence mechanism because she'd already grown closer to Rhys than she'd intended; she'd already allowed him to creep into her heart and she wouldn't give him hope that what they'd shared in Sardinia could be anything more than a happy memory, because how could it when she was heading back to her fast-paced London life, while he was navigating his way to his future in Europe? She pressed her hand tighter against his chest, feeling his heart thudding beneath her fingertips. 'It's not that I don't want to go to Europe with you because I'd love to travel properly, but my work schedule is manic. However much I'd like to continue what we have here, it's...' She trailed off, the word 'temporary' on her lips belittling what they had. Yet she knew it wouldn't be possible to hold on to it either. Even if she said yes, it would only delay the inevitable.

'I understand, I only asked because I hoped.' He shook his head. 'I'm going to miss you.'

'Then we keep in touch.'

As friends. The words screeched into her head when it felt so much more than that because she was going to miss him like crazy too.

'And stay friends,' he said with a resigned tone that didn't quite match the smile he was trying to hold.

'Friends, always,' she agreed, although she couldn't keep the tone of resignation from her voice either. She did not want to end their time on Sardinia on a subdued note. She shifted closer to him, her breath teasing across the top of his chest. 'But right now we can be a little bit more than just friends.'

'Oh, I like that idea.' Rhys's grin reached his eyes this time as he pulled her on top of him, any further conversation cut short through action rather than words.

* * *

The sense of loss was stark on the flight home. Lola stared out of the window. She'd gone to Sardinia anticipating time with her friends, to switch off and celebrate Mirabel getting married, but it had ended up being so much more. The best bit of it was on another flight and she was struggling to process her feelings about leaving Rhys.

They'd said a private goodbye in bed that morning. The taxis to the airport were staggered, and Lola and her friends had said goodbye to Rhys and the others a couple of hours later with hugs and tears all round. Friendships had formed, Sarah in particular hitting it off with both Gareth and Zoe.

And Lola's last hug with Rhys. She hadn't wanted to let go. Perhaps their friends knew, because Barnaby and Gareth had joked around, clamping their arms around Rhys's shoulders and marching him to the waiting taxi. Her friends had swarmed her, talking a hundred miles an hour as their final couple of hours at the villa were filled with last-minute packing, then they too were in a taxi whizzing off to the airport.

Despite Polly's insistence to give them all the gossip, none of her friends pushed Lola for details. After breakfast, Polly's quiet 'So, did you have a good night?' within earshot of Deni and Sarah was answered by Lola's flushed-cheeked smile, nod and a whispered 'The best.' Polly had hugged her, Deni had grinned and Sarah had knocked her shoulder against hers, commenting 'About time too.'

Perhaps they sensed she was hurting, sad and confused even if she had the delicious memory of the night before. Rhys had been worth it; not only did he make her feel worthy and wonderful, but he was gentle and passionate, thoughtful, sexy and open. His suggestion to go travelling with him had surprised her. It was tempting, but she couldn't upend her life, not when she had a job and responsibilities. It wasn't as if there was a realistic future for them.

She squashed that thought, unwilling to imagine a different

path, one that included Rhys. She didn't want the burden of conflict, not when she needed to focus on ensuring her ex stayed out of her life. That was her priority before she could think about anything else.

On the plane with Deni and Mark sitting quietly next to her, and Sarah and Polly in the row behind, she had too much time to mull over the last couple of weeks while she was in limbo between Sardinia and home.

There was no pretence with Rhys; he was willing to talk about his feelings, his hopes and dreams as much as his fears and regrets. Going travelling was his way to heal and figure out what he wanted. He was at a crossroads and perhaps she was too, she just hadn't realised it till now. Life was a merry-go-round of adult responsibilities, work and friends, relationships and big dreams. But what was her dream? She had ambition, but what did she want long term? In the early days of her relationship with Jarek when she'd been swept up in love, her imagination had run away with her thinking about their future, and her focus had shifted from being totally career-minded to settling down and starting a family. A shudder stole through her. How trapped she would have been if their relationship had become serious – she couldn't even bear to think about the horror of having had a child with him.

Lola gazed out of the window to a silver streak of a river winding through a mountainous region far below. A thought had been seeded a while ago of what shape her life could take with someone she loved, with someone who treated her right and loved her unconditionally. She hadn't dared believe it could be more than a fantasy. Her days revolved around work and a social life, yet she wanted more, but she hadn't realised what it was she was missing out on.

Her friends were all growing, moving on and pursuing things

that enriched their lives. For Lola, a feeling of loss had been building following the end of a destructive relationship, then witnessing her best friend changing her life so drastically for Fabs and their future, but Mirabel was doing it for love. When Lola really thought about it, what was more important than that?

39

The Eurostar train leaving London St Pancras and heading for the Channel Tunnel felt much like a metaphor for what Rhys was doing; careering headfirst into the dark and unknown. He wasn't running away, but trying to find his way back to the person he used to be.

It was ironic that his first stop was Paris, the city of love. He'd been brave and made a romantic gesture by inviting Lola; he had to remind himself she hadn't shot him down, she just wasn't in a position to pause her life for an adventure with someone she had only just met, however intense, eye-opening and emotional their time together had been.

However jumbled their emotions had become, their love pact had been just that, a pact. The love bit wasn't real, even if it had felt like it at times and things had developed between them physically. She was more than just a good memory, though. He was going to keep in touch with her; he just hoped she'd meant it when she'd reciprocated his desire to stay friends.

Rhys rested his forehead against the window as the countryside outside of London passed by in a brown-green blur. He was on his way to Paris, while Lola had been dealing with a huge headache back in London, reporting Jarek and pursuing a legal route to ensure he stayed out of her life. She had Barnaby on the case, supporting her legally as her representative but as a friend too – a role Rhys himself had wanted. He'd even considered delaying the start of his travelling, but what use would he be in Bristol while she was in London? She didn't need any handholding, plus during their last morning in Sardinia she'd encouraged him to reshape his life. They'd erased their sadness with one last tumble in the sheets, a memory that resurfaced frequently. He just wished they'd had more time, more of each other, more everything. They'd messaged each other a few times since they'd returned from Sardinia, and he'd suggested they meet up in London ahead of him leaving for Paris, but unfortunately that had coincided with her working away.

He sighed deeply and his breath fogged the window. Travelling was supposed to be the start of his journey to renewal, so why did it feel like he was leaving everything important to him behind?

* * *

Rhys had been craving time alone, but he'd underestimated just how alone he'd feel ambling along the streets of Paris. Of course there were plenty of other people on their own, but that didn't stop him from noticing the couples walking hand in hand. He really had nothing to be sad about when his time was his own and he was free of the mundaneness of everyday life, a freedom that would continue till almost the end of the year. He'd head home refreshed, revitalised and raring to go again. At least that was the plan.

The Eiffel Tower soared into the sky, bold against the rain-grey clouds. The air was damp and the trees were autumn-tinged: gold and red and wintery brown. Underfoot, the paths were carpeted by soggy leaves. It was a long way from the perfect sunny days they'd experienced in Sardinia; it was as if the flight home had switched the seasons from summer to autumn. The view was iconic, but it seemed less romantic on a grey day. Holding his phone up, he captured the whole of the Eiffel Tower and took a picture. After Sardinia, he believed he was in a better place emotionally, but he felt adrift without Lola; being on his own again only highlighted how wonderful their time together had been. He hadn't had much time to dwell on things when he'd been back in Bristol unpacking, repacking and getting his house ready for his cousin, but he had all the time in the world now to think.

Sarah and Gareth had set up a Sardinia WhatsApp group for them to all keep in touch. There'd been so many messages wishing him well as he'd set off to catch the Eurostar, but it had been Lola's 'bon voyage' that had meant the most.

After pounding the Parisian streets, Rhys returned to Montmartre. Before heading to his hotel on one of the winding cobbled streets, he detoured to a restaurant he'd put on his list of places to visit.

Large boughs of red, white and purple flowers decorated the wall above the canopy that covered the typically Parisian tables and chairs. The day had slowly brightened, and now it was early evening, the sky had cleared, bringing with it a glimpse of sunshine.

He nabbed a table on the pavement which enabled him to watch the world go by to a backdrop of crisp autumn colour. A breeze tunnelled along the street, sending leaves spiralling down from the trees. He ordered and sipped a glass of Sauvignon Blanc while he waited for his food. It was hard to believe it was a week day. The stab of guilt that he wasn't teaching his Year 5 class was expected and, on day one of travelling, he felt like he was skiving. Doing what he pleased would take some getting used to.

His phone buzzed. He turned it over and his heart did a flip when he saw who the message was from. Lola. He clicked on it.

> Bonjour Rhys! Es-tu arrives? That's the extent of my French, desolee! How is Paris? I've been thinking about you all day. I was gutted to be up in Yorkshire while you were in London yesterday, but hey ho work calls (not that I can really call the last couple of days work!). I think what you're doing is brave, adventurous and just darn wonderful – enjoy every minute of it, even the bits that you struggle with, because I'm sure the good will outweigh the bad. Send me pics! x

That little voice of worry became a lot smaller and his heart flickered back to life. He shouldn't have questioned if she'd really wanted to remain friends when her message was effortlessly breezy. The warm tingle in his heart grew. He'd chosen to go travelling by himself, but that didn't mean he was alone. If the time in Sardinia had taught him anything, it was that he had some good friends. He'd also been surprised by the connection he'd had with the people he hadn't been that close to, because when he returned he would meet up with Gareth for that drink. While there would always be a distance between himself, Freddie and Zoe, it didn't mean they couldn't have a tentative friendship. Even with Fabs living in another country, they would always be best friends. Of course there would be challenges as their lives veered in different directions, but that didn't have to change anything if Rhys didn't let it. He'd see more of Barnaby too, because comparing himself to his friend's success both professionally and personally was futile; there was true friendship there and a connection that had been strengthened by their time away.

And as for Lola, his feelings and thoughts may have been scrambled when it came to her, but in his heart he knew how he felt and he wasn't scared. It was a feeling he would embrace as he strolled the streets of Paris and continued on to Barcelona, Lyon, Milan and beyond. Rebuilding his confidence, learning to accept who he was and focus on the good in his life was within grasping distance. He just needed to let go of his fear, his worries and that nagging thought that he didn't deserve happiness or was worthy of finding love.

A waiter brought him a plate of chicken supreme and topped up his wine. The rich creamy smell of the mushroom sauce spiralled into the chill air; people strode by, their heels clipping the pavement, and the early-evening sun made the shuttered buildings opposite gleam in the retreating light.

He turned his focus to Lola's message and started a reply.

> Paris is wonderful

Rhys's fingers hovered over the keys. He knew what he wanted to say, but he wasn't sure if he should. But why hide what he was thinking and feeling? Burying his emotions and worrying had done him no good. Wasn't it better to be brave and say what he meant, rather than wonder what could have happened?

He finished writing the message and sent it.

> Paris is wonderful, much like you.

40

Lola stared at Rhys's reply for a long time, not because she was trying to understand the meaning behind his words, but because she was trying to figure out how his words made her feel. Their relationship had shifted dramatically in the short time they'd known each other and now it was happening again, a transition that was as confusing as it was wonderful.

A thundering pop beat shook the walls, pulling Lola back to the here and now: on location at a stately home in Yorkshire where Starlight's video was being shot. Lola was there with MTV, who were doing a fly-on-the-wall-type documentary about the band. As she'd told Rhys, this was a perk of the job; the downside had been missing out on seeing him before he went travelling. She'd been telling the truth when she'd said she'd been thinking about him all day, even with the distractions of a bustling pop video set. Simon Cowell had dropped by to say hello to the girls before lunch, and there'd been semi-clad dancers wandering around all day. The make-up artists had been none too subtle about eyeing up the sexy male models, while one of the runners had looked up the forty-something-year-old owner of the house to discover with glee that he was a bona fide eligible bachelor. None of that had stopped Lola from daydreaming about Rhys. And now after that message... So few words, yet with her heart racing and palms sweating, they'd *physically* done something to her.

After coming home from Sardinia, it had been straight back to work. She'd had little time to consider the what-ifs with Rhys. Lola shouldn't have had to make concessions or change anything about her life, but if it meant she was safer and further away from Jarek's damaging influence, then she was willing to take action. On her first day back home, she changed her number and saved all of the screenshots and photos to do with Jarek into a folder. Barnaby had been an absolute godsend, giving her legal advice and starting the process of applying to the civil courts to get an injunction to stop Jarek's harassment and stalking or face the consequences.

Now, just over a week after returning from Sardinia, she was in Yorkshire for work, while Rhys was in Paris sending messages like that. The longer she left it to send a reply, the more she knew he'd be freaking out, wondering if he'd been too honest. Yet wasn't their ability to talk about everything the reason they'd both left Sardinia happier and more positive?

She bit her lip and studied his message again. She missed talking and laughing with him as much as she missed being with him romantically. Most of all, she missed his friendship – a friendship they could maintain long distance *if* they continued to be open and honest with each other.

Lola glanced around the entrance hall with its stone pillars and gothic touches, the driving beats at odds with the history. She was wearing a jumpsuit and high heels, and felt sure of herself and confident in an environment she was comfortable in. Yet this wasn't real life. Everything the band was projecting was a dream, something to aspire to – a glitzy side of life that was all for show. Real life wasn't as polished and perfect as the biggest girl band in the world was portraying it to be. Lola bought into this lifestyle, though – she helped to showcase it to the millions of fans around the world. Not that there was anything wrong with being swept up in the fantasy, but it was make-believe.

While Jarek had shown her all that was wrong, Rhys had opened her eyes to new possibilities and opportunities, a new path to happiness. That was why she was struggling to know what to reply. 'Thank you' was lame, and gushing about how wonderful he was would seem like an afterthought, even if she meant it.

Clutching her phone, she strode outside, away from the thumping beat. The gardens were spectacular, the formal one in front of the house all clean lines and sculptured hedges, but it was the view beyond to a silver-grey lake surrounded by trees flaming gold, red and yellow that captured her attention. Rhys would love it here. It was funny how she was somewhere like this while his first stop was a city she'd love to visit. His whole trip through Europe was peppered with cities; he was moving from place to place with the opportunity to meet new people and take stock of what he wanted while exploring and discovering. It sounded idyllic and something she'd have jumped at before—

She cut that thought short. It would be something she wanted to do now, but she had responsibilities and stuff to sort out. Turning down Rhys's offer had been sensible, even if it hadn't felt right.

The air was damp and Lola shivered despite her long-sleeved jumpsuit. She dragged her eyes away from the countryside view and scrolled through the photos she'd taken in Sardinia until she reached the selfies of her and Rhys on the evening they'd made their love pact. She hadn't realised it then, but Rhys's smile was different to the smile he'd woken up with on their last morning together. That one had been a real smile that reached his eyes and made her heart swell with all sorts of feelings that she still couldn't put into words but had meant everything.

Attaching the photo to her reply, she added a few words:

> This was perfect, the start of us x

She faltered for just a moment, wondering if that promised too much, because there wasn't really 'an us'; they hadn't talked about the possibility of them being more than just friends. Even if she had accepted his offer to go travelling with him, it would only have been an extension of what they'd had on Sardinia. They'd probably have ended up broken-hearted. It would be extra time, nothing more, and yet she'd promised herself to be open and honest, not just with herself but her friends, and wasn't Rhys a friend? Someone she'd grown incredibly close to in a short space of time, who she'd shared so much of herself with, so perhaps she should be honest with him even now.

Be brave, Lola, she thought and sent it.

41

Those first couple of messages reconnected Lola and Rhys through honest vulnerability and they started messaging frequently. They shared the mundane things about their day; not that there was anything mundane about Rhys visiting the Louvre and watching a show at the Moulin Rouge, or Lola showcasing one of the hottest pop bands in the world to a film crew.

After two more days in Yorkshire, Lola was on the train to London, and Starlight were off on the European leg of their tour. Rhys said *au revoir* to Paris and started his journey to Barcelona. Their days were punctuated with messages from each other. Lola sensed that Rhys preferred their contact through texts so she never phoned him. Anyway, it suited her because she got a thrill every time a message pinged onto her phone and she rarely wondered where he was or what he was doing because he told her everything.

12 OCTOBER

> I thought I'd like Barcelona, but wow, I love it more than I thought possible. Think it's the mix of the architecture, being by the sea and the Gothic quarter. Oh and tapas. And wine! Off to the vineyards of Penedès for a guided tour of wineries tomorrow. May be too sozzled to message. ;)

Way to go to make me jealous! Although I will be having dinner with Deni, Sarah and Polly tomorrow at a Thai place we've wanted to go to for ages, followed by cocktails, so it's not all bad here. At least that's what I'm trying to tell myself. Have you heard from Fabs at all?

> Not a thing. Has Mirabel been in touch?

Nope, not that I expected her to. It's very strange now I'm back in the London office without Mirabel here. Her replacement is great, I mean she's a dream to work with and I know her a bit anyway, so it's all good, but she's not Mirabel.

> How are you coping with everything?

Dealing with it day by day. Barnaby's been a star keeping me updated, although Jarek doesn't seem to be in London any more. His apartment has been put up for sale. Barnaby's on the case and doing some investigating. I'm just tentatively hoping that after his antics in Sardinia he's realised he's taken things too far and is finally out of my life like his last message suggested. I won't hold my breath until I know something concrete, but I have hope.

> I hope that's the case too x

23 OCTOBER

Florence is my favourite city so far. The hostel is in the centre so it's easy to get everywhere and I'm more than happy with pasta and pizza for dinner every evening. I think you'd love it. I got chatting to a fellow traveller who's staying at the hostel, an Irish guy in his 40s who's taking time out post-divorce, and we're taking the train to Arezzo, a hilltop town that feels a bit more off the beaten track. Photos will follow, I'm sure. :)

> Glad you have company and Arezzo sounds right up your street. Although I'm surprised you've not got a wine tour of the Chianti region booked since you LOVED the winery outside Barcelona so much!

I didn't bang on about it that much.

> Or send me a million selfies of you quaffing copious amounts of wine – no, of course you didn't! Anyway, I thought at these wine tastings you had to spit it out afterwards. Seems a waste of wine...

My thought exactly. That's why I ended up tipsy.

> Tipsy?! You looked completely and utterly drunk to me.

I'll try to behave tomorrow.

> Like hell you will! Please don't go all boring on me, Rhys. I'm enjoying hearing what you're getting up to. ;)

25 OCTOBER

> Mirabel messaged after they got back yesterday and sent a couple of photos of their honeymoon. It's been so strange not hearing a thing from her for a month – the longest we've ever not talked or messaged. They sound blissfully happy. Just hope that lasts now they're back on Sardinia.

She'll be so busy looking for a home for her and Fabs alongside building her business she won't have time to worry that she has to live with her in-laws for a while longer.

> Well, she might mind about that, but as she's got a handful of her old clients signing with her, she will definitely have no free time.

And then when they start talking about having kids.

> Oh Mirabel's been talking about starting a family for ages. She's going to have her hands full. I can see you as godfather though.

And you as godmother.

> Now there's a thought. Night, Rhys.

Night, Lola. Or should I say buona notte.

30 OCTOBER

> Have you met any more interesting people?

The Island of Hopes and Dreams

Yeah, I've met some amazing people and had plenty of interesting conversations while in Rome so I've not been completely alone. I've been out all day exploring the Colosseum and Roman Forum. I like the time to myself, choosing where to eat and what I want to do. Feels weird at times though, but there's a freedom to it that's refreshing. The days are going by quickly and I can't believe it's been more than three weeks already. The time's slipping away. There's so much to do and take in. I'm loving it...

> I feel there's a but to that?

Yeah there is because the longer I'm away, the more I keep thinking how good it would be to share this experience with you.

> You are in a way, Rhys. I love hearing about where you are and what you're up to.

It's not the same as physically sharing all the special moments with you. What I'm trying to say in a roundabout way is I miss you.

> I miss you too.

5 NOVEMBER

> Apparently Barnaby's got some news for me. It's all gone quiet over the last week or two, which worries me because every time I feel like Jarek is out of my life he comes back like a bad smell. I'm hoping Barnaby has positive news to share – he's video calling me this evening.

> Let me know how it goes, although I might not have service later as I'll be on the train to the Dolomites. Should get to the Harmony Hotel by eight, then I'll finally be in one place for the next week. I really hope Barnaby gives you good news x

* * *

With so many nerves attacking her stomach, Lola struggled to eat her dinner. By the time she sat down to talk to Barnaby she felt wrung out.

'So I got a private investigator friend on the case.' Sitting in his study in Bristol, Barnaby's face filled the screen. Lola perched, tense, on the edge of her sofa in her loft apartment. There was a whizz, then a bang from an early firework being let off nearby. 'The simplified version is, I had a suspicion that Jarek had upped and left the country, but I wanted to be sure. I kept running into dead ends. You already knew his apartment had been listed for sale, but my PI friend discovered he's relocated to New York – still working for the same investment bank – but it was when he did some further digging that the extent of his deceit when it came to you and his other life was discovered.'

'What do you mean "his other life"?' Lola froze, watching Barnaby carefully.

Barnaby clasped his hands together. 'There's no easy way of saying this, but he duped you – to some extent he's been hiding a lot of who he is from his employer, his colleagues, pretty much everyone in the UK.'

'Because he has a life in the US?'

'Yes, a wife and—'

'He's *married*?' Lola heard her voice go up a notch. Although actually that nugget of information didn't throw her as much as she thought it should. He'd kept so much hidden, why would this be any different?

Lola thought back. In the early days of their relationship, she hadn't thought much about him travelling to the US for work or him being away for a week or two at a time. A year or so later, it had begun to feel like a reprieve, even if he had called her every day. But she'd never once considered he was already married.

Barnaby's calm and authoritative voice broke through her thoughts. 'He has a wife and a child. From the digging that was done, she seems content to be a homemaker living off him in a multi-million-dollar New York apartment.'

'So, very much the quiet, subservient partner he craves, leaving him free to do what the hell he wanted in another country...' Lola's voice petered out. She pulled her cardigan tight.

Barnaby nodded. 'I think it's impossible to understand someone's psyche when it's the opposite of how a sane person would treat someone. He obviously likes the control and the freedom of doing what he pleases. Perhaps he gets off on the thrill of seducing someone new—'

'And trying to control them too? It's not as if he could really have tied me down with marriage if he's already married to someone else.'

'In another country. From what we've found out, I wouldn't put it past him. Who knows what we'd find if we continued to dig.'

'Shit.' Lola rubbed her fingers across her forehead and grabbed the throw next to her, clenching it tight. 'How could I have been so naïve?'

Barnaby leaned closer, resting his arms on the polished wood of his desk, and looked intently at her through the screen. 'You weren't naïve, Lola, he was just good at lying and manipulating you. The upside to all of this is he seems to have cut his losses here and gone back to the US.'

'You think permanently?'

'I believe so, because whatever he was trying to get from you didn't work – or perhaps you proved to be too much work. His last message to you said as much.' He gave her a grave smile. 'You didn't play ball; you didn't submit to pressure. However much he tried to unsettle and control, you were having none of it. He's obviously someone who enjoys playing games and getting the upper hand, but you never let him.'

'Thanks to you lot too; thanks to Rhys.'

'Exactly.' Barnaby nodded. 'But most of it has to do with your strength and your ability to follow your gut. I'm confident that Jarek's out of your life because he's returned to his old one. Previous one, whatever you want to call it.'

'And his wife and child? Are they okay?'

'From everything the PI found out, his wife seems happy—'

'That could all be on the surface, though.'

'True. But it could also be that this desire to control and play games is achieved through having an affair. You just happened to be his victim.'

Lola breathed out slowly and stared out of the steel-framed window with its view across the rooftops of Islington. A firework glittered red, then gold as it lit up the darkness. 'Why would his wife put up with it?'

'Because of the lifestyle he gives her,' Barnaby suggested. 'A New York address with a Central Park view; money is power and perhaps she's fine with that. There's no sign or suggestion of physical abuse; obviously emotional abuse is harder to define. All I can assure you is that *you're* finally free of him.'

Lola had assumed it would feel like a weight lifting, but it was more complicated than that. The hidden scars remained and would take time to heal. Perhaps they would always be there. She just needed to learn to live with them, to thrive despite them.

She released her hold on the throw and met Barnaby's steady gaze. 'I can't thank you enough.'

'I saw first-hand what sort of man he is – we all did, so I'm glad I could help in some way and give you the assurance that he's finally out of your life. The date for the court hearing has come through for the injunction and I doubt very much he's going to contest it. You can rest easy, Lola.' He cleared his throat and leaned back in his chair. 'You've been keeping in touch with Rhys?'

He was fishing for something. Lola knew that he and Rhys were in contact.

'Yeah,' she said smoothly. 'I like hearing about his European escapades.' What she didn't say was that they messaged frequently, she caught herself thinking about him more times than she could count, and her heart would do that little fluttery thing every time she received a text from him. If missing someone, thinking about them constantly and wishing she was with them meant she was obsessed, then Rhys was an obsession.

'He's been worried about you dealing with this all alone.'

'I'm not alone, not really.' She heard it for the lie it was when she was at home by herself. 'My friends have all been fabulously supportive; Rhys too from afar. And you, Barnaby, you've been amazing, thank you.'

'I'm just glad you're okay.' He frowned, looking unsure if he should say something more, then added, 'And Rhys will be happy that this difficult chapter is over for you, because it is, Lola. I promise you it is.'

Lola didn't quite know what she felt after saying goodbye to Barnaby. She'd hoped for the impossible and it seemed to have come true. Not that the news Barnaby had given her had erased the hurt Jarek had caused, but that constant tightness in her chest now had a real chance of healing and she could look forward rather than constantly over her shoulder. She was free from a mentally abusive relationship that had echoed long after she'd ended it.

Lola closed her laptop and took out her phone. She clicked on the message thread she had with Rhys.

> There's too much to explain in a text, but it seems Jarek is well and truly out of my life. Hope you've arrived safely. X

She sent the message knowing he might not receive it until he was in his hotel in the Dolomites, then she rang Mirabel. They'd already had a couple of long catch-ups about her honeymoon and house hunting in Sardinia, while Lola had told her the truth about Jarek and him turning up at the wedding, kept her in the loop about life at Rhythm continuing without her and the ongoing situation with her ex, so it filled her with joy to relay all that Barnaby had told her.

'For the first time I feel like I can actually shut the door on him and breathe easy again. Although his poor wife—'

'*He's* out of *your* life, Lola,' Mirabel pressed upon her. 'That's what you need to focus on. And, by the sounds of it, she may well be aware of what he's like but has chosen the security of money and the comfort of a multi-million-dollar apartment over a decent, faithful husband, while you, my lovely, have got out. You're free and can finally live your life on your own terms.'

Lola gazed across her apartment, the dark-stained wooden floor and exposed red-brick and white walls softened by a deep-pile rug and framed pictures of iconic album covers; her own private space. It had been her haven away from Jarek, and it still was to some extent. Yet since returning from Sardinia, she felt like a different person with a fresh outlook on life, new desires, hopes and dreams.

'You're completely right,' Lola said as a stream of fireworks exploded into the night sky. 'But I can't shake off the feeling that something's missing.'

'Me!' Mirabel screeched with glee.

'Well, yeah, of course there's that; I miss you like crazy. Work's busy and exciting and filling my time. Friends are busy with their own lives and I just keep thinking there should be more to my life than what I have, which seems incredibly greedy because everything's good...' She trailed off, not really knowing how to put into words what she was feeling.

'Is it discontent or something more?' Mirabel paused, allowing the silence and thoughts to grow. 'Something along the lines of missing a certain someone?'

Lola's heart battered her chest just thinking about Rhys. 'I do miss him. But I miss you too, and I miss being with Deni and Sarah on Sardinia. I miss seeing Polly regularly because she's understandably busy with her kids.'

'Mmn,' Mirabel said in a non-committal way. 'Think of the news Barnaby's given you as a fresh start. Really think about what will make you happy, then follow that path, however scary it might seem.'

'Like you did following Fabs to Sardinia.'

'I want to be here. I just want it to be on our own terms; with our own space, leading our life together. We'll get there. Good things are worth the wait, isn't that the saying? It'll be the same for you with... well, with whatever you decide will make you happy.'

* * *

Lola pondered her conversation with Mirabel for the rest of the evening and it was only when a message from Rhys popped on to her phone after she'd gone to bed that an idea began to take shape.

> I can't tell you how glad I am that he's out of your life. If you want to talk, call me. I arrived late in Cortina d'Ampezzo but at the hotel now. Hopefully you can sleep easy tonight. xx

She did want to talk to him desperately, but not late at night when she knew she wouldn't be able to put into words how she was feeling. Instead, she slept fitfully because her head and her heart were at odds with each other. When she woke after the alarm, she didn't have time to reply to Rhys. She could have messaged him while on the Tube, but she wasn't sure what to say, not when her head was firing off a dozen preposterous, crazy, exciting and enticing ideas. Wired on coffee, she started work late, feeling drained and hyper at the same time.

At least she was kept busy throughout the morning, lining up radio and TV interviews for a debut artist. By the time she left the office at lunchtime, she'd worked herself into such a state over the possibilities racing through her head that she needed to get out.

She walked from St Katharine Docks across Tower Bridge, which was jostling with tourists taking pictures, and followed the path alongside the river towards Borough Market. Clouds of varying shades of pewter filled the sky above the equally grey Thames. Across the other side of the river, the trees in front of the stone walls of the Tower of London were the only colour in an otherwise dismal day, yet even they were muted without a hint of sunshine. Beyond, metallic and glass skyscrapers dominated the skyline – a view she knew well. London was a place she'd thought of as home for so long and yet her heart was trying to tug her in a different direction. Home didn't have to be a place, it could also be a person.

Tears slipped down Lola's cheeks, which were already damp from the incessant drizzle. The combination of the view, the weather and her thoughts should have been downright depressing, but none of that really mattered, not when, on a grey Thursday in November, her heart was elsewhere entirely and, if she was brave enough, she was finally free to follow it.

42

Lola obviously hadn't wanted to talk the night before because she hadn't phoned him, but then they hadn't actually spoken to each other since they'd said goodbye in Sardinia. All of their communication had been through messages, which he found far easier. He wasn't sure he'd know what to say to Lola if they talked, not when he was in such a muddle emotionally. He longed to talk properly like they had on Sardinia, but he knew it wouldn't be the same over the phone, and a video call would be torturous when all he wanted to do was hold her in his arms again.

After his train journey and late arrival at the hotel the day before, Rhys woke refreshed. He took a cup of coffee out onto his balcony and breathed in the fresh mountain air. The town lay in the Cortina valley, the surrounding mountain peaks of the Dolomites dusted with snow, while the lower slopes were carpeted with evergreens and larches, a muted dusky gold where the sun didn't yet reach.

It was the right time to be somewhere like this, to take a breath, think and reflect. Up until now, travelling from place to place exploring the old parts of cities, soaking up the atmosphere and culture had been what he'd needed. He craved this kind of space in his everyday life and he was itching to pull on his walking boots and get lost in the wilderness. Metaphorically speaking. He smiled wryly; he was far too organised and planned things to the minutest detail to get lost or accidentally stray too far, but a hike to explore the surrounding area was on the agenda.

After breakfast, Rhys set off on a four-hour walk starting and ending in Cortina that took him beneath towering spruce, across rocky terrain and into the shadow of soaring mountain peaks. Back at the hotel, he ate a late lunch on his own in a restaurant with an uninterrupted view over the town. Eating breakfast and lunch on his own was fine, it was dinner he struggled with while surrounded by couples, families and groups of friends enjoying each other's company.

But sitting staring at his phone wasn't going to make Lola call or message. She'd likely phoned Mirabel yesterday evening. Of course she'd call her best friend over him. She had probably celebrated with her friends too and was in full-on back-to-work mode today. They'd messaged each other every day he'd been travelling, so he was sure today would be no different, but it didn't mean he had to wait for her to make contact. They were friends, there was no need to play games. He drained his coffee and composed a message.

> Everywhere has been incredible in its own way, but this place... Maybe I like the space when the sky seems so vast, or perhaps it's because I'm surrounded by trees and mountains. Whatever it is, it's awe-inspiring and no words or even photos will do it justice (although I'm sending you the photo I took from my balcony this morning).

He sent it, not expecting her to reply straight away when she'd be at work, but his heart lifted when she did.

> Well that's stunning. Beats a damp, miserable London. Wish I was there x

Rhys studied those last few words, turning them over and over in his head, wondering what tone she would have said them with if they'd been talking on the phone. She could simply mean she'd much rather be in the Dolomites than London, but she could also have meant that she wished she was sharing the view with *him*. He replied simply with the truth.

> I wish you were here too x

Pocketing his phone, he left the restaurant and went via his room to grab his swim things before heading to the outdoor pool to front-crawl away his worries while reminding himself that this time away was to focus on his dreams and future.

The air chilled his face as he bobbed up and down in the warm water, catching glimpses of ice-blue sky and mauve mountains as he swam. Dusk fell and Cortina erupted with hundreds of twinkling lights as windows lit up. For Rhys it was the perfect place to hope and plan and dream.

* * *

Rhys woke early again the next morning to drink his coffee on the balcony and watch the sun rise. Perhaps it was the comfort of a routine he liked after weeks of travelling with little structure to his days, something he had lots of in his real life. What he didn't have back home was this sort of freedom or the joy of the outdoors within strolling distance. That gaping hole needed to be fixed somehow, a hole that had grown since saying goodbye to Lola in Sardinia. One that wasn't filled even when he received a message from her over breakfast.

> Got any plans for today?

No, a message from her didn't fix the hole, but he felt less alone sitting in the spacious restaurant eating his continental breakfast and listening to the international chatter from the other guests. He smiled as he wrote a reply.

> A repeat of yesterday. Off for a hike, although I might take lunch with me this time. Back to the hotel for a swim, then dinner.

> Sounds perfect.

> What are you up to?

> Oh, nothing special. Busy day though and prob not contactable for most of it. Will catch up with you this evening x

Rhys put his phone face down on the table. While Lola was off to work, he would be striding beneath autumn-gold trees and soaking up the awe-inspiring sight of jagged mountain peaks. Turning his attention away from his ever-growing melancholy over missing Lola, he spread a map of the area out on the table and began to work out his hiking route for the day.

* * *

Rhys returned to the hotel just before dusk. His thighs burned and his cheeks were flushed from the cold. He'd pounded away his worries beneath the forest as he'd navigated the steep slopes.

Winding his way back down had been the best bit, knowing he'd be able to ease his aching muscles with a swim in a warm pool before feasting on venison and falling into bed. His long-term dream of moving away from Bristol to somewhere he could wake up surrounded by trees had been brought sharply into focus here. He'd love to work for himself rather than have the rigidity of school hours and term time. He thought back to one of his first conversations with Lola and her suggestion of turning his woodworking hobby into an actual job. He'd always considered it to be a pipe dream, something he'd do when he was older, because what he was doing now was sensible and safe. Teaching was an important profession and one he liked; he had his own home that he'd worked hard for. Of course there were plenty of things missing – while he couldn't magic up a loving relationship, he could make his long-term dream come true if he had the guts to.

Earlier in the day he'd taken a photo of his picnic spot with the lake framed between trees, the surface smooth and milky-turquoise, Punta Sorapis jutting towards the pale, sun-bleached sky. The sense of contentment he'd felt there had been absolute. Without the summer crowds, he'd only passed a handful of other hikers along the way. He sent the photo to Lola, the only person he'd wanted to share the moment with. He liked his own company, but he longed for Lola's more.

43

Lola cupped her hands around her G&T and gazed out through the window. It had been a hellishly long day, but one filled with excitement and anticipation, as well as nerves and a dash of uncertainty. Now, sitting in the warmth of the bar, all of those feelings still jostled together, but her overriding thought was sometimes you had to be brave and step out of your comfort zone, shake off the fear and make a sweeping gesture to be able to move forward.

Flames spat and crackled in the bar's fireplace, but even wearing her chunkiest winter jumper she was only just beginning to warm up. At least her travel sickness had eased now. The bar was mostly filled with couples having pre-dinner drinks, but Lola had managed to grab a free table by one of the huge picture windows and had settled herself so she could see across the bar to the entrance hall and archway to the restaurant. Candlelight flickered across the table. She turned back to the window, shivering at the coolness seeping through the glass.

Rhys had been spot on about the view. Tomorrow, she hoped she'd be able to see the mountain peaks he'd talked so enthusiastically about, but for now she'd make do with the lights twinkling from the picture-perfect village in the valley below.

She knew there was a chance that turning up unexpectedly could backfire, but after a month of messaging back and forth she was almost certain that Rhys would welcome her with open arms. Over the last few weeks, there'd been a constant tug at her heart. She'd felt like a lovestruck teenager, obsessing over a man she couldn't have a relationship with, yet as the days, then weeks had marched on, she began to question this. Those jumbled thoughts and feelings had intensified until the night before last when they'd come to a head because she realised she was free and shouldn't allow her heart to remain in the shadows. Of course there was a risk that they'd been so swept up in the romanticism of Sardinia and the freedom of a place far from real life that in reality they wouldn't work. She was willing to give it a try, even if she was well aware that a hotel in the Dolomites was far from real life either. She wouldn't judge anything on that, but on Rhys's reaction and the way he made her feel when they finally got to hold each other again.

Rhys had messaged her earlier from the pool, so she'd been camped out in the bar in the hope that he'd follow his plan of heading to the restaurant for dinner after he'd had a swim. She was considering ordering another G&T to combat her churning nerves when she spotted him waiting behind a family at the doorway of the restaurant.

With her heart thudding so hard she had trouble focusing, she wrote a quick message.

> Have you got time for that catch-up I promised earlier?

She was shaking as she clicked send. She watched him take

his phone from his back pocket and click on the message. Was that a slight smile as he thumbed a reply?

> Just about to have dinner. Can chat after if you're free?

Lola felt light-headed as she sent another message.

> I'm free right now. Mind if I join you?

At his obvious confusion, laughter escaped from Lola. She felt drunk on fluttery nerves as he stared at his phone. Even though she couldn't make out his facial expression, she imagined his frown growing, followed by slow realisation.

He looked up and swung around, his eyes searching. And when they landed on her, his look of surprise edged with delight stirred something deep inside.

Lola's heart battered her chest as she made her way across the bar towards him. He stepped away from the small queue that was forming at the restaurant door.

'What on earth are you...' His words petered out as he shook his head, although his smile gave away his feelings.

'I thought I'd surprise you.' She gave a little shrug that belied the emotions whirling through her. 'Figured you might fancy company at dinner for once.'

He reached for her, his eyes not leaving her face as if he'd blink and she'd be gone again. 'Forget about a table here,' he said quietly. 'Let's order room service.'

'I actually booked a room for tonight, I didn't want to assume—'

He cut her off with a kiss and, with his arms encircling her waist, tugged her close. They were standing in the hotel's entrance hall in full view of the bar and a handful of the diners in the restaurant, but Rhys didn't seem to care one bit. The shy teacher had morphed into a confident, passionate man who seemed to finally know what he wanted. He pulled away from their kiss with a look of joy. Taking her hand and flashing a grin at the bemused hostess, he led Lola away from the restaurant towards the lifts.

'You haven't come all this way to spend the night alone in your room.'

Her heart spun out at his words, and his tone. Heat pooled into the pit of Lola's stomach at the unspoken promise of what the night would entail. She was certain her decision to make a romantic gesture by taking urgent leave from work and getting a last-minute flight from Heathrow to Venice, then a coach into the heart of the Dolomites had been the right one. Everything about Rhys and the way he made her feel was so incredibly right and she was going to prove just how much he meant to her the second they reached his room.

* * *

Snow dusted the grey mountain peaks, which were jagged against the pale-blue sky. The sun shone on the larch trees that decorated the edge of the lake, turning them a vibrant yellow. Rhys had always intended to walk to Lake Federa today, but to do so with Lola was more than he'd dreamed of.

He still couldn't quite believe she was here. The message she'd sent the evening before asking if she could join him for dinner had taken his breath away and then when he'd realised what it meant. He'd never felt anything like it before, yet the word to describe how he felt in his head and heart, he knew exactly what that was.

They'd fallen into bed the moment they'd got to his room.

They were still getting to know each other, yet he already felt as if he knew her intimately, and the way they were instantly so comfortable and at ease with each other was everything. Eventually, they'd ordered room service and sat wrapped in sheets on the bed together eating pizza and just talking and talking until desire snuck back. The plates were discarded and they'd had sex again before falling asleep, happily exhausted in each other's arms.

It was dark when they'd woken in the early hours. Rhys had suggested they go for a hike to watch the sunrise, and Lola had immediately agreed, jumping out of bed to shower, dress and pull on hiking boots. He didn't think he'd ever loved anyone more...

Love. That was the right word to describe what he was feeling as they sat together by the lake in the pink-tinged dawn watching the landscape come alive. They weren't alone; there were a couple of photographers capturing the rising sun in all its glory, as the trees glowed golden and the dark surface of the lake transformed into a reflective watercolour of trees, mountain and sky.

Lola's face was flushed. Whether it was from the bracing walk in the semi-darkness of a cold morning, or from the beauty that was materialising in front of them, he wasn't sure. But with his arms around her as they watched the sun rising, nothing else mattered. It was only when she turned to him with tears tracking down her pink cheeks that he realised she was crying.

'I always thought something was missing in my life, and then I met you,' Lola said quietly, as if she didn't want to break the stillness of the morning. 'You make me whole.'

She wiped away her tears with her fingers and turned back to look at the lake. He remained quiet, allowing time for her words to sink in, giving her the opportunity to say more.

'Believe it or not, I am incredibly happy right now.' She gestured to her still-damp cheeks and laughed. 'I'm fed up of bottling up my emotions and being scared to admit how I feel in here.' She pressed her fingers over her heart. 'Which is why I wanted you to know that. Know how much I've missed you and thought about you. I don't expect anything in return, I just need to be honest and open with you. I've pretty much felt that way since we first met on the jetty. Do you know I was about to creep away when I saw you because I thought you wanted to be on your own. Then you invited me to join you.'

Rhys folded his hands over hers. 'I'm just glad you stayed.'

And made a love pact that had come full circle to them watching the sunrise in the Dolomites; a love pact where there was no longer any pretence, just a heady feeling of love.

'I learnt quite a lot about myself in Sardinia thanks to you.' Rhys took a deep breath of the cold, pine-tinged air. 'I'd been afraid to really live, because to do so, to fall in love and have those magical life experiences, could invite heartache and disappointment.'

'It also invites possibility and hope. True happiness.'

'Oh, I know that now, because I felt all of those emotions the minute we met, but I didn't dare believe those feelings were real.'

'When did you realise?'

Rhys smiled and a chuckle escaped. 'I realised our love pact was no longer pretend the moment you thumped your feet against the headboard in our hotel room in Bosa.' Lola stifled a laugh as her cheeks flushed. 'But the moment I realised I was in love with you was when I saw you walking towards me yesterday.'

'Because you understood I love you too.'

They gazed at each other with an openness that had always been there but meant so much more now their feelings were out in the open. A quiet happiness thrummed through Lola and she seemed at peace.

She snuggled closer. 'I don't quite know how we're going to make us work, but I'd like to give it a try if you do too?'

Rhys cupped her face in his hands and kissed her. He knew without a doubt that the smile he gave when he pulled away reached his eyes.

'More than anything,' he said as they gazed together at the sky, mountain and golden larches mirrored in the glass-like surface of the lake.

EPILOGUE
THREE YEARS LATER

The rock was warm and barnacle-rough through Lola's thin trousers. With her feet dipped in the cool water of the rock pool and the September sun on her shoulders, being on the beach took her back to her childhood, to the freedom of growing up on the coast and the peace she felt by the ocean. Sandymouth Bay was one of her favourite places, with its huge swathe of sand, and rock pools of varying shapes and sizes, backed by crumbling cliffs. The only other people in sight were dog walkers and young families, antlike on the vast beach. The dramatic landscape reminded her a little of the Cane Malu tidal pool in Sardinia, but rather than being otherworldly, this place evoked a sense of freedom and joy.

Lola tilted her face to the sun and relished the warmth. Soon, the long days of summer would be over and she'd have to swap her sandals for wellies and salads for hearty soups. But at least then the wood burner could be lit; there was nothing better than spending the day outdoors and returning cold and exhausted to the warmth and comfort of home. That thought alone was enough to motivate her to move. Even though she was a relatively new driver, she'd become confident quickly out of necessity, yet she'd still prefer not to have to navigate the narrow lanes near home in the dark.

Standing up, she searched the edge of the rock pool and spotted Archie's wagging tail. She whistled and grinned as he looked up and bounded over. He charged through the shallow rock pool, splashing water over her legs, then snuffled his sand-covered nose into her hand. She stroked behind his ears and kissed the top of his head. He was an eighteen-month-old Beagle cross and they'd fallen in love with him the moment they'd laid eyes on him at the rescue centre. Her childhood dream of having a dog had finally come true.

'Come on then, Arch, let's go home.'

An overnight stay with her parents had ended up being longer because her dad had insisted she stay an extra day so he could fire up his new gas barbecue and cook her a meal. Making an effort to see her parents more often was one of the best things she'd done. They'd all benefitted from quality time together, their relationship revitalised by openness and effort, bringing all three of them closer. It made Lola happy that the drive back up the M5 was now familiar because she'd done it enough times. The changes in her life over the past three years had been monumental and good for her. She loved visiting her parents and making the most of coastal living for a few days, but she adored returning home.

Home. Just the thought filled her with joy, the same way heading west onto the M4 towards Wales rather than east to London ignited something in her heart. Rhys was often with her, but he had to work this time, so she'd visited her parents on her own, although she was never alone now she had Archie for company.

As she passed the 'Croeso i Gymru' sign after crossing the

Prince of Wales Bridge, she rang Rhys to say they were less than an hour from home.

* * *

The two nights that Lola had intended to stay at the Harmony Hotel in the Dolomites had turned into five and even then she'd been reluctant to leave. While she'd returned to London, Rhys had continued on to Salzburg. But promises had been made, truths shared and hearts given, so Lola had gone home with a renewed purpose and her mind made up over Rhys, because she was certain he was her future.

As Rhys journeyed through Europe and Lola threw herself back into work, their frequent messages were interspersed with long phone calls late into the night. Their chats became less about missing each other and more about their hopes and dreams and taking chances, made less scary if they did it together.

In mid-December, Rhys had returned to the UK a new man... well, not exactly 'new' because he was still the wonderfully open, kind and delicious man Lola had fallen in love with, but he'd regained a sense of who he was and what he wanted. His passion fuelled Lola's own desire to reshape her life. Mirabel had transformed her life with her marriage to Fabs and her move to Sardinia along with a U-turn of her successful career. Deni too was an example of how reassessing priorities and regaining perspective led to a healthier relationship and a happier balance. Lola remembered Deni's advice about following in Mirabel's footsteps when it came to love, so she chose to put happiness ahead of everything else, something she realised was tied up in Rhys.

They knew they wanted to spend Christmas together even if it wouldn't be alone. Lola had vowed to make amends with her parents, while Rhys was desperate to introduce Lola to his family. They saw Fabs and Mirabel at a pre-Christmas party hosted by Deni and Mark, before their friends went to Mirabel's parents for Christmas. On Christmas Eve, they took the train to Bristol and Rhys gave Lola a whistlestop tour of his house before they drove to Wales to spend Christmas Day with his parents, brothers and their families. Growing up an only child with family spread far and wide, Lola had never experienced a big family Christmas. Rhys had said his parents were reserved compared to Fabs's, but a house full of children injected excitement and love into the festivities. A chaotic, noisy and merry few hours on Christmas Day was a first for Lola, but she knew she wanted more of it in her life. More Rhys, more love, more family, more joy. More everything. Having children had never been a serious consideration, but seeing how good Rhys was with his nieces and nephews, the possibility of starting a family with him in the future became more than just an idea, but a hope, a dream, a desire.

The time with Rhys's parents was as impactful as it was fleeting. On Boxing Day, they drove down to Devon. As her mum and dad welcomed them, Lola realised it was the first time she'd brought a boyfriend home to meet her parents. She was involving them in her life and introducing them to the person who meant the most. Rhys was her olive branch offering and he charmed them, but not in the way Jarek would have, rather in his effortlessly honest way.

She was glad her parents had never met Jarek and she was even happier that he was out of her life. The messages had stopped, she had an injunction against him and, like Barnaby had said, he'd cut his losses and left. If there was a silver lining, his damaging influence had altered her opinion of what was important when it came to love and life.

Rhys's talent for crafting beautiful things was apparent. She'd only had to look at the quality of the work in his house to know it could be more than a hobby and when he talked to her about turning it into a job, she wholeheartedly encouraged him. Continuing to do what was expected was relatively risk-free, but to invite possibility and a better way of life by following your heart, well, wasn't that the ultimate dream? Because although Lola and Rhys were opposites in many ways, they were united about building a life together. Of course, compromises would have to be made, but when they talked about what they wanted, many of their dreams aligned. Lola had spent her teens dreaming about an exciting career in London and she'd believed she'd had it all, until she hadn't. Her friends had kept her going through the hard times, but she'd been drifting, unsettled and lost, much like Rhys had been in Bristol, albeit for a different reason.

The following spring when Rhys took Lola to see a sizeable plot of land in Wales that contained a wood, a stream and a house that had seen better days but had plenty of potential, the fluttering in her stomach matched the excitement in Rhys's eyes. Neither of them had said much as they'd been shown around, but during the drive back to Bristol they'd fired off ideas, talking non-stop, their passion palpable as they planned their future.

While Lola was happy in her job, Rhys was discontented in his. He longed to move away from the city to follow his dream of countryside living and the possibility of turning his hobby into a business. Lola enjoyed the unpredictability of her job and the travelling, but she wanted more freedom and to put the past behind her. An honest chat with her boss at Rhythm paved the way to flexible working. Suddenly, their hopes and dreams could become a reality if they were brave enough to take the chance.

Nine months later, a tumble-down house with five acres of land in the Vale of Glamorgan surrounded by woodland, countryside walks and within driving distance of the coast became the place they would call home.

* * *

The Hideaway was a fitting name for their house in the woods. Compromises were a part of life and relationships, but Lola and Rhys had managed to attain something that made them both happy. There was no sea view but there were beaches a short drive away. Cardiff was commutable too, which made it possible for Lola to travel to London or wherever else for work.

After handing in his notice at the school in Bristol, Rhys moved to Wales to start doing the house up before Lola joined him. He found part-time work as a supply teacher and spent every spare minute gutting the house, rebuilding and decorating. He put his woodwork skills to good use, transforming the kitchen and building shelving in the living spaces and wardrobes in the bedrooms. Lola joined him at the weekends, swapping her heels and make-up for dungarees and a paintbrush. With four bedrooms, there was enough space for her to turn one into a snug with a whole wall filled with bookshelves.

Once the house was liveable and Lola had learnt to drive – discovering her travel sickness was significantly eased by being the driver rather than a passenger – she rented out her apartment and made the permanent move to Wales.

Rhys started on the next phase of their long-term plan, building the first of three wooden glamping cabins to rent out as holiday lets. He had grand ideas of eventually adding two tree-houses as well, which would be an extra source of income while he swapped teaching for his own woodworking business.

Now, three years later in mid-September, the Hideaway was filled with their friends, who were all sitting around the clearing at the heart of the wood, their chatter joining the birdsong. Freddie and Barnaby were in charge of the barbecue and smoke twirled into the air along with the delicious aroma of grilling burgers. The weather had been kind, with an Indian summer reminiscent of their time in Sardinia. Not everyone was staying, as even with two cabins completed, there wasn't enough space. Polly and Barnaby had brought their families with them, while Deni, Sarah and Gareth were with their partners. Fabs and Mirabel were joined by their seven-month-old son Enzo, plus Freddie and Zoe had their cheeky two-year-old in tow. A baby had arrived before Freddie and Zoe had managed to get married. Lola was certain they'd never get round to tying the knot because their son was as much of a handful as he was adorable. Everyone had been in agreement that a baby would make or break them and Lola was quietly pleased that they were somehow muddling along. Rhys had forgiven them and Lola wasn't going to hold a grudge, not when she and Rhys were happy. As both Sarah and Polly had stressed on more than one occasion, being in a permanent sleep-deprived state of anxiety with a young child came hand in hand with parenthood. Lola and Rhys hadn't reached that stage yet; starting a family was something they'd talked about and hoped would be on the horizon, but for now they were focused on the here and now and the things that made them happy. The Hideaway was a huge part of that.

Fabs and Mirabel had managed to achieve a decent work/life balance, but then it was a little easier in Sardinia with a host of family to help out with the baby, and at least they had their own modest coastal home to retreat to when things got too much.

Mirabel had her struggles, though, and missed her own family and friends; the compromise was lots of time spent in the UK. Work as well as family brought her back. Her own talent agency had gone from strength to strength and she needed help, so a change was on the cards for Lola too. Going into partnership with Mirabel was an exciting step for both of them. Fabs and Rhys referred to them as the dream team.

Lola cast her eyes over their friends filling the sun-drenched clearing. Fabs was bouncing a chubby-cheeked Enzo on his knee, while Rhys was pulling silly faces at his godson, making him giggle. It was a joyous sound that made Lola's heart yearn. She smiled as Rhys hid behind his hands and went 'peekaboo', setting off another wave of giggles as Enzo rocked back against his dad. She really was ready for the next stage of her and Rhys's life.

Catching Mirabel looking at her husband and son with a mix of pride and love, Lola gestured towards them. 'They're just too cute together.'

'I'm completely biased, but yes, I have to agree.' Mirabel put her arm around Lola's waist. 'This weekend with everyone means so much; I can't put into words how amazing this place is. I'm blown away by what you two have achieved in such a short time.'

'It's mostly been down to Rhys, and anyway, it's no different to what you've blinking well created over the past three years either: your own successful agency and a baby.'

'Both of our lives have changed beyond all recognition,' Mirabel said wistfully. 'Can we take a walk?'

'Of course.'

They left the clearing, the adult conversation muted against Enzo's continuing giggles and the screeches of Barnaby's daughter playing hide-and-seek with Polly's children. Archie barked and spun round in circles, then chased after them. The path meandered beneath the trees and the only sounds besides the distant ones of their friends was the sigh of the wind through the leaves and the bubbling water as they neared the stream.

'I don't think I've ever been anywhere quite so peaceful or beautiful,' Mirabel said as they continued walking.

'You live on Sardinia,' Lola said pointedly.

'It's a different kind of beauty. Maybe it's because both you and Rhys are so happy, it's fed into everything here.'

'This place is Rhys's dream,' Lola said softly. 'His happiness makes me beyond happy.'

'What about you, though?' Mirabel glanced at her. 'Are you not torn between here and London?'

'It's the best of both. Here there's peace and freedom and the sea on the doorstep – something I've always craved – but I can go back to London when I need to, the same way I can escape back here.'

'Is it *your* dream, though?'

'It's our dream, Mirabel. That's what makes this all so special. I honestly didn't know what I wanted and then I met Rhys and everything slotted into place. I wasn't looking for love; it found me.' Lola clasped Mirabel's arm as they strolled down to the stream. The cool clear water rushed over the rocky riverbed, and flickers of sunshine and shade danced across the surface. 'Of course, if you'd told me four years ago that I'd be living in Wales in the middle of a wood with dodgy Wi-Fi and no coffee shop in walking distance, I'd have laughed in your face, but four years ago I was downright terrified, felt incredibly alone despite being surrounded by friends and was still reeling from a destructive relationship that had undone me completely. Everything I thought was important wasn't. I don't care if I can't easily pop out for a latte or a cocktail with friends, get my nails done or go clothes shopping. I've discovered so much more, not least of all happiness.'

'Oh Lola, I'm literally going to cry all weekend.' Mirabel hugged her tight, then wiped her eyes. 'My hormones are shot to pieces anyway – ever since I got pregnant with Enzo, I've been an emotional wreck and it's not gone away. Maybe it never will. Motherhood's made me happy yet permanently weepy!'

'At least you have an excuse,' Lola said as her own eyes began to well. 'Come on, let's go and join everyone. I'm overdue a cuddle with my godson.'

* * *

Once the sun had set, Lola brought blankets out to combat the chill in the air. Everyone gathered around the firepit at the centre of the clearing and the cool night was banished by firelight and laughter, beer and burgers, chatter and friendship.

Lola loved how all of their friends were with them, both hers and Rhys's, because they'd become a friendship group that had only grown stronger with the challenges of life. After Sardinia, they'd made a pact to get together at least once a year and so far they'd managed it despite everyone living in different parts of the country and Fabs and Mirabel in Sardinia. But to have everyone together at the Hideaway, to be able to show off what she and Rhys had created, was extra special, particularly now.

The fluttering in Lola's chest intensified as Rhys stood up and raised his glass. Archie whined and shifted close to Lola, nudging her hand with his damp nose so she would stroke him. Rhys glanced towards them as he waited for the conversations around the firepit to stop.

'I can't begin to tell you how good it is to have you all here, to share this place with you, somewhere that has made Lola and me incredibly happy.' The firelight flickered across his face and Lola noticed his cheeks had flushed, and it wasn't just from standing up in front of everyone, but because of what he was about to say. He glanced at her again and raised his glass higher. 'And we have a bit of an announcement to make.'

'Uh-oh, here we go!' Freddie said. Zoe slapped his arm, but everyone laughed.

A hush descended and all of their friends looked expectantly between her and Rhys.

'So, Lola and I are engaged,' he said with a huge grin.

'About bloody time too!' Deni called, instigating another trickle of laughter from the group.

'I knew it!' Gareth turned to Sarah. 'Didn't I say they'd announce their engagement this weekend?'

'Yeah, yeah, the king of predictions strikes again.' Sarah rolled her eyes at Gareth, then turned to Lola and Rhys. 'This has been a long time coming, you two. I think I can speak for everyone when I say we'd have been more surprised if you *hadn't* announced you were engaged.' Sarah raised her glass. 'I'm delighted for you, as I'm sure we all are.'

'Hear, hear!' echoed around the group.

'The best news.' Tears tracked down Mirabel's cheeks, even though Lola had phoned her the day after Rhys had proposed in this very clearing a week before.

'When's the big day?' Barnaby asked. 'Or are we getting ahead of ourselves?'

'Oh, we've not thought that far ahead yet,' Lola said as she scratched Archie beneath his ears. 'We've been rather busy getting this place up and running.'

'Sardinia is a wonderful destination for a wedding.' Mirabel flashed them a gleeful smile.

'It certainly is,' Rhys agreed. He sat down next to Lola and took her free hand. 'But here is pretty special too.'

Yes, Sardinia was a stunning place to get married and of course it was a possibility, but as suggestions of where they should or shouldn't get married were offered, it was Fabs who made the most sense; a low-key wedding with a big party afterwards would suit them both, and where better to host it than the Hideaway, a place they'd created through love, hard work and passion. It was where they lived and had grown together, where their fledgling relationship had developed into something so much more, it was their livelihood and their future, somewhere that held possibility and promise.

The Hideaway was home, yet Sardinia would always be special because it was where they'd opened up their hearts and souls to each other, where they'd met and made their love pact on that moon-bathed jetty and had fallen in love for real.

* * *

MORE FROM KATE FROST

Another book from Kate Frost, *A Love Like No Other*, is available to order now here:

https://mybook.to/LoveLikeNoOtherBackAd

ACKNOWLEDGEMENTS

The Island of Hopes and Dreams was a joy to write, a virtual escape to beautiful Sardinia as I fell in love with both the island and Lola and Rhys as I wrote their story. Like many of my books, this one has a cast of supporting characters who were equally challenging and wonderful to write – Deni, Gareth, Zoe and Giada were particular favourites. Many of the locations in the book are real: the towns of Bosa, Porto Cervo, Porto Rotondo and Costa Paradiso, the Cane Malu tidal pool and the beaches Cala Brandinchi and Spiaggia di Cala li Cossi. Villa Capparis and Villa Sereno – the two luxurious villas where the friends stay and the family live – are fictional but an amalgamation of some of the stunning villas I found through rather enjoyable online research! For Il Giardino, where the wedding takes place, I took inspiration from Su Gologone Experience Hotel, which really is nestled among juniper trees in the foothills of majestic mountains.

From cover design to editing there are plenty of people to thank: the Team Boldwood super stars Amanda Ridout, Nia Beynon, Wendy Neale, Jenna Houston, the whole of the production and marketing team, and of course my brilliant editor Caroline Ridding. Many thanks to cover designer Alexandra Allden, copyeditor Jade Craddock and proofreader Jennifer Davies. Thank you to writer friends and the wonderful blogger and bookish community for reading, reviewing and championing books. Thank you as always, Judith, for reading an early draft, for your insightful thoughts and for spotting all those pesky repeated words! To my family, thank you for the endless support and encouragement. Last but not least, a big thank you to YOU for reading one of my books and for making my own hopes and dreams come true!

ABOUT THE AUTHOR

Kate Frost is the author of several bestselling romantic escape novels including *A Greek Island Escape*, and *An Island in the Sun*. She lives in Bristol and is the Director of Storytale Festival, a book festival for children and teens she co-founded in 2019.

Sign up to Kate Frost's newsletter to read an EXCLUSIVE short story!

Visit Kate's website: www.kate-frost.co.uk

Follow Kate on social media:

- facebook.com/katefrostauthor
- x.com/katefrostauthor
- instagram.com/katefrostauthor
- bookbub.com/authors/kate-frost

ALSO BY KATE FROST

One Greek Summer

An Italian Dream

An Island in the Sun

One Winter's Night

A Greek Island Escape

An Island Promise

A Love Like No Other

The Island of Hopes and Dreams

BECOME A MEMBER OF
THE SHELF CARE CLUB

The home of Boldwood's book club reads.

Find uplifting reads, sunny escapes, cosy romances, family dramas and more!

Sign up to the newsletter
https://bit.ly/theshelfcareclub

Boldwood

Boldwood Books is an award-winning fiction publishing company seeking out the best stories from around the world.

Find out more at www.boldwoodbooks.com

Join our reader community for brilliant books, competitions and offers!

Follow us
@BoldwoodBooks
@TheBoldBookClub

Sign up to our weekly deals newsletter

https://bit.ly/BoldwoodBNewsletter